LUCY COURTENAY

♥MOViE
NIG#T★

h
Hodder
Children's
Books

A division of Hachette

HODDER CHILDREN'S BOOKS

First published in Great Britain in 2018 by Hodder and Stoughton

1 3 5 7 9 10 8 6 4 2

A CIP catalogue record for this book
is available from the British Library.

ISBN 978 1 444 93073 3

Typeset in Berkeley Oldstyle by Hewer Text UK Ltd, Edinburgh
Printed and bound in Great Britain by CPI Group (UK) Ltd, Croydon, CR0 4YY

Hodder Children's Books
An imprint of
Hachette Children's Group
Part of Hodder and Stoughton
Carmelite House
50 Victoria Embankment
London EC4Y 0DZ

An Hachette UK Company
www.hachette.co.uk

www.hachettechildrens.co.uk

For Caroline Pia Dauphine Robert

31 DECEMBER

I am dancing and I am happy and I have hiccups.

I always dance at New Year. Even as a kid I was doing the Macarena at midnight. Tonight, thanks to the awesome blue lights that Dan has rigged up in his great glassy living room, I feel like a sea serpent in an aquarium, wafting and swaying so smoothly that you can't see the joins. I am Miss Price and Professor Whatsisname in *Bedbrooms and Knobsticks* all rolled into one.

My white dress sparks to life as the strobes flash. Vashti and Laura look in my direction as I blind half the room, lighting up like a crane at Christmas. Wow. I am a *luminous* sea serpent.

'Hanna.'

'Not now, babes,' I say, eyes closed and arms mid-wave. 'I'm in the zone.'

'Han, you just whacked me in the face.'

Sol is rubbing his cheekbone and trying not to get trampled by the rest of the dancing crowd. I know he wishes he wasn't here. He's not a party king.

'Call it an affectionate punch,' I suggest.

'You're drunk.'

'I am not drunk. I am awesome.' I squint around the floor, trying to spot Dan Danny Dan my man manny man. I want to run my hands all over his ripped torso and tweak his floppy earlobes. I want to *bite* him. Four weeks in and I'm obsessed.

'You're drunk,' Sol repeats.

'You all right, Han?' says Laura, reaching for me – or my dress, it's hard to tell which – with her long purple nails.

'She's fine,' says Sol. 'Just needs a bit of air.'

He threads me through the pumping room to where a set of shiny glass doors open on to a big deck-like balcony overlooking the garden. There are solar lights edging the lawn and a lion water feature. Dan has the best house ever. Dan is the best boyfriend ever.

'I'm the king of the world,' I say.

I spread out my arms and attempt to lean over the balustrade like Kate Winslet in *Titanic*. Sol hauls me back into an upright position. I press him on the nose to keep him from sliding around, but no matter how hard I press, he won't stay still.

'You're going to give me a nosebleed if you keep doing that,' he says.

I take my finger away. I do not want Sol's nose blood all over this dress because then people will be talking about my outfit for all the wrong reasons in the morning.

My boyfriend is clearly outlined in the window upstairs. I feel a rush of pride, shortly followed by an urgent need to run upstairs and kiss his knuckle-chewingly handsome

2

face. From down here I can see his lovely raven-black hair sticking up and his beautiful Greek profile and his white shiny teeth as he breaks into his killer smile and turns to talk to whoever he's talking to.

Sol claps like someone getting the attention of a kid on a bouncy castle. 'Let's get you a drink of water,' he says, in a tone that can only be described as brisk. His eyes are normally murky-pond green, but right now the strobing lights coming through the glass doors of the living room are making them flicker like flames.

'Outside, inside,' I grumble. 'Make up your mind.'

I throw one more glance up at Dan's window as Sol tows me back to the house.

And that's when I see Lizzie Banks kissing my boyfriend.

Sol is now saying something else in his best calming-small-animals voice. I can't hear the words clearly. He sounds a long way away, like he's at the other end of a great tunnel. I dig my very high heels into the deck and stare at the way Lizzie's got Dan squished up to the window, with her chipped nails in his perfect hair. Her nails are flaky red, like the blood that is now draining out of my heart. The shock has knocked the hiccups clean out of my body.

'Lizzie Banks is kissing Dan,' I say, in a voice that feels thick and odd and not mine at all. 'SHE'S KISSING HIM.'

'Who's kissing who?' says Trixie, whirling by in blue sequins and false lashes so long that I feel the extra drag of air at eye level as she passes.

3

I rush through the dancing crowd, passing my brother and his girlfriend Leah PDAing away as usual. I have to reach the stairs and climb them so I can fetch Dan to safety. *Lizzie . . . Anyone but Lizzie*. My dress is so tight that I can't rush as fast as I would like. Sol keeps a tight grip on my arm.

'Don't make a scene, Han,' he says. 'It won't end well.'

'Damn right it won't end well,' I grunt in fury. I've got to the bottom of the steel and glass stairs, and am now considering how best to climb them in knee-length body-con. A stair lift would be good. 'Trixie says Lizzie Banks has been after Dan ever since we started college.' I feel hot as I say Lizzie's name. 'It's embarrassing, actually. I'm embarrassed for her. I mean, what a *joke*. Lizzie Banks is a JOKE.'

Sol is stoutly refusing to let go of me as I attempt to hop up the steps. Every time someone comes past, he nods at them with a nonchalant 'All right?' in a bid to defuse suspicion that all is not well. Dimly I feel grateful. Mainly I feel like something very large has just been dropped on me from a great height.

Trixie appears at the living-room door. As she assesses my third enraged attempt to climb the staircase without ripping my dress, I can see the cogs whirring beneath her coal-black extensions.

'Everything all right?' she says, fixing Sol with large glitter-lashed eyes.

'Everything's fine, Trixie, thanks for asking,' says Sol. 'Han, the door's *this* way.'

Vashti and Laura appear, drawn by the promise of drama.

'You're *leaving*?' says Vashti.

She doesn't have to say anything else. I know. Only lunatics and losers would leave Dan's party half an hour before the clock ticks over into the new year.

Sol gives my arm an extra-hard tug. 'Yup.'

I have no choice but to give up on the staircase and pant quietly by his side, a defeated dog in a white tube bandage. The tears are beginning to rise.

'Hanna?' says Sol. 'Come *on*.'

Hanna

The party muffles to nothing as Sol shuts the huge front door behind us with a click. I take a shuddering breath. God, it's cold out here. I realise I have forgotten my coat. Wait – I didn't bring a coat. Only geeks wear coats to parties.

'I had this dream that Dan and I were going to get married in Singö,' I gasp, grasping Sol's coat lapels as he hustles me down the drive. It's hard going in these shoes. 'We were going to ride bicycles in matching fisherman's jumpers and have beautiful children who spoke three languages. My heart skips like a lamb on Red Bull every time I think of him. This isn't over, Sol. Lizzie Banks is just a blip on the radar screen of our love.'

Who knew this much emotion could make you feel sick? My stomach has started boiling like a pan of overheated soup. I'm impressed with myself for taking rage to this level.

Why did it have to be Lizzie?

'How can I get him back?' I wail.

And then I'm sick on Sol's shoes.

It's incredible how much less emotional you feel the moment after you vomit. Instead of rage and grief, I now feel exhaustion. I lean against the nearest lamp post as Sol tries to wipe his shoes clean on the sparkly, crunchy grass beside Dan's gate. My eye make-up should be acting like a wall of potato salad at an all-you-can-eat buffet, but it isn't. I can't keep the tears from spilling over.

'Welcome to the Dump Club,' Sol says.

I'm so shocked that I almost stop crying on the spot.

I have *never* been dumped.

I have, in fact, been the dumpee my whole dating career, from the twenty-three minutes I spent with Hugo Jackson at the Year Seven Christmas disco before moving smoothly to the other side of the dancefloor with Andrew Gillespie, to Dan Dukas wafting two tickets to *Fantastic Beasts and Where to Find Them* under my nose a month ago while I was waiting for Stevie O'Shea to buy us into *Inferno*.

'I have NOT been dumped,' I say, appalled. 'Lizzie Banks took advantage of the situation, that's all.' *And not for the first time*, I think bitterly.

Sol looks at me through his over-long ginger fringe. 'Kissing involves two people. Or one person and a melon, if you're desperate.'

I snort with miserable laughter as I stare at my mascara-smudged palms. Then I start crying again because the world has never looked so bleak.

'A person's first dumping shouldn't happen on New Year's Eve,' I sob. 'It's against the rules in every movie ever made.'

'Life isn't a movie, Han.'

As we pass the bus shelter, the memory of Lizzie's hands running through Dan's hair assails me again, in an overflowing toilet of horror that makes me gasp for breath. No one tells you this stuff destroys your breathing apparatus as well as your heart.

'I feel like an excavator has dug out my lungs,' I gasp, sinking on to the plastic bus shelter bench. I thump my chest to demonstrate.

'I know.'

Sol has always tried so hard to empathise, but how can he really understand a situation like this?

'You've never had a girlfriend,' I point out. 'You have no idea.'

Sitting down beside me, Sol opens his coat and lets me snuggle up against him. 'Shows how much you know,' he says over my head.

'You *have* had a girlfriend?'

I don't mean to sound disbelieving. It's just . . . Sol with a girlfriend doesn't compute.

'A lot can happen between the ages of twelve and sixteen,' he reminds me.

'Like growing three feet and a voice like a foghorn.'

'I don't have three feet,' he says seriously.

It's three months now since Sol Adams scooped me off the college canteen lino with half a pint of strawberry yoghurt splattered across my backside as I screamed, 'I can't believe you're here! Why didn't I know you were here?' at

8

my best friend from primary school while he mopped me down. It's true what they say about only missing stuff when it comes back again, armed with serviettes. I realise I am feeling better. Sol always had the knack of lifting my mood. How I survived for years without him is beyond me.

'I would know if you'd been out with anyone *recently* though,' I say, wiping my nose. 'Approximately seventy per cent of our daylight hours have been spent together since September.'

'There's always the other thirty per cent of my time to account for.'

I force my mind away from the dark places and think about this. Sol has always been the stealthy type, sneaking about like a crapping cat. Could he have been seeing someone without me knowing?

'Who is she?' I say with sudden interest. 'When did she dump you? Why don't I know about her?'

'How do you know it's a she?'

Dan goes clean out of my head. A lot *can* happen between the ages of twelve and sixteen.

'No,' I say.

'No,' he agrees. 'She's someone you don't know.'

I am dumbfounded. 'I am the world's worst friend,' I say, when I can find my voice. 'You've been dumped and I didn't even know you were going out with anyone.'

'You know now.'

'Why did she dump you?' I say indignantly. Sol is lovely. Sol is perfect. Sol might not be fanciable, but Sol is *everything* else. Then I pale. 'It wasn't because of me, was it? I know we spend loads of time together but it's never been like that. She does know that, doesn't she? She does know we don't fancy each other?'

Sol stands up. 'Let's keep walking or we'll freeze to death.'

I stagger to my feet, mainly to stay in contact with Sol's lovely, warm, geeky coat, and bang my nose right into his back. He has stopped dead in the middle of the road.

Tiny white sparkles are floating in the icy haze over our heads. They grow thicker and busier, twirling away like a million glittering Cinderellas at the Prince's ball.

Snow.

I'm not cold any more. I'm in that scene in *Serendipity* minus the glove twirling down from the sky. I've always wanted to be in that scene.

'*This* is a movie,' I say, spreading out my arms and not even minding the pinpricks of cold as the flakes land on my almost-blue arms. 'It's snowing on New Year's Eve!' I check my watch. 'It's snowing on New Year's Eve at *midnight*,' I add ecstatically – if you can be ecstatic and heartbroken at the same time. 'We have actually gone beyond the celluloid here.'

'No one makes films on celluloid any more.'

'All right, Steven Spielberg.' He's being deliberately obtuse. 'What I'm trying to say is that we have moved beyond movies and into the realm of *signs*.' I say this in hushed tones to match the rapidly whitening scene around us.

'Don't tell me,' he says. '*Serendipity?*'

I wriggle under his coat so that my arm winds more snugly around his tummy. We walk on down the empty road, enjoying the feeling of our very own snow globe, our perfect cocoon of calm. And it's an amazing feeling, given the circumstances of the evening.

At my gate, I pull my arms free from his warmth.

'Home sweet home,' I say. I make a weak rocker sign with my fingers. 'Party on. Thanks for looking after me. I'll return the favour one day when you forget to be sensible. If that day ever comes.'

Something flits across Sol's gaze.

'Happy New Year, Hanna,' he says.

There is the weirdest moment, like the rest of the world has somehow stopped turning. There isn't a sound anywhere. There is a kind of halo around Sol as he stands in front of me in the dancing snow below the streetlight, flakes on his ginger lashes and something I don't recognise in his pondy eyes.

And in that moment, I have a perfectly brilliant idea. The kind of idea that only ever becomes reality if you come up with it on New Year's Eve, preferably while drunkenly standing in the snow in four-inch heels with your best friend.

'You know what we should do?' I say with sudden excitement.

The unrecognisable thing vanishes from Sol's eyes. 'Oh God,' he mutters.

'We should watch a movie together on the last day of every month for a whole year, right round until next New Year's Eve. Twelve movies, total.'

Sol looks up at the sky again. 'What is it with you and movies?'

'They hold *answers*.' I prod him in the chest. 'We need answers, Sol. Why did we both get dumped? What did we do wrong? Don't you think it's time we learned from the greats? I bet Audrey Hepburn never failed to hop up a flight of stairs to confront a boyfriend-stealing witch. And I can guarantee you that Amy Adams never fell flat on her arse in yoghurt. We should start tonight. Mum and James are at a party, Raz is still snogging Leah at Dan's, and my little brother is at a sleepover. So we'd have the house to ourselves.'

Sol brushes a snowflake away just under my eye. 'You're bone cold and you're miserable and you're drunk,' he says. 'And I'd quite like to wash your sick off my shoes. Go to sleep, Hanna. We'll do it another time.'

I yawn on cue. He's right. I'm totally knackered. Thoughts of taking off this infuriatingly tight dress and these agonising heels, washing my face and then crying my way through all the Facebook pictures of me and Dan, without being disturbed until dawn, begin to feel quite appealing.

'The end of this month at mine, then,' I say, fumbling in my purse for my keys. 'My place, my choice. You choose the next movie at yours. I promise I won't interfere. Unless you choose *Star Wars*. Don't choose *Star Wars*. I can't stand *Star*

Wars. I mean, I've never seen *Star Wars*, but I can't stand the thought of *Star Wars*.'

Sol is walking away, his hand raised as the snow swirls around his head.

'Oh, and Happy New Year to you too,' I say, a little belatedly.

But he's already gone.

SOL

1 JANUARY

I am *such* an idiot. There was even falling snow. It was like that film she's probably crazy about, Bridget Bloody Jones, with Renée Zellweger in leopard pants and Colin Firth being ineffably cool and wrapping her up in his coat and kissing her.

I groan out loud. Partly at the thought of Hanna in leopard pants. Mainly because I hate myself utterly right now. Because tonight I have realised three things. One: I am hopelessly in love with Hanna Bergdahl. Two: for the first time since our recent reunion, Hanna Bergdahl appears to be single. And three: I am stuck in that inescapable netherworld of demons and acne – the Friend Zone.

For a second, through the haze of snow and streetlight back there on what I will now for ever think of as Loser's Corner, as I was gazing at her lips and I thought, maybe, she was gazing back at mine, the exit door was plainly marked. One arm slipped around her back, maybe the old rest-foreheads technique, and the way out was right there.

14

Maybe it's because I came so close this time, the Friend Zone is feeling more inescapable than ever.

She might have thrown up again while we were kissing, I suppose. And I would never have known whether it was through revulsion or what remained of Dan Dukas's rum punch. So maybe it's for the best.

It doesn't feel like the best, that's all.

Nigel is waiting as I turn the latch. I don't see him exactly. More *sense* his devil eyes gleaming underneath the stairs. So I barely flinch when he launches himself at my ankle and savages my puke-flavoured sock.

'How did it go?' Gareth shouts from the kitchen.

I steady myself on the post at the bottom of the stairs as I heel off my vomity shoes. Nigel is still hanging on. 'Great,' I say. 'Best party ever. Yay for parties.'

'Any girls?'

'Just Hanna.' Even her name makes me ache.

'Any boys?'

Andrew sticks his head round the kitchen door. 'Solomon? Get in here now and tell us everything.'

'No one gave me a second look,' I say.

Andrew pulls a face, assessing my outfit. 'No wonder. Coat like that.'

'Leave him alone, Andrew,' says Gareth.

I take off my coat, snuffle my nose into its creased depths to breathe in the non-pukey parts of Hanna, then hang it up. 'What are you doing in tonight anyway?' I ask. 'I thought you were going to a party.'

15

Gareth wanders out of the kitchen in his favourite old-man PJs. 'Nigel wouldn't let us leave,' he says.

Nigel has still got my ankle between his teeth. His tail is lashing around like an incensed garden hose.

'That damn cat held us hostage until nine,' Andrew explains. 'I had my best trousers on and he was in no mood to spare them. By the time he gave up we'd both drunk too much to drive. Happy New Year to us.'

'You sad individuals,' I say. 'Held hostage by the cat.'

'He needs therapy,' says Gareth.

'He needs neutering,' I say.

I can see Gareth retracing the conversation to where it all began.

'*Just* Hanna?' he says a little beadily.

Here we go.

'We're friends, Gareth,' I say.

'Friends at four doesn't mean just friends for ever. Friendship is the best foundation for a relationship.'

'I don't know about that,' says Andrew. 'I've never liked you much.'

As Gareth knuckles Andrew on his faintly balding head, I find myself wishing – and not for the first time – that I hadn't met Hanna Bergdahl aged four, over the sugar paper and crayons. Then maybe I would have had a chance to start again. I could have been all mysterious, instead of the kid she remembers getting locked in the school toilets when we were seven. I could have been cool, not the boy whose ninth birthday party had us all whittling wooden spoons at the Museum of Agricultural Life. There is no way back from this place.

'Get *off*, Nigel,' I say and shake my foot.

Nigel explodes from my leg like a jet-black bomb and hurtles for the cat flap. Which is closed. We all hear the sound of his skull smacking against solid plastic.

'Justice,' says Andrew darkly.

For a while there, I think I had the Lost Years on my side. You know, the mysterious-past thing. A lot *does* happen between twelve and sixteen. But four years in the States didn't even equip me with that basic cool-kid essential: an American accent. Any mystery I might have had has already glimmered and died like a cub scouts' bonfire.

Hanna, on the other hand, has grown into herself. Particularly, she has grown into her teeth. And her hair, once a bit frizzy, is now as smooth as a wedge of butter. Long too, and thick, and cool to the touch. She's always had blue eyes but now, they are bluer. Somehow.

I kick my bedroom door shut irritably, lift up the box covering the paper figures on my table – I haven't figured out how to light them to best advantage yet – and flip on my computer. The FaceTime light is already green and Frank is grinning at me. Four years of mutually getting the shit kicked out of us has built some kind of telepathy across the ocean.

'Happy New Year, Frank,' I say, flopping back on my bed.

Frank lifts a long, slim finger. 'Eight more hours to go here, bud. Five more hours of Mom asking me if I have a date for tonight or if I would prefer to watch reruns of *I Love Lucy* with her and Dad and the dog.'

We share a wince. Lucy Shapiro is a touchy subject.

'Ironic,' I say.

'Ironic,' agrees Frank. 'But I haven't been hanging here waiting for your return to talk about my non-existent love life. I want to know if you and Hanna finally—'

I hold up my hand. Frank stops. There is a silent moment of empathy.

'She asked me in to watch a movie but I said no,' I tell him.

'You said *no*? Are you insane? Movie plus couch spells a sure thing, my friend, did no one ever tell you this? I'm guessing her parents were in.'

'They were out. Her brothers too.'

'You total asshole,' Frank breathes.

I hadn't fully considered my assholery on the movie front. But now Frank has pointed it out, it's hard to ignore. I could have spent two hours with Hanna, alone, on a couch. Instead, I chose to return home, get savaged by a psychopathic cat, endure a well-meaning conversation with my parents and get insulted by my best mate from five thousand miles away.

'Go back round there and say you changed your mind,' Frank orders.

'She was drunk,' I say. 'I said we'd do it another time.'

'Rein in your ambitions, man.'

'Do it as in *watch a movie* another time. We have a date at the end of January.'

At least, I'm *telling* myself it's a date. Except of course that Hanna will have another guy by the end of January. She might even have made up with Dan the Douche, although his track record suggests that's unlikely. I try and fail to take heart from this. A girl like Hanna doesn't stay single for four and a half weeks.

Frank is so close to the screen now that I can count his eyebrow hairs. He has a *lot* of eyebrow hairs. 'If you're telling me I have to wait a whole month,' he says, 'your movie date had better come up with the goods.'

'You need to sort your own love life out,' I tell him. 'Then maybe my own wouldn't be so interesting.'

'If only it were so simple,' sighs Frank.

As I slide my computer shut, one more good thing occurs to me about a very, very bad evening. If I had gone back to Hanna's to watch a movie – *Don't think about how we could have been alone, don't think about it* – I would have had to explain about my supposed ex. Hanna is the type of girl who doesn't give up easily, and I haven't given her nearly enough information to satisfy her curiosity. She would have talked through half the movie, squirrelling away, digging for details, and details on details. There's no way my spur-of-the-moment fib would have stood up to Hanna's level of scrutiny. I would have been a Friend with Delusions, not simply a Friend. I'll just have to hope she's forgotten all about it the next time we see each other.

SOL

Morning doesn't so much dawn, as spill over the horizon in a pool of pale white light. The snow from last night has settled, leaching the few colours on the other side of the bathroom window to subtle shades of pastel. As I shave, I wonder if I can be bothered with New Year resolutions. I wonder much the same every January, then make a couple anyway.

'I will kiss Hanna Bergdahl this year,' I say, pointing my razor at the mirror. 'Failing that, I will stop my Haribo habit. No more sour cherries. They make that shit with hooves.'

I should probably be making resolutions about bigger stuff than Haribo, but I can't think much past Hanna at the moment. This is a big year, as Gareth and Andrew are fond of telling me. Six months before the questions start to matter.

To take my mind off this fact, I spend five careful minutes adjusting my paper figures, then play with the desk lamp for a while, trying once again to work out the best way to light them. If I position them in a certain way, their shadows are kissing while their bodies aren't. I may be able to do something with that. I place the upended box back over the scene, protecting them from breeze and Nigel and prying eyes, and resolve to give them my full attention later.

'Coffee with or without cat hairs?' offers Andrew as I reach the kitchen. 'Nigel's had the filters again.'

'I'll pass, thanks.' I grab my coat and check my keys and phone are in my pocket.

'Off out already?' asks Gareth from behind one of the endless Christmas papers he's catching up on.

'Stuff to do,' I say.

'Anything we can help with?'

'No,' I say. 'Thanks.'

'Are you going to see Hanna?'

I don't feel like discussing Hanna with my parents this morning. How long do I have to make polite conversation before I can slide away?

'He's checking his phone again,' says Andrew.

'What do you have to do at seven o'clock in the morning on New Year's Day?' Gareth asks, lowering his paper.

'Bye,' I say firmly before Andrew can jump in again.

Pulling the door closed behind me, I relax as I breathe in the brand new air. There is a muffled quality to everything today, as if someone has clamped a large pair of ear defenders around the world. The year is seven hours old, new and clean and full of every kind of possibility. Once a year I get to feel this way. The past is erased. No Friend Zone, no badly whittled cutlery. There is no reason why today can't be the best day of my life.

The route to the railway station takes me past the end of Hanna's road. I stop for a moment, shivering in the early morning cold, and gaze at the sleepy windows that climb the street. It's possible she's not been asleep long, spending all night thinking about Dan Dukas.

I don't like to think of Hanna crying.

There is a sudden explosion from a nearby privet hedge and the sensation of teeth clamping around my calf. My yell dislodges a clump of snow from a tree branch overhead, which hits me with pinpoint accuracy. Curtains twitch along the road. I'm wet, cold, shocked and furious.

'Bloody cat,' I say, grabbing Nigel and wrapping him tightly in my arms so that he can neither bite nor scratch me. I am basically a cat straitjacket.

The train is due in eight minutes. If I dump Nigel back in the hedge, I can make it in five and take up position on the footbridge. While I am considering this course of action, a car flies past, throwing up a plume of brown snow from beneath its filthy wheels. Under my chin, Nigel starts purring like a smug motorbike. He knows I can't leave him here.

I march back home.

'Stalking birds, fine.' I deposit Nigel in Andrew's lap. 'Stalking humans, not fine.'

'He has a thing about main roads,' says Andrew.

'It's called a death wish,' I say. 'You *need* to neuter him.'

I storm upstairs. Thanks to Nigel I have missed the first train of the year. The one that *starts* everything. That brings people home from night shifts and parties, reunites families and friends. The blank canvas ready for the perfect frame, the perfect shot, the perfect story. The second train isn't the same.

Seven and a half hours into the new year, and I have already failed on two counts. That has to be some kind of record, even for me.

Hanna

My head hurts almost as much as my heart right now. My eyes are stuck shut with salt crystals and all the mascara I couldn't get off last night. My stomach still has crease marks on it from that stupid dress. My toes are fused together from my shoes.

'You have to stop crying at some point, sis.'

'You don't understand,' I sob, my head buried beneath my pillow. 'I'm never going to be happy again.'

Raz shifts his weight on the end of my bed. I hear the crunch of his apple. 'Is Dan Dukas really worth this level of grief?'

'Imagine if this was you and Leah,' I hiss. 'Imagine how you would be feeling now.'

Raz rolls his eyes in that way people have when they think they're rock-solid in love. Mum rolled her eyes like that once, before Dad upped and left with no word of warning.

'Leah isn't Dan,' he says.

'I don't know what you've got against him,' I sniff. 'Oh wait, yes I do. He's rich, and that goes against all your socialist principles.'

'I don't like him because he's a shit. He went out with Jono's sister last year. That didn't end well either.'

'You can't believe everything Jono tells you,' I say.

Raz shrugs. 'My best friend isn't the one embarrassing you on social media today.'

I sit up in horror. 'What?'

'I hate to kick over your sandcastle, but you should probably know,' says Raz. 'Dan Dukas kissing Lizzie was all over Insta before the last stroke of midnight last night.'

I usually appreciate the direct approach. Just as well, because it's Raz's default setting. But this morning, I feel like my brother just pulled all my guts out in a slithering grey pile on the duvet.

'Dan did NOT kiss Lizzie Banks,' I spit. 'Lizzie Banks kissed HIM.'

'That's just semantics. Dan kissed Lizzie, he Instagrammed the news and he hasn't called today. These are the facts. He's not a nice guy.'

My eyes fill up again as I think of Lizzie's lips gobbling Dan like he's chocolate. Her fingernails in his hair. I used to paint those fingernails dayglo colours after Brownies every week.

'She's a bitch,' I say dully.

My brother holds up a second apple. *'Gott Nytt År, sis.'*

I take the apple out of habit. Good luck and health and all that. It tastes of dust and broken relationships.

'Mum's gone to fetch Linus from Isaac's house,' Raz says, getting off the bed and tossing his own apple core into my bin. 'James is on a run. I'm going over to Leah's to help her dad clear the garden and earn approximately a thousand boyfriend points, which I intend to cash in this evening.'

'Gross,' I say.

Raz grins. 'Wash your face, you look like you ran up a chimney.'

I crawl to the bathroom. Bloody mascara. They make the stuff with indelible ink. I scrub at my face so hard that my eyelids feel sore and baggy, and still there's black stuff coming off on the cotton wool. I slather my aching face in moisturiser and hobble back to bed. I don't have the energy to do much else today, so I grab my laptop and hit Netflix. Thank God for movies. Movies are my safe place, my perfect world, where nothing goes wrong that can't be fixed by the ninetieth minute.

When I switch my phone on without thinking, it vents like an enraged elephant. Dan and Lizzie have broken the internet. I genuinely feel as if I'm going to be sick again, like I was on Sol's shoes.

Disabling every social app I have is a wrench, but it's better than the alternative. I'm left with about fifteen text messages from the girls, all saying more or less the same thing: that Lizzie Banks is a two-faced slut who doesn't deserve Dan, that I did nothing wrong (except I did, clearly, or none of this would have happened), that he's crazy to prefer her over me.

GOD I HATE MY LIFE.

My phone rings.

'Sol,' I say. And I burst into tears.

One of the many good things about Sol is that he doesn't say stuff like 'It's going to be OK' or 'There, there' or any of that meaningless crap people say to fill space. He just listens. After about five minutes of me gasping and snotting and cursing and him saying nothing at all, I prod my computer wanly.

'Want to come over and watch *No Country for Old Men*?' I say.

'You really know how to pick the cheerful ones.'

'It's the first one I thought of that doesn't involve any romance. Do you want to?'

'Can't. Gareth is making lunch. Family time.'

I lie back on my pillow and close my sad, tired eyes. 'Sol, I *have* to get Dan back.'

'You have seen Insta?'

'That'll be Lizzie Banks.' Her name tastes like cold Brussels sprouts in my mouth. 'Dan never knows which buttons to press.'

'Must be all those phone upgrades he gets. Tough having to relearn phone protocol four times a year with a brain like a pea.'

'Dan's brain is bigger than a pea,' I say with dignity.

'A brain like a cabbage then. A cabbage is bigger than a pea.'

'Sol—'

'I was with you last night, Hanna. I saw what happened. Just ask my shoes.'

I lie back on my bed. 'Stick 'em in the wash,' I tell the ceiling. 'They'll be grand.'

'*Leap Year*.'

Sol is the only boy I know who recognises every single film quote I ever put out there. Even the really rubbish ones, the ones from movies that most guys would rather wax off their own leg hair than watch.

'I'm going to do it, you know,' I say, wiping my nose with the back of my hand. 'Get him back. It'll be like in *Leap Year* when Amy Adams goes back to Matthew Goode's pub and tells him she loves him.'

Sol sounds surprised. 'Dan Dukas is Matthew Goode in this scenario?'

'*Obviously* Dan is Matthew Goode,' I say. 'They both have dark hair, they're both tall, they both have cute accents. What's Gareth cooking anyway?'

'Something super elaborate that will use every pan in the kitchen and drive Nigel insane. Well, even more insane. You know, he hijacked me on my way to— when I was out today.'

'On your way to what?'

'This place,' Sol says in his usual evasive manner. 'Where I went this morning. To think.'

'To think about her?'

'Who?'

I'm glad *he* can forget. 'The girl who dumped you,' I remind him a little caustically.

'Oh. Yes. Hanna, this idea you had about watching movies every month. Were you serious?'

'I'm always serious when I'm talking about movies,' I say. 'Except when I'm talking about serious movies.'

'Fine,' he says. 'As long as we take turns.'

I feel happier. 'I'll choose the first one.'

'Don't choose *Bridget Jones*.'

'Might do, might not. Don't worry about her, OK?'

'Who's worried?'

'You. You sound weird.' My phone bleeps. 'Ooh, sorry, call waiting, can you hold a sec? Loveyoubye. Hello?'

'Hanna babes,' breathes Trixie. 'You must be feeling *awful*. I can't *believe* Dan would do that to you. Do you want to talk about it?'

If Trixie had called first, the invitation would have been tempting. Now I just feel drained, and a little edgy. I need a plan that will make me look less pathetic than I do right now. The girls have certain standards, and I can't disappoint. I need to ask Sol's advice. Sol, who is right on the other line, waiting like the angel that he is.

'Sorry Trix, call waiting. Can you hold?'

I flip across.

'It's Trixie, Sol,' I say. 'It's really important that I don't sound needy with her because it'll get back to Vashti and Laura, who already think I'm a bit weird, but I have to tell her something to get her off my back about the Dan fiasco. What should I say?'

'Why do they think you're weird?'

Because I hang around with you more than I hang around with them. I don't tell him this. 'This isn't the time to question my social agenda. This is the time to help me out.'

Sol sighs. 'Tell Trixie that you had dumped Dan earlier in the evening, so him and Lizzie mean nothing to you. Remember how we left before midnight? Use that.'

'But—'

'Tell her. And be convincing. If you can convince Trixie Logan, she'll convince Vashti and Laura for you. Problem solved.'

Sol is a genius.

Flip.

'It's *so* nice of you to call, Trix,' I say. 'But basically unnecessary.'

'Hanna, I totally understand if you can't talk right now. I would be the same if I knew everyone knew I had been dumped on New Year's Eve and there had been pictures posted to prove it and *everything*.'

'Don't believe everything you hear.' I even laugh, although it sounds like a canary being fed into a lawnmower. 'You see, Dan and me? We were over before midnight. So him and Lizzie . . . him and Lizzie Banks are fine by me.'

'Hon!' gasps Trixie. 'Are you telling me he ended it *before* he got with Lizzie Banks?'

Why should Dan get to be the dumpee in every version of this?

'*He* didn't end anything,' I protest. '*I* ended it. With *him*.'

'You dumped the hottest guy in college?' Trixie says disbelievingly.

'You know what it's like,' I say, turning the bright button up as high as it will go. 'It was time to move on.'

'Oh my gosh,' Trixie says suddenly. 'I know who you dumped Dan for!'

'I— You do?'

'Don't get coy with me, babe. I'm like, *so* pleased for you guys! You are *made* for each other.'

Now I'm confused. 'I didn't dump Dan for anyone,' I say. 'Can't a girl enjoy being single just for the sake of being single?'

'So are you guys public knowledge or a secret?'

This conversation has galloped out of my control. 'I think Instagram has taken care of any public announcements, don't you?' I say.

'Not you and Dan. You and *Sol*.'

'Trixie,' I say, 'I have no idea what you're talking about.'

'You and Sol have been inseparable since September. Everyone's noticed.'

The penny drops.

'NO WAY,' I say loudly. 'I'm not into Sol! Are you *insane*?' I'm not having *that* on the Trixie Logan grapevine. It would endanger my friendship with Sol like some kind of rainforest frog.

'Oh,' says Trixie, with a tutting noise. 'Of course. I forgot he's gay.'

'He's not gay,' I say.

31

'He lives with two guys, Hanna. If that's not the route to being gay, I don't know what is.'

'Hi,' says Sol.

Trixie gives a little shriek. I almost drop the phone.

'I think you pressed the wrong button, Han,' says Sol.

29 JANUARY

Tell me now or I'm not coming.

Took AGES 2 decide but finally gone 4 . . . Breakfast at Tiffanys. Feeling the Hepburn vibe. Even bought the bk!!!

Reasonable choice but the film is different from the book.

Still a happy ending . . .?

Audrey Hepburn gets pregnant, goes to Brazil and doesn't end up with George Peppard.

OMG totes not reading it now

BREAKFAST AT
TIFFANY'S (1961)

DIRECTOR BLAKE EDWARDS

WRITERS TRUMAN CAPOTE
and GEORGE AXELROD

Holly Golightly (Audrey Hepburn) lives by herself in a half-empty apartment in New York. She spends her time on expensive dates and at high-class parties with rich men, and plans to marry for money. Holly's life changes when she meets her neighbour, aspiring writer Paul Varjak (George Peppard).

The film won Oscars for Best Score for Henry Mancini and Best Song for Johnny Mercer's classic tune 'Moon River'.

31 JANUARY

I have changed my shirt three times in the past half hour.

'This is not a date,' I tell my reflection. 'Hanna isn't *insane* enough to fancy you. Hanna isn't that *insane*. Keep the *insanity* at a distance.'

I return to my room, rip off shirt number four and select a black T-shirt. Skinny jeans, Converse, done. There's no point in making more effort. My stress levels can't take it.

I go downstairs, open the fridge and rest my burning face next to the butter on the top shelf. I have to calm down. Hanna is expecting her best friend for a movie night tonight, not a hyperventilating weirdo.

'Dates always made me lose my appetite,' Andrew observes from his laptop, set up as usual on the kitchen table. 'What *have* you done to your hair?'

'Dyed it,' I mumble at the butter.

'On purpose?'

'It's not like when a pair of red pants winds up in the white wash, Andrew, naming no names,' Gareth says. 'Of course on purpose. I think it looks *great*,' he adds, in a discouragingly hearty tone.

I remove my face from the fridge. 'It's just a bit darker, OK? No big deal.'

'It makes your eyes look bigger,' says Andrew. 'I had no idea hair dye did that.'

Gareth looks at me more closely. 'Have you borrowed Andrew's guyliner?'

'That's so adorable!' says Andrew.

Even Hanna's blank indifference is better than this.

'I'm not wearing guyliner,' I say.

I am in fact wearing guyliner. It has become clear to me that I need reinventing if I'm ever to stand a chance with Hanna. I'm already regretting the hair dye, which will take at least a week to wash out. I remove my head from the fridge and check the area for immediate danger to life and limb.

'Where's Nigel?'

'In the bathroom, stalking spiders.' Andrew scrolls down his laptop screen. 'Do we think a cat muzzle is the answer to Nigel's anger issues?'

'Neutering is the answer to Nigel's anger issues.' I pull my coat from its hook and regard myself briefly in the hallway mirror. The eyes are OK but the hair is a disaster. I snatch up one of Andrew's beanies and cram it on my head. I'll have to keep it on.

'Be good,' says Gareth.

'And if you can't be good,' Andrew adds, 'be Russell Brand.'

I shut the door on my parents' cackling, turn up the collar on my coat and breathe. When I am satisfied that I have finally stopped sweating, I allow myself to set off.

Incredibly, Hanna is still single. Dan Dukas has been wearing Lizzie Banks like a poncho for four weeks now, but it hasn't stopped Hanna from hanging around college like a lovelorn sheep and crying on my shoulder most break times. Several guys have tried asking her out, but she's turned them all down. I know this because I was there when they came up to her and asked. Good to know I'm not perceived as any kind of threat.

I catch sight of myself in a window. The beanie makes me look like maybe I snowboard. That's good. Except I don't think snowboarders wear guyliner. Am I giving out mixed messages here? I wish I had a sister. Or a mother. Just occasionally in my life, like today, a woman's opinion might be useful.

She's never going to fancy you, I remind myself as I try to walk like maybe a snowboarder would walk. *This is just watching a movie, OK? Just a stupid, bloody movie.*

Hanna opens the door in a little black dress with a thick chain of pearls round her neck before I've pressed the button. She's even done her hair in a huge Holly Golightly beehive.

'You dressed up too!' she squeals, hugging me. 'I *love* it! You do know the beatnik look is *Funny Face* though?'

'It's all the same period,' I say, struggling to formulate a sentence. She smells the way love should smell. I'm going to

37

have to do something about this addiction because it's going to *kill* me. 'And it also has Audrey Hepburn in it. So I figured . . . yeah. Beatnik.' Beatnik. Snowboarder. Whatever.

Hanna takes my hands and drags me inside, her perfect teeth gleaming at me in the low hallway lighting, already chattering about I don't know what. Her brother Raz regards me with amusement from the kitchen door, a book of intense Russian literature dangling from his hand.

'How's it going, Captain Sparrow?' he says.

'That's *Pirates of the Carribean,* you idiot,' Hanna fires off as she manhandles me up the stairs to the snug.

'Catch you later, Solzhenitsyn,' Raz calls after us, grinning.

There's a bowl of Twiglets on the table. Champagne glasses and lemonade. The lights are dimmed. There is a stuffed ginger cat sitting on top of the TV.

'It belongs to Linus,' says Hanna, snatching up the cat and throwing it at me. 'Seemed appropriate seeing how there's a cat in the film. Aren't you going to take off your hat? Not that it doesn't look good but, you know, we're indoors and everything, so maybe you don't need it.'

'Um,' I say, 'I wasn't planning—'

Hanna takes the beanie between her painted fingernails and plucks it from my head before I can protest.

'What do you think?' I say nervously as she gapes at me.

'I don't know,' she says at last. 'You don't . . . look like you.'

This is good, isn't it? Because Hanna would have to be *insane* to fancy someone who looks like me? Losing my

38

nerve beneath her scrutiny, I remove the hat from her fingers and cram it back on again.

'Better?'

She pats my hand like I'm a dog. 'Concentrate now, the opening scene is my favourite part.'

I can't relax with her leaning against me. I feel all hot down one side of my body. Any minute now and I'll start sweating again. I stare rigidly at the screen, at Audrey Hepburn climbing out of the scruffy yellow cab in her long black gown on an empty New York street, jewellery so heavy that it looks as if it'll snap her swan neck, chowing on a danish and takeout coffee. Hanna snuggles closer. Her hair is like a spun-gold vase on her head.

'I didn't know they did takeout coffee in the sixties. I thought that was a nineties thing,' I blurt.

'I've always wanted to know how she does her hair,' Hanna says. 'I've got a teacosy stuffed with socks under mine.'

I reassess her beehive.

'Linus's socks. They're really tiny,' Hanna explains. 'I put the stuffed teacosy on my head and then sort of wound my hair around it. That's how I got it up so high, like in the film. You wouldn't believe how many pins are in this thing.'

I start laughing. Well, gulping really. Then laughing because the gulping sounds so completely stupid.

'I'm sorry,' I manage between gusts. 'It's just . . . a tea cosy with socks?'

I mustn't cry because that'll make the guyliner run. I should know this because I've seen it happen to Hanna a hundred times.

'Don't do that laugh,' Hanna warns, her face breaking into pieces. 'Don't Sol, I can't . . . you know it makes me . . .'

We're both helpless on the floor in front of the TV by the time Holly Golightly is running up the steps to her New York brownstone with the sleazy fat guy pursuing her. Thank you, whichever gods are watching. I'm fine now.

Fine-ish, anyway.

Hanna

Sol looks completely different with darker hair. I'm glad he put his hat back on. He's done something to his eyes as well, for the beatnik thing. I didn't have him down as someone so into theme-dressing. It makes me wonder what he'll dress up as next time.

'Do you know,' I tell him as we munch through the Twiglets, 'that the guy who wrote the book wanted Marilyn Monroe to play Holly Golightly?'

'Too curvy,' says Sol.

'What's wrong with curvy?'

'Nothing's wrong with curvy, it's just . . . Holly Golightly shouldn't be curvy. That's all.'

'That's just you superimposing Audrey Hepburn on the character,' I tell him grandly.

We eat a few more snacks and neck the lemonade before it goes any flatter. I belch comfortably.

'I love the smell of half-digested Twiglets in the evening,' Sol says, wafting his hand around.

We reach the party scene. I have been swotting up about this film all week, so I now tell Sol in detail all about how the scene was a real party, with champagne and everything, and how the director just told them all to make it up as they went along.

'This lot would give Trixie and the other vixens a run for their money,' Sol says as New York's finest laugh and pose and play to the camera.

'Trixie's not a vixen,' I say. 'She's not clever enough.'

Sol raises his eyebrows at me.

'I don't mean that in a nasty way,' I say flushing. 'Trixie's all right.'

'Apart from when she airs her views on contagious homosexuality?'

'She doesn't mean any harm,' I say. 'She's just not majorly brainy.'

'I don't get how you two were ever friends at school.'

'We weren't, particularly. She mainly hung around with a bunch of girls who ended up at the private college out of town. You wouldn't have recognised her then. Her hair was mousy and she hadn't discovered fake tan.'

The chaos on the screen reminds me of Dan's New Year's Eve party.

'Dan wouldn't have dumped Holly Golightly for Lizzie Banks,' I say. 'Not that it was an actual *dumping*,' I add quickly. 'More of a *stealing*. Everyone knows Lizzie Banks is a maneater.'

'*I* don't know Lizzie Banks is a maneater,' says Sol. 'I barely know Lizzie Banks at all.'

I don't want to think about Lizzie right now.

'Shut up and watch the film,' I tell him.

When it's just us like this, the ache I feel for Dan fades a little. It would be nice if we could just shut the curtains and stop all the clocks, like in that poem in *Four Weddings and a Funeral*, and stay in here for ever, dressed like this, eating Twiglets and drinking flat lemonade from Mum's champagne glasses.

'We never did it, you know,' I tell Sol in a sudden burst of confidence. 'Me and Dan. We did other stuff but never . . . it.'

Sol screws up his face.

'I don't know why, because I'm totally into Dan and everything,' I go on. 'Maybe because I thought we had plenty of time. It's probably why he and Lizzie Banks hooked up. Do you know, Trixie caught her with my last-but-one boyfriend in the summer?'

'Stevie?'

I lean my head back on the sofa. Carefully. I don't want the tea cosy to collapse. 'Jake Molino. The summer before you showed up. *Stevie* was my last boyfriend. *Jake* was my last-but-one.'

'I thought Dan was your last boyfriend.'

I grab more Twiglets. 'Dan is not in the past. Not yet.'

'Is there anyone in our year you *haven't* been out with?'

I pull a face. 'I know it sounds bad, but it's just what we did. Don't tell me you weren't saliva-swapping with the best of them in California.'

43

God this film is good. It's amazing that it was made over fifty years ago. I don't say anything else until it gets to the part where Holly and Paul agree to spend a day doing stuff they've never done before. This is when I sit up and pay real attention, perhaps for the first time this evening.

'I *knew* Audrey Hepburn would have the answer!' I say triumphantly. 'We need to do a few things we've never done before, Sol. Just like they do in the film.'

Sol is still wearing the scrunched-up face he had on when I started talking about me and Dan and sex. 'Hanna—'

'I've been too passive about this whole Dan thing,' I continue. 'Nothing changes if you're passive about it. We have to get *active*.' I prod Sol in the belly to make my point. My fingers spring back at me like they just hit a trampoline. 'I could get Dan back. You could get . . . whatshername back. Assuming,' I add, 'you want to. Do you want to?'

'Mm,' he says.

I have been trying to get Sol to tell me about his ex ever since his New Year bombshell, but he never rises to the bait. It's really frustrating. Seizing his hand, I stare deep into his eyes. They are mossy tonight, not pondy. I think it's the guyliner.

'We're going out,' I say. 'Right after the film. Dressed as we are, to do things we have never done before. It doesn't have to be big stuff. Just to get the idea. You know, before we do anything life-altering. Say no and you're a chicken.'

SOL

Which is how I have ended up in the confectionery aisle of the supermarket at half past nine in the evening with two fingers of Fudge up my nostrils.

Hanna is peering round the corner into the main aisle. 'Someone's coming. I dare you to keep them in your nose until they go past.'

I'm enjoying this, in a weird kind of way. So far, we have juggled with cucumbers in the grocery section and played flip with packs of cheese slices. Hanna has pocketed three scourers and I have a copy of *Men's World* down the back of my trousers. If my confidence continues to build in this dizzying direction, I might take Hanna up on her challenge for real. I'm not bad at kissing, if Lucy Shapiro was telling the truth.

'There's two people,' Han tells me breathlessly. 'I can't see if they . . .'

She stops.

'What?' I ask thickly, fighting the urge to sneeze.

Her eyes are very wide when she turns round to look at me.

'It's Dan,' she says in a funny voice.

I whip the fingers of Fudge out of my nose. 'Is he alone?'

Hanna shakes her head.

'Is he with Lizzie?'

She shakes her head again. Like extras from *Mission: Impossible*, we peer round the end of the aisle.

Dan Dukas is wearing a beanie hat not dissimilar to mine, except that it looks good. His hair is dark and shiny, a few curls resting on his shoulders, and I can see his thick black eyelashes from here. He is holding a glossy magazine with dirt bikes on the front. The *Men's World* in my trousers makes me squirm as I realise how close I must have come to meeting him in the magazine aisle. Looking at him in all his manliness makes me remember that I am nothing but a skinny ginger loser, more likely to win the lottery than ever kiss his ex-girlfriend. I am relieved to be reminded of my status in the pecking order before I do something so stupid as to try.

Like Hanna said, the girl with Dan is not Lizzie Banks, who is dark and pale and tall. This girl is more fragile-looking, with burned caramel skin and long black hair pulled into a thick plait over one shoulder. She is looking up at Dan with big, disbelieving brown eyes as he winds her plait around his broad wrist and strokes her cheek with his thumb.

'I'm going to be sick,' Hanna says.

I check which shoes I'm wearing. 'You're not going to be sick,' I instruct. 'You and I are going to leave and not look back.'

'I have to talk to him. We agreed to take risks tonight. This . . . this is my chance to take that risk.'

'You said we were starting small,' I remind her. 'That we weren't doing anything life-altering tonight.'

Hanna looks pale but horribly determined. 'I know what I said.'

Juggling cucumbers is one thing. Talking to the object of her desire is something else. A sense of rebellion rises in my gut. *Hanna is mine tonight, Duck Ass.*

'You can't talk to him,' I say stubbornly.

Hanna is moving towards the main aisle. She mustn't walk into view in that black dress and remind Dan the Douche how gorgeous she is.

'Don't,' I say a little more loudly.

'I'm going to,' Hanna says. 'I have to.'

'You can't, because he's with *her*!' I hiss.

She stops in her tracks and gawps at me as if I have said something earth-shattering. I'm not quite sure what.

'Oh my God,' she says.

I . . . What?

She is by my side again, Dan apparently forgotten. 'Sol, I'm so sorry,' she says. Her hands are on my shoulders and her big blue eyes are full of concern. 'I know this is hard for you because you're so private and everything, but I want you to know that I totally support you here.'

47

'Right,' I say carefully.

'It's your ex-girlfriend, isn't it? With Dan? I can tell by your face.'

Hanna standing here, holding me and giving me the full force of her attention, is better than her going up to Dan Dukas. Much better. I feel myself relax.

'Mm,' I say.

Hanna closes her eyes. When she opens them again, I'm not entirely sure I like what I see.

'But this is incredible, Sol. Don't you realise, I *know* Carmen? We were at school together. She went to that private college I mentioned the other day, the one that's out of town, I haven't seen her in ages. Oh my GOD! You were dating *Carmen*? Why didn't you tell me before? Why didn't we all go out *together*, you and me and Dan and Carmen? You total idiot!'

I seriously did not think this through. This is a small town. Everyone knows everyone. I've been away for four years. Four long, extremely stupid years. Of course Hanna knows her. What was I *thinking*?

'So can we go?' I say, trying to recover.

'Then again,' Hanna continues, 'throwing Dan and Carmen together – oh my GOD I can't believe you were dating CARMEN! – any earlier and who knows what might have happened? So maybe it's for the best . . . Sol, I can't believe this!'

Dan Dukas is so close now that I can hear his voice. His conversation is a lot easier to focus on than my own right now. It's also unbelievably boring.

'. . . bought this carburettor, see, because my bike needed a new carburettor, because I totally *wrecked* it out in the woods, I just totally had the track pinned the whole way. Did I mention that I ride most weekends, I'm pretty good? You should come watch me, it would be fun.'

Carmen's voice is as quiet and shy as Dan's is loud and confident.

'I'd like that.'

Dan laughs a husky laugh. 'Of course you would.'

I have an awful feeling that they're snogging now, approximately six feet from our aisle. We have about ten seconds to get out of here.

'*Please*, Hanna!' I would get down on my knees, only that would slow our exit.

Hanna sighs. 'We've both had a shock so we'll head back to mine.' She juts out her chin. 'But this isn't over, you know.'

And by the time Dan and my 'ex-girlfriend' make it to the confectionery aisle, all that remains of our presence are two fingers of Fudge, a crumpled magazine and three pan scourers spinning gently on the floor tiles.

Hanna

7 FEBRUARY

I am still reeling about Sol and Carmen. I mean, *Carmen!*

She was sweet, Carmen. She was a person who always had time for you in the toilets when your hairspray jammed and you accidentally sprayed yourself in the eyes. I haven't thought of her in ages.

You know what the strangest thing is? Picturing my best friend kissing Carmen while I'm simultaneously talking to him on the phone. I'm honestly not *trying* to picture it, it's just – there. In my brain. Weirding me out.

Sol continues true to form. Not saying a word about it, no matter how many different ways I approach the subject. I swear, if you were to cut him, little padlocks would come pouring out of his veins instead of blood. He would never have told me about Carmen if I hadn't worked it out. I'm sure of it. This boy has taken mysteriousness to a whole new level.

'Anyway, I have a plan which should benefit us both. It involves Linus's ukulele and Dan's garage. It should be a guitar really, but Linus doesn't have one of those.'

'Look, Hanna, please don't.'

I attempt to push the image of Sol gently kissing Carmen – I know it would be gentle – out of my head. 'It's fine,' I say, adjusting the phone against my ear. I'm walking along the pavement towards Dan's house, the ukulele slung over my shoulder. 'It's not a hard song, and the uke is way easier to play than the guitar. I've practised it all week and it's sounding good. I even recorded it on my phone to double check I had the chords right. Do you know, they nearly cut it out of the film? Apparently Audrey's reaction was, "Over my dead body" so they kept it.'

'I'm coming over.'

'No need. Anyway, I'm at Dan's now. Fingers crossed, I'll have Carmen free for you again before this evening is out. Talk about win-win.'

I slide my phone into my pocket and stare up at Dan's house, with its big glassy wrap-around windows, and its huge double garage with the doors open to display Mr Dukas's convertible Porsche, Dan's dirt bike and Mrs Dukas's personalised silver Range Rover Evoque, all lit up for the street to admire. In all the time I've known Dan, I've never once seen the doors closed. I think the Dukas family consider it more of a showroom than a garage.

Dan has always had another purpose for it, sneaking out at night by climbing out of his bedroom window, across the garage roof and down the tree. He always promised to show me how to do it. Now I'm here, I reckon I can figure it out for myself.

I walk around the dark end of the garage and consider the climb. If I can make it on to the side wall, it should only be a brief scramble up to the lowest branch of the tree. I bend down to tighten the laces on my trainers, sling the ukulele a bit further back over my shoulder, and attempt to heave myself up the wall. It's harder than it looks, and I bark my shin.

I squint at the tree again. My leg is throbbing. If I jump and grab the branch I could heave myself up without using the wall at all. Maybe that's better.

I take a leap and grab the branch. It breaks off in my fist and I fall back, grazing my other shin on the way down. I almost land on the ukulele as I hit the ground with a lung-busting thump.

For the first time, I reconsider what I'm attempting here. It's certainly an active approach to getting Dan back. I have never serenaded anyone with a ukulele before, so Holly Golightly would approve. Then again, it *could* go wrong. But with only a week to go until Valentine's Day, it's my best option for getting Dan's attention. I have never been without a boyfriend on Valentine's Day, not since it started mattering. I'm not starting now. Plus, of course, when I get Dan back, that means Carmen is free for Sol to kiss, gently, once again.

I examine my bleeding shins and stand up.

'You know you could be had for breaking and entering. Not to mention a whole raft of health and safety issues pertaining to garage roofs.'

Sol is wheezing and panting and leaning forward with his hands on his knees by Dan's gate. He's clearly run the whole way here.

'Sol, thank God,' I say.

He straightens up with his hand resting on one side of his ribs. 'You're pleased to see me?' he gasps, a bit doubtfully.

'I need a leg up into this tree. It's harder than I thought to climb it.'

'Han—'

I put my hands on my hips. 'I'm doing this for both of us, you know. I get Dan, you get Carmen, assuming you want her, and seeing how she's completely gorgeous I'll assume you do. Dates for Valentine's Day. It's less than a week away now.'

'So?'

He's such a *boy*. Doesn't he understand how these things matter? I can just imagine what Vashti and Laura and Trixie would say if I was single on the most important day of the year.

'Fine,' I say. 'I'll do it by myself.'

I take another running jump at the tree. This time I am more successful, getting a firm grip at the base of a thicker branch. I swing my bottom up, and triumphantly wiggle my feet into the crook of the branches. There is a dull thud and the sound of splintering wood. My shoulder feels oddly unencumbered.

'You dropped your ukulele,' says Sol at the foot of the tree.

From my position in the tree, I contemplate the shattered instrument on the chequered brickwork of Dan's drive. I hope Linus didn't like it too much.

'It doesn't matter,' I say heroically. 'I'll use the phone recording instead. It might work better, actually. There's this tricky bit which I amazingly got right when I recorded it. This way, at least the song part of my plan will work out.'

Sol paces below, muttering incantations like some sort of druid, as I reach for the top of the garage and heave myself on to the felt roof. Dan's bedroom window is closed, and the light is on. My stomach fizzes.

'Still time to change your mind!' Sol implores from below.

'Over my dead body,' I say, channelling Audrey.

'Could happen!'

Loud music is pouring from Dan's bedroom window. I wonder a little nervously whether *Moon River* on a recorded ukulele will penetrate the booming bass. Still, I'm here now. Better give it a try.

I step out into the middle part of the garage roof. There is a ripping, tearing sound beneath my feet. Before I can even press play on my phone, I am plummeting into the garage, where I bounce off the roof of Mr Dukas's Porsche, slide sideways and downwards and smack my feet into Dan's dirt bike. There's an awful clang of metal as the bike keels straight into the passenger side of the Evoque and rips a hole right through the customised paint job. The level of destruction is instant and extraordinary, and on some level rather impressive. The sound of car alarms is deafening.

I am so shocked and winded, lying there sprawled on the garage floor, that for a moment, I think I'm dead.

Sol skids in through the open garage door.

'Ow,' I say in a small, breathless voice, looking at the blood on the palms of my hands.

'Han, look at me, are you OK, are you broken? Thank God for the Porsche's soft top, what's left of it. Can you get up?'

I stagger to my feet. 'My hands hurt,' I choke out.

Sol takes them gently. 'To call you stupid would be an insult to stupid people,' he says, tugging me out through the open garage doors.

'*A Fish Called Wanda*,' I say through my tears, stumbling after him. Everything else is starting to hurt now. 'Sol, I can't run this fast.'

'If you can recognise film quotes, you can run.'

The car alarms are still shrieking. Unbelievably, no one is running out of the house to scream at us. There are no blue police lights, no barking dogs. Not even a twitching curtain over the road. The neighbours in Imperial Avenue are plainly not into each other's business.

'Stop,' I beg as he tows me along.

I could let go of his hand. But making a decision like that is too much for me right now, plus I'm not sure my hand would hear my instructions through its own trauma. We keep running. I suppose I'm not dead, and nothing is

55

broken, except my pride and my palms and Linus's ukulele. So there's that.

Sol shoves me through his front gate and into his house. He practically gives me a fireman's lift into the kitchen, hurls me into a chair and dives for a First Aid box sitting by the sink. His parents look up, startled, from their dinner.

'Good night?' asks Andrew, his fork halfway to his mouth.

SOL

Through all of Hanna's pain, I can't help wondering what would have happened if Carmen had been at Dan's tonight. What if I'd had to explain about our non-existent relationship? Plus Hanna could have *killed* herself. I want to rant and rave and jackboot up and down the room. But it's hard to yell when she's looking so tearful and apologetic and pale, sprawled all over my duvet and shakily examining her bandaged hands.

'I'm really sorry about spoiling your parents' dinner,' she says.

'I think they enjoyed it,' I say. 'Listen, it's late and you're in shock. I'm going to call your mum and ask her to fetch you.'

Hanna looks at me with her big, blue, teary eyes. 'Is it OK if I stay?'

My brain skitters like an excitable horse. Hanna wants to stay? Here? Tonight? She hasn't stayed in my house since we were eleven years old.

'I think you got away with it,' I say out loud. 'I don't think anyone was in.'

She looks shocked. 'But Dan's music was on—'

'I don't imagine Dan Dukas ever gives his parents' electricity bill much thought,' I say. 'And no one came running at the noise, did they?'

Hanna examines her palms again. 'Please can I stay?' she repeats, a little more quietly. 'Mum will want to know how I ended up with hands like these and I've always been rubbish at lying. Oh God, I must have caused thousands of pounds' worth of damage in that garage.'

'Mr Dukas can afford it,' I say. I'm not feeling very charitable towards the Dukas family right now. 'Of course you can stay.'

I leave her texting her mum as I hurry out of the bedroom to track down the blow-up bed. *Don't get ambitious*, I tell myself. *She just avoided serious injury in pursuit of someone considerably further up the food chain than you. She doesn't need you slobbering all over her. She just needs you to fix her hands and talk to her about movies.*

I open the loft and climb up the ladder to get the bed, thinking hazy thoughts of me and Hanna alone in my bedroom. In a crucial moment of inattention, Nigel rockets past me on the ladder and vanishes into the loft.

'Last time he went up there,' Gareth says, coming up the stairs, 'it was three days before we got him down again.'

It takes me, Gareth *and* Andrew to fetch Nigel down from the gloom of the loft space. We only succeed because he shoots inside the sleeping bag I need for Hanna's bedding. By the time my parents have locked the cat in the kitchen and I have brushed my teeth so hard that I have made my gums bleed and returned up the ladder for the blow-up bed I should have fetched twenty minutes earlier, Hanna is out cold.

For one appalling moment, I wonder if she got an invisible head injury in that garage and has actually died. You hear about stuff like that happening all the time. My heart blams in my chest as I press my fingers against the base of her neck to check her pulse. I leave my fingers where they are for a few seconds longer than strictly necessary, then snatch them away because that is unacceptable, stalkerish behaviour.

'Is that who I think it is?'

I glance up at my laptop and its winking FaceTime light. Frank is peering with interest down the webcam.

'Well, it's not Lucy Shapiro,' I say. 'Oh, and keep your voice down. It's been a tough day and I don't want to wake her up.'

'Don't tell me, you're going to let her sleep there without making even the teeniest, tiniest move on her,' Frank says, a little more quietly.

'Some of us are gentlemen round here,' I say, and reach for the off button.

An artist once filmed David Beckham sleeping, for the National Portrait Gallery. I would love to do the same thing. Only not with David Beckham, obviously.

I apply myself to taking off Hanna's trainers and socks. No one should have to sleep in their trainers. Then I wrap my duvet around her as best I can, drop on to the blow-up bed and stare at the ceiling. It's going to be a long night.

SOL

10 FEBRUARY

Han and I see Lizzie Banks walking home from college, her shoulders rounded in on themselves and her head bowed to her chest.

'Hey Lizzie,' I say as we pass.

Hanna says nothing.

Lizzie walks on, her gaze firmly fastened to the pavement. Her long dark hair, normally worthy of comment, looks as lifeless as she does. I still struggle to match what Hanna has said about her with my own impressions. Guys talk about the 'easy' girls at college all the time, and it's not Lizzie Banks they talk about. Although she has been a topic in recent days.

We clear the railway crossing and take the road towards my house. I try not to stare at the passengers on the platforms, and do my best to ignore the way their stories are calling me: the shambling students and school kids at the end of their day among the older people dressed up for an evening in the city. It's probably the only time the two worlds collide.

'Lizzie looked awful,' Han says.

This is the first time I've ever heard Hanna *not* use Lizzie's surname. The alpha girls at college, the Trixies and the Vashtis, do it all the time when they talk about girls outside their own sphere. Is it a power thing? A way to define 'them' and 'us'? I've never liked it, and I'm glad Hanna's not doing it now.

Hanna fiddles with her fingerless gloves. She's taken to wearing them everywhere, to prevent questions about the plasters on her hands. I can tell she is chewing something over because she is uncharacteristically silent.

'Spit it out,' I say, as we reach my front gate.

Hanna brings her eyes back into focus. 'What?'

'Whatever's bothering you.'

'Nothing's bothering me.'

I unlatch my gate. 'Fine. See you tomorrow.'

'I should have said something to Lizzie,' Hanna blurts as I reach my front door. 'You don't know her, but you still said hi. I should at least have said that. We used to be friends when we were at school. Before she stole my boyfriend, anyway.'

This is news to me. Not once in the whole of last term did I see Hanna and Lizzie exchange a single word. Now I think about it though, Lizzie is a far more obvious friend for Hanna than Trixie. She's got more than one brain cell for starters.

'You and Lizzie?' I repeat.

'School was a long time ago,' Hanna says defensively. 'Can you even remember what you were doing in June?'

Running away from our favourite quarterback, after one of Mr Yamauchi's classes. Me and Frank spent most of the summer legging it through the scrub behind the high school, Frank's terror of scrub-dwelling snakes receding in the face of the more immediate threat of Chet Langdale's fists.

'Yes,' I say.

'Well, I can't,' Hanna says. 'School is a world away.'

'It's five minutes down the road,' I say. 'If I can remember California, surely you can remember Gordon Lane?'

'Shut up, Sol! And stop looking at me like that.'

'I'm not looking at you in any way other than my eyeballs are looking at your eyeballs,' I protest.

'You *are* looking at me,' Hanna mutters. 'I just wanted to say that I feel bad about not saying hi to Lizzie, and I don't expect to be judged, not by you.'

I let myself into the house thoughtfully. My figures are waiting for me, tucked beneath their protective box, precisely where I left them this morning. Her and him, neatly posed on the steps I have fashioned out of cereal-packet cardboard, against my painstakingly assembled background. I rig up the tripod, fix my phone to the base, check that it can take the whole scene from left to right. The desk lamp is angled, the paper car set to approach. I run the sequence one more time, test the minute adjustments I will have to make, assess the shadow play and work out the timings. Sixteen frames a second. Eight seconds should do it. A hundred and twenty shots, or so.

I think I know what my choice of movie is going to be this month.

It's got to be worth a try.

23 FEBRUARY

You've never *seen* it?

Nope. Any good?

An 80s classic. Molly Ringwald, Andrew McCarthy. Jon Cryer.

The uptight 1 from 2 and a 1/2 Men?

You'll like it.

Thought U wd pick Leap Year L

That piece of crap?

U love Leap Year!!!!

No Han, YOU love Leap Year.

Tell it 2 the hand! R we dressing up?

PRETTY IN PINK
(1986)

DIRECTOR HOWARD DEUTCH

WRITER JOHN HUGHES

Andie (Molly Ringwald) comes from the wrong side of the tracks, works in a record store for her older boss (Annie Potts), and hangs out with her best friend Duckie (Jon Cryer), who has a crush on her. When rich kid Blane (Andrew McCarthy) asks Andie out, she can't believe her luck. But as their relationship progresses, Andie realises that being with someone from such a different social sphere is not easy.

The filmtrack showcases many classics of the Eighties, including 'Pretty in Pink' by the Psychedelic Furs.

Hanna

29 FEBRUARY

'They arrested who?' I ask, midway through applying my electric-blue eyeliner.

'This Mexican band player,' Trixie repeats. 'You know those Mexican bands that go around playing in restaurants in big hats?'

'Mariachi?'

'*Mexican*, Hanna. Not Japanese. So I told Laura that I'd seen this band in town, and Laura told Vashti, and Vashti told Dan – sorry babes, hate to mention his name because I know it must still totally *kill* you to hear it – and the next thing this band player's like, being *questioned* about the garage break-in. God. *Mexicans*. You know, Laura's dad's wife's brother had his watch nicked in Mexico?'

'Trixie,' I say, trying to change the subject, 'does this outfit say real Eighties to you, or just Topshop revival?'

Trixie assesses my fingerless lace gloves, the boxy jacket I got out of the back of Mum's wardrobe, the frilly skirt.

'Totes for real,' she confirms. 'What is it for anyway, Dan's party? Oops, there I go again!'

I concentrate on adjusting my gloves. 'Dan's party is still some way off,' I say as casually as I can. 'I'm not planning for that yet.'

Trixie flaps her blue enamelled fingers. 'There's still *plenty* of time to get a date. You mustn't worry about it. It would be *awful* if you had to turn up to your ex-boyf's party without anyone else, but I'm sure that won't happen. Was Valentine's totally hideous?'

'I enjoyed it, actually,' I lie. 'I got an anonymous red rose and some chocolate.' I think Mum and James sorted out the rose and chocs. I haven't asked them because I want to think they were from Dan and I don't want to torpedo the dream.

'Stevie got me a cuddly bear,' says Trixie. 'It was so cute of him. Vashti thinks it's from this really expensive shop on the other side of town.'

I feel the sudden urge to compete. 'I got this homemade film,' I say. 'Totally anonymous.'

Trix looks interested. 'Like, a sext thing?'

I think about the little film on my phone, the anonymous email address that sent it. Eight seconds of stop-animation magic. The way the headlights from the tiny car move over the paper figures on the steps so that their shadows are apart, then together as if they are kissing, then apart again. It makes me feel soft and strange inside, thinking that someone made it for me. It must have taken *hours*. I've played it so many times, looking for clues. Slow-mo, backwards. Sol has forbidden me from showing it to him again or quizzing him on who he thinks sent it.

'Definitely not a sext thing,' I say.

Trixie reapplies herself to the blue nail polish. 'Chocs and roses and films are cute, hon,' she says, wafting her hand around to dry the polish. 'But they're not the same as an actual kiss from an actual boyfriend, are they? Stevie and I . . .' She looks coy. 'Things just got a little more serious at Valentine's, shall we say?'

I feel a flash of jealousy. I haven't been kissed in weeks. My lips are forgetting how to do it.

'Don't say anything to Vashti though,' adds Trixie. 'I don't want to get a reputation like Lizzie Banks.'

At least I avoided any activity that might show me in a bad light with the girls. I also avoided standing on a muddy slope in the polar-cold woods, waiting for three seconds of Dan Dukas to whip past and shower me with sand from his back tyre – assuming he's replaced the dirt bike I trashed just under two weeks ago.

I feel a teensy bit disloyal for thinking this.

'It is perfectly possible to live a normal life without a boyfriend,' I say.

'Course it is, babes,' says Trixie doubtfully. She has been dating Stevie O'Shea since the *Inferno* situation. 'What's this dress-up for anyway?'

'Movie night at Sol's.' I study the lippy that Mum's lent me. It's called Sweet Ice and is the weirdest blue-purple-white colour I've ever seen. She probably last wore it in

1987. 'We're watching this Eighties movie *Pretty in Pink* tonight. Have you seen it?'

'My mum is mad for Andrew McCarthy, he's the hero.'

'What does he look like?'

'Tall and dark,' says Trixie. 'A bit like Dan, really. Oops, you can't take me anywhere!'

I grit my teeth. 'Mariachi isn't Japanese, by the way,' I say.

'Mexican, Japanese,' says Trixie. 'What's the difference?'

SOL

'I was expecting a mullet at the very least,' says Hanna, getting comfortable on the sofa amid a crinkle of synthetic lace.

She's looking a bit odd tonight, curled and frosted like a toilet-roll cover in an old people's home, and with these awful pale lips like some kind of New Romantic zombie.

'What, the perm isn't enough?' I return, peering at her over the top of Andrew's old round sunnies. I almost ditched the pork-pie hat in a last-minute panic.

'Trixie's mum fancies the lead guy,' Hanna tells me as I try to calm myself by arranging the snacks: Walkers crisps, Smarties for the multi-coloured Rubik's Cube vibe and a fruit juice called Um Bongo. 'Andrew McCaffrey.'

'McCarthy,' I say.

'Is he hot? Do you think I'll fancy him?'

I adjust my round sunglasses and put a fistful of Smarties in my mouth as the credits roll.

For the first five minutes, Hanna is silent, her parted, shimmering lips resembling the belly of an exotic lizard as

Molly Ringwald picks out the weirdest outfit I have ever seen for a day at school. The soundtrack is good. Really good. Better than I remember.

'Is that him?' she asks, sitting up as the rich love interest appears at the top of the high-school stairs. 'Trixie's right. He does look like Dan.'

'This other guy is about to show up,' I try to say, with my mouth full of Smarties.

'I know you told me not to talk about it any more,' she says, turning away from the screen to look at me, 'but do you honestly think there is no way on *earth* that Dan sent me that beautiful little film? He is good with his hands, he could have made that little car, he's into cars.'

I swallow the Smarties. I don't want to know how good Dan Dukas is with his hands.

'He's not into cars,' I say. 'He's into bikes, or what's left of them when you've finished smashing them up.'

We have missed Duckie's entrance. The Um Bongo tastes like the contents of a chemical toilet and turns my tongue a strange and unattractive colour. I'm not sure I can face too many more Smarties.

'Ooh, James Spader! What a doll,' says Andrew, appearing with fresh supplies of crisps as the villain makes his appearance in a cloud of hairspray and a jacket so sharp he could whet his cheekbones on it.

I remove my sunnies and polish them glumly on the hem of my shirt. 'Go away, Andrew.'

'Must I?'

Hanna giggles at Molly Ringwald's enormous glasses.

'Andrew?' Gareth calls from the kitchen. 'Your cat won't let me near the fridge.'

'Always *my* cat at the most inopportune moments,' grumbles Andrew, getting up from the back of the sofa.

We have silence for the next half an hour. I snatch a glance at Hanna every now and again. I should tell her about the film. My film, I mean. She loves it; she's obviously keen to know who sent it. I dwell hopefully on the notion that she gasps, and wells up, and then maybe runs away because she's confused, before running back again (in the rain, ideally) and—

'God he *is* like Dan,' Hanna says as Blane asks Andie for a date.

Scrap that. It's too much of a risk. Much better to stay mysterious. Maybe she'll work it out for herself. Oh God, there's another load of anxiety right there. How long until she works it out? What if she loves the film but doesn't like the guy? What then? The best relationship in my life, gone.

Duckie is now professing his love for Andie on the screen.

'Face it, you little weirdo,' says Han. 'You don't stand a chance. Listen Sol, you know Lizzie?'

I take a deep, calming breath. 'What about Lizzie?'

Hanna studies her fingerless gloves. 'Everyone's saying she slept with Dan.'

I think about recent conversations I have heard. 'I know,' I tell her.

Hanna frowns. 'I don't have sex with him and I get

71

dumped. Lizzie does, and she gets dumped. What does Dan want?'

'The hunt,' I say.

Dirtbags like Dan Dukas hunt, catch, discard. Either because the quarry won't have sex, or because the quarry will. There is no middle ground. Nice guys hope sex comes along when it comes along. Sooner rather than later, of course, but still – they have the manners to wait. If the one they want is worth it.

'He didn't hunt me,' Hanna says.

'He scooped you from under Stevie O'Shea's nose.'

'The other bit of the hunt, though,' Hanna says. 'The sex bit of the hunt.'

I take off my sunnies and rub the bridge of my nose. 'Did he ask you to sleep with him?'

'He didn't ask, exactly. He just acted like he thought I would. And I would have,' she adds. 'Eventually.'

'Dan Dukas doesn't understand long words like "eventually",' I say. 'Sex or no sex, the boy has the attention span of a goldfish.' Saying 'sex' to Hanna is making me feel odd.

'Do you think if I slept with him now, he'd like me again?'

'For an intelligent person,' I tell her, 'you ask some very stupid questions.'

We're quiet for a while. The movie rolls on.

'I feel bad for saying this,' Hanna confides, 'but Trixie's really thick.'

'You and I both know Trixie Logan is the dimmest lightbulb in the building, Hanna.'

'Am I being really snobby?' Hanna looks worried. 'We've been friends since we were twelve, and all I can think about at the moment is how stupid she is.'

'I thought you said she hung out with a different group at school.'

'She did, but a bit with me and Lizzie too. Then, when college started, she was the only person I knew apart from you.'

'And Lizzie,' I say.

'And Trixie knew Laura and Vashti and everyone.'

Hanna has a thing about that word. *Everyone*. Like Vashti Wong and Laura Hamilton represent the entirety of the world.

'A lot can happen between the ages of twelve and sixteen,' I say. 'As I think we have already established. Is Trixie annoying you because she's thick, or is she annoying you because she's annoying?'

Hanna gives this deep thought. 'Annoying,' she concludes. 'Do you remember what she said on the phone that time?'

'I'm hardly likely to forget,' I say.

'She had a go at Mexicans earlier too.'

'Right,' I say slowly. 'Because . . .?'

'According to Trixie, they're interviewing a local Mexican band about the Dukas garage thing.'

'You can't take a ukulele anywhere these days,' I say.

Hanna puts her arms round me. 'Thanks,' she says into my neck. 'You always know what to say.'

73

I savour the moment, breathe her in, and choke a little at the hairspray fumes. Would it be weird if I kissed her now?

She releases me before I can decide. We get back to the film. Somehow we are already at the part when Andie is chopping up her best friend's dress. Hanna squints at the mess of pink satin and lace.

'That dress is awful,' she says. 'Truly *awful*. I know this is the Eighties, but was that a good dress even then? She looks like Barbie's laundry bag.'

Within ten minutes, the Psychedelic Furs are blasting away any final remnants of hope that I may have had of making this evening a turning point in my relationship with Hanna Bergdahl.

'Good choice,' Hanna says, stretching like a cat. 'Not sure what life lessons we learned though, other than "avoid spectacle lenses the size of frisbees". Andrew McCarthy's hair looked weird at the end, don't you think?'

'It was a wig,' I tell her sadly. 'They had to reshoot the ending and he'd already cut his hair for another part.'

'I *knew* it looked weird. Why did they reshoot it?'

'In the original ending, Duckie got the girl.'

'Duckie is so clearly gay,' Andrew says, drifting past the living-room door. Nigel is tightly wedged under his arm and not looking happy about it.

'He isn't gay,' I protest.

'He's gay, Solomon. The gay best friend. So obvious.' Andrew hands Hanna her coat with his free hand. Nigel hisses and squirms.

74

Hanna pulls on her coat and presses a cloud of rock-hard frosted curls against my cheek. 'Are you going to Dan's birthday party?' she asks on the doorstep. 'Will you go with me? Please Sol, I know I'm always asking you to parties you don't want to go to, but I really need your support. Trixie and Vashti and everyone are going, there's going to be a live band and real champagne and everything.'

'You're on your own with that one,' I say with feeling.

Hanna makes a funny gasping sound. 'Oh God, I'm so sorry! You're worried Dan is still with Carmen, aren't you? I'll find out for you, OK? If he is, then I totally understand if you don't want to come. If he isn't, will you come with me then? Please?'

'Who's Carmen?' asks Gareth, appearing at the top of the stairs.

Han gives me a look that says a thousand different things: sorry for landing you in it by mentioning a girl your parents know nothing about (funny, that), please please change your mind about my ex-boyfriend's party and help me out, thanks for the conversation about my thick friend, I remain completely ignorant that I love you in the wrong way.

'Who's Carmen?' Gareth repeats.

'Bye, Han,' I say as I shut the door.

In my room, I pick up the box containing my paper figures, my cardboard steps, my little car, my collaged background, and I put on the lid, and with some force I shove it as far into the back of my wardrobe as it can go.

Hanna

27 MARCH

Mum is in my room, holding what remains of a black velvet dress. She's normally so cool and calm, never a hair out of place, make up just so. Now she has two pink spots in her normally pale cheeks and there is a line of sweat on her top lip. This roughly translates as: the angriest I've ever seen her.

'What were you thinking?'

I try to formulate an answer. 'It . . . you . . . I needed . . .'

Mum shakes the black velvet at me. 'I *loved* this dress.'

'You never wore it,' I say anxiously. 'I didn't think you'd mind.'

The pink spots on Mum's cheeks grow pinker. 'I wore it on one of the most precious evenings of my life. The night I first went out with your stepfather. The night which began this whole phase of our lives, Hanna! You may not remember that, but I *do*.'

Right. Not good, then.

'You're always going on about how we buy too many clothes and why don't we just use the clothes we've got, and

76

I thought it would be nice to give that dress a new lease of life,' I say, in the most placating voice I can manage.

'By cutting half of it off?'

The dress is a lot shorter. Not quite half the dress it was, but almost. I feel thin ice cracking beneath my feet.

'Mum,' I plead, 'I honestly thought you wouldn't mind. It was right at the back of your cupboard where you keep the stuff you don't wear any more.'

Mum buries her face in the black velvet bodice and doesn't say anything.

'And you're normally really cool about me borrowing your clothes and everything.'

'Borrowing,' says Mum in a muffled voice. 'Not *destroying*.'

'I haven't destroyed it,' I say. 'I've customised it. I needed something classic for Dan's party tomorrow night and I can't turn up wearing the same as everyone else, and so I thought—'

Mum looks up. 'You cut up my favourite dress for your ex-boyfriend's party?'

'Not *totally* ex,' I say, scenting danger. 'I mean, he's not out of my life all together. We still talk.' In the corridor at college for two seconds as he walks past and I say hi and he says hi and a bit more of me dies inside.

'You cut up my favourite dress for your *semi* ex-boyfriend?'

The ice is caving. My feet are slipping.

'I know it sounds bad when you put it like that, but—'

Mum's voice is deadly quiet. 'And you think you are going to this party?'

I gulp. 'I . . . Yes?'

Mum folds the dress over her arm. She strokes it like it's a wounded animal. 'No party,' she says.

Crack. I actually do feel as if I have just plunged into the coldest water in the world. I can't breathe from the chill. Mum is banning me from the most important party of the year?

'But,' I manage to say, 'I *have* to go, it's unbelievably important that I'm there because it's Dan's . . . because . . . everyone is going—'

There is icy blue fire burning deep in Mum's eyes.

'No party,' she repeats.

No. NO NO NO.

'I'll sew the dress back together!' I say helplessly. 'It'll be like those broken plates that Chinese people consider extra special—'

'It is not a plate, Hanna. It is a Donna Karan.' Mum pauses. '*Was* a Donna Karan. There will be no party. You will stay at home while all your friends are out, and you will think about how other people's possessions matter just as much as your own.' She frowns. 'You used to know that.'

I can't move. I can't even close my mouth.

Mum gives the dress over her arm one last sorrowful stroke.

'I'll wash James's car for a month if you let me go,' I beg.

But my bedroom door shuts as quietly as the door of a tomb.

I sit down on my bed and try to keep my hammering heart under control. I shouldn't have cut up the dress, that

78

much is clear. The trouble is, I have been seeing Vashti and Laura and Trixie in new dresses in my head for *weeks*. Every outfit I saw on the high street last weekend had little whispering goblins all over them saying, *Vashti got me in the blue*. The thought of appearing in the same dress as Vashti made me feel too ill for shopping. I've got enough to worry about with the Dan thing.

Had enough to worry about.

My life is officially over.

SOL

28 MARCH

'I feel,' I insist, 'like an absolute idiot.'

'You look fantastic,' says Gareth, patting me on my white-tuxedoed shoulder. 'Like a young James Bond.'

'I look like a kid in a grown man's clothes. Wait,' I add, pointing at Andrew. 'I *am* a kid in a grown man's clothes. *Your* clothes.'

'It fits like it was made for you,' Andrew says smugly.

I silently pull Andrew's beanie on. I'm growing quite fond of it.

'It'll do you good,' Gareth says. 'Get you out of the house.'

'I'm not a dog or a pensioner,' I say.

'Come on, Sol! You might have fun. And you promised Hanna you'd go.'

Yup. I did. Sol the doormat, the Bond-alike in the glitzy white jacket, ready for action once again. And I won't even have Hanna by my side to sugar the pill this time. I glare ferociously at myself in the hall mirror. Only Dan Dukas would be so pretentious as to insist on white tuxes tonight.

'Is Carmen going to be there?' Gareth asks casually.

This whole Carmen comedy routine is something else Han owes me for.

'Probably,' I say, seeing no other way round the question. 'Given that she's going out with the host.'

'You'll be fine,' Andrew says in a soothing voice.

'Yeah,' I say awkwardly. 'Thanks.' Even I'm starting to believe that I once had a relationship with this girl.

Gareth tucks something crinkly into my tux pocket and pats it. 'Can't be too safe,' he says.

'Go tiger,' Andrew adds.

Oh God. My parents have just given me contraception.

'Never wink at me again,' I say. 'Either of you.'

As I pull the door shut, I hear Nigel yowling like the Cat of the Baskervilles in the kitchen. Andrew and Gareth have promised the neighbours they'll keep him in tonight because he sprayed on their front door yesterday. The answer to all of this is obvious, but Nigel's balls remain sacrosanct.

Thank you so much, Sol, you're a total hero, I love you beyond words, have I told you that?

'She loves me beyond words,' I repeat to myself, turning down the street and past Hanna's road and past the station and up Imperial Avenue, where cars are slowly turning in and out of the Dukas driveway like a great steel and rubber carousel. The driveway is full of white jackets and brightly coloured dresses, the garage doors wide open to display the Dukas family toys, whole again: a Porsche with a new roof, an Evoque with a fresh paint job and a dirt bike with very little dirt on it.

Beep.

On FaceTime, Hanna's eyes are large and red-rimmed and there's a spot on her chin.

'Have you seen Dan yet?' Her eyes dart all over the screen. 'Has Vashti asked where I am? Is Dan with Carmen? Are you OK?'

'I've just arrived, Hanna. Give me a chance.'

Hanna cranes her neck as two girls in short black dresses wiggle past me. 'It looks awesome,' she says in despair. 'I can't believe I'm not there. I'd sneak out, only Raz is in charge tonight and in the worst mood I've ever seen. He's acting even tougher about this grounding than Mum. Honestly Sol, I think I'm going mad. I didn't sleep a wink last night, worrying about all this. Not a *wink*.'

I'm still annoyed that I've come here tonight. Why am I such a sap? I need to grow a backbone, and soon, or there will be way too many more parties just like this one on my horizon.

'Have you been worrying about the party, or your mum's feelings about her dress?' I demand.

'Don't lecture me, OK? I feel awful enough about everything without you going on at me too.'

I'm in no mood to cut Hanna any slack. 'Imagine how you'd feel if someone came in and cut up one of your most precious possessions. Have you even said sorry?'

'Of *course* I've said sorry! Who do you think—'

She stops, bites her lip. Falls silent.

'I can't believe I'm having to point this out,' I say.

'Nor can I,' she says, in the smallest voice I've ever heard her use. 'I'm a really horrible person, aren't I? I don't deserve to be at the party. I don't deserve to be at another party, ever again.'

'Apologise to your mum or I won't tell you anything about tonight,' I say. 'Not a word.'

I slide the phone back into my pocket, where it crinkles embarrassingly against Gareth's condom.

I realise, as I approach the front door, that people are looking at me strangely. Glancing around, I see that I'm surrounded by couples. I'm so used to going places either by myself or with Han that bringing someone else didn't occur to me. I don't mind being alone, personally. It's other people who seem to have a problem with it.

'Hey, gay boy! No date tonight?'

Dan Dukas is raising a slopping champagne glass to me. Carmen is standing beside him, in a jawdropping red dress that clings to every part of her. She looks a bit lost.

'Your mates were all busy,' I say. 'Hi,' I add to my not-ex-girlfriend as Dan tries to work out how to respond.

'Hello,' says Carmen shyly.

I feel as if I ought to know her. If it weren't for our not-relationship, I'm sure I wouldn't have said hello. Now I'm grinning at her and she's grinning back.

Dan indicates me with his glass. 'This guy has two dads,' he tells Carmen.

'I have two penises as well,' I say. 'You can have one if you like.'

I just said 'penises' in front of a pretty girl I've had a non-relationship with. The irritation I'm feeling for Hanna is giving me wings.

Dan looks puzzled. 'I already have one, thanks.'

'Good to hear the rumours aren't true,' I say. 'Nice to meet you, Carmen.'

'What did you say, gay boy?' Dan calls after me as I move into the hallway. 'What rumours?'

There's an air of suppressed wildness in this crowd as they stand around waiting for the adults to leave so the party can really get started. The white tuxes look universally terrible. I sneak a glance at myself in a hallway mirror, and feel glad that I've kept the beanie on.

Stevie is by the champagne. 'You seen Trixie?' he asks me.

I shake my head.

He looks relieved. 'Me neither,' he says. 'Where's Han?'

'Grounded,' I tell him, taking a glass of juice. Carnage is always around the corner at Dan's parties. I like to stay sober in case I need to find a fire exit.

'Nice one,' Stevie says, though I'm not sure what's so nice about it. 'Sol mate, Trix has told me to get her a drink and join her in the other room but some of the boys are having a kick-around in the garden. Will you do the honours?'

I dutifully take Trixie's glass to the other room. It gives me a sense of purpose. All the girls at the party seem to have

84

decamped in here. I can see one other guy, looking panicked by the fireplace in the overcrowded room. There's no way out from over there.

Trixie looks like a tin can, all corrugated steel pleats and glittery cheekbones. She's right in the thick of a group of girls in other metallic shades: gold, silver, bronze. I feel like I'm at the modern equivalent of a joust.

'Where's Stevie?' says Trixie as I hand her the champagne.

'In the little boys' room.' I like Stevie, as far as these things ever go. 'He won't be long.'

'Hi Sol,' says Vashti Wong.

The other girls giggle.

'Hi,' I say cautiously.

Vashti's coal-black eyes are glittering. Maybe it's the silver eyelashes reflecting in her pupils. 'Loving the tux,' she says. 'It fits you really well.'

She reaches out with silver talons and squeezes my arm like she's testing it for ripeness. The other girls giggle harder.

'No Hanna tonight?' Vashti asks me.

'Didn't you hear, Vash?' says Trixie in hushed tones. 'Hanna Bergdahl has been grounded for cutting up her mother's most expensive dress, it was, like, a thousand pounds or something.'

Again with the surname thing. How many Hannas does Trixie know?

'She wanted to impress Dan,' Trixie continues. 'It's a bit sad really because Dan is *so* over her.'

Vashti is still standing uncomfortably close. 'It's nice to see you by yourself for once, Sol,' she says, her fingers trailing up and down my tux sleeve. '*Are* you by yourself?'

'I didn't bring a date, if that's what you mean.'

She leans a little closer. Her breath is hot against my ear. 'Got to love a lone wolf,' she whispers.

I feel more like a rabbit in the glittering headlights of an oncoming car. Vashti is pretty, but there's something hard about these girls that makes me nervous. I know if I don't leave now, I'll be trapped in here for ever like the poor bastard by the fireplace.

I attempt to leave. Vashti places her palm flat against my chest, right on my tux pocket. The condom crinkles cheerfully. I know that she knows that's what it is.

'What's the rush?' she says, holding my gaze.

This girl is practically asking me to sleep with her. I've hardly spoken three words to her in my entire life. Who says the guys are always the predators?

SOL

It's a relief to get back into the hallway. All I want to do right now is go home and plan a set of paper figures for a new film. I think I'll make them joust, but instead of lances they are going to use guys like me.

I take another juice and head out on to the wide deck with its view of the back garden. The guys are playing football around the lion fountain, which stands squarely in a space otherwise perfect for a pitch.

Stevie's tux has been tossed into a nearby flowerbed. 'Keeping Trix out of trouble?' he calls up at me. 'I owe you.'

If you piled up everything everyone owes me right now, I think, *it would make a decent heap*. 'No worries,' I say.

'That girl's more trouble than she's worth,' someone else shouts across the gloom.

'Piss off,' says Stevie cheerily.

Jake Molino jumps up and down by the fountain, clapping his arms to his sides to keep warm. 'Has anyone seen Vash tonight?' he asks. 'Apparently she's acting like one of those heatseeking missiles off *Octopussy*. Once she's locked you in her sights, you won't get away. I need to find that girl.'

Some of the boys cheer, and boot the ball a bit harder.

'She just locked on to me,' I say.

They all laugh uproariously.

'On to a winner there, isn't she?' Stevie says.

'I'm not gay,' I say. Only I don't say it loudly because, frankly, I can't be bothered with another conversation about my sexuality.

Vashti doesn't think I'm gay, I remind myself. *Or if she does, she thinks she can bring about a miraculous conversion.*

Beep.

I take out my phone.

'I've been crying my eyes out for nearly an hour,' Hanna says wanly. 'I need to talk to Mum only she's out tonight until late so I have to wait. It's like torture.'

'You'll cope,' I tell her.

She nods and wipes her nose. Snot trails across her face. Sometimes I wish FaceTime hadn't been invented.

'How's the party anyway?' she asks.

'Terrible. Do I have to stay much longer?'

'Leave whenever you want. You don't have to do anything I ask, ever again. Is Dan still with Carmen?'

'He was when I arrived. That's not to say he still is.'

'Thanks,' she says forlornly. 'You know. For putting up with me.'

'I'm not the one whose dress you cut up,' I point out.

88

'I realise that,' she says with a grimace. 'Are you still up for movie night this month, by the way?'

'Why?' I say, suddenly anxious. 'Do you want to cancel?'

Hanna shakes her head. 'No. Do you?'

'No,' I say.

'Good. I thought maybe you wouldn't want to hang out with me after . . . you know. Everything.'

'Han,' I say, 'don't you know me at all?'

'I don't think I do, really,' she says.

I wonder what she means. 'So we're still on for the movie?' I prompt.

'Yes,' she says. 'I picked it ages ago, but I'm thinking maybe of changing to something else. *The Fisher King* or *Atonement* or something like that.'

'Don't drown in remorse here,' I say. 'Pick whatever you like. I'll be there.'

I head back inside through the big glass doors, where I see Vashti Wong with her arms around Dan Dukas, her face buried in his neck and his hands firmly round her bum. They seem oblivious to the fact that Trixie and the other girls are gathered nearby in a tight circle, pretending not to watch. Carmen is nowhere. The atmosphere is uneasy, excitable. Everyone knows something important is happening.

My blood amps up to boiling hot. I don't know if it's because I'm jealous, Vashti having made it clear that she wanted me half an hour ago, or just furious on my not-ex-girlfriend's behalf. Maybe it's both. Or maybe it all goes back to Han and New Year. Whatever the cause, I find that I am utterly blind with rage, and Dan Dukas is the focus.

Life in the States may have failed to give me an accent, but it taught me two things: how to run, and how to fight. When you're the skinny ginger English kid with gay parents, these are useful skills. My calf muscles propel me through the crowd like I'm attached to some kind of gas canister. I feel my hand bunching up, my elbow pulling back. I am powerless to stop whatever the hell I think I'm doing as I power my fist into Dan Dukas's jaw.

Dan squeals. Vashti springs backwards, her mouth open in a shiny plum-coloured O. Trixie and the girls are screaming. I push through everyone as though they are paper figures of my own making, intent on leaving as fast as I can. What was I thinking, coming here in the first place, acting as Hanna bloody Bergdahl's personal love scout?

I cannon into someone right outside the front door. She's crying and her eyes are almost as red as her dress. She's all alone. Horrified, I catch her before she crashes into the shrubbery.

'Carmen?' I say. 'God, I'm so sorry, I wasn't looking where I was going. Are you OK?'

Carmen doesn't recognise me at first. Of course, she's only met me once, briefly, when I told her I had two willies.

'How do you know my name?' she says, wiping her eyes.

Interesting point. Dan didn't actually introduce us.

'I'm a friend of Hanna's.' Whom I hate and love in equal measure right now.

Carmen opens her beautiful, sad eyes very wide. 'Hanna from school? Hanna Bergdahl?'

The shouting inside the house is getting louder. Now that the red rage has faded, and my hand has started killing me, I realise that I ought to leave before I get slapped with a charge of GBH.

I take Carmen's arm. 'I'll walk you home if you want,' I say, glancing a little anxiously over my shoulder. 'I'm guessing you don't want to stay?'

She shakes her head. 'I have a coat,' she says. 'Red. It's inside.'

Of course it's inside. Taking a deep breath, I dive back into the confusion, keeping my head down, getting flashbacks to New Year. Damn, my hand is throbbing like Dan's dirt bike at full throttle. Thank God the coat's red. I spot it immediately, and drag it from the pile before anyone sees me and lynches me from the banister.

'Here,' I say, as I sling the coat round Carmen's shivering shoulders. 'Let's go.'

'What's happening now?' she asks, glancing back at the chaos inside.

'Something we're best out of.'

Carmen walks quickly. She's not wearing ridiculous heels like the ones Hanna and the other girls insist on wearing to parties like this. Her shoes are flat and sparkly instead, and sit neatly on her long brown legs. It's only a matter of moments before we reach the same bus stop where Hanna and I stopped in the snow at New Year. When . . . nothing happened.

'Nice shoes,' I say. Could I remind her any more plainly that I have grown up in a single-sex household?

Carmen looks at the way I'm flexing my fingers by my side. 'What's the matter with your hand?'

'I kind of . . . punched your boyfriend,' I confess.

She gasps and puts her hands to her face. 'Does it hurt?'

'It's nothing,' I say, even though the bloody thing's killing me. I'll have to wrap it in ice as soon as I get home.

We walk on. Carmen is looking at me with more and more interest. I'm feeling a little heady with the attention.

'You know my name,' she says. 'But I don't know yours.'

'Sol,' I say. 'Solomon.'

'Solomon,' she says, as if testing the sound.

My name sounds exotic in her very beautiful mouth. Did Hanna honestly think I could have dated someone this gorgeous? I feel almost proud.

'Did you punch Dan for me, Solomon?' she says next.

I think carefully about how to answer this.

'If I say yes,' I say at last, 'will you think I'm violent and weird? Because I'm not. I don't know what happened back there, to be honest.'

Oh my God. One of the prettiest girls I have ever met has just slid her hand into mine. She's keeping it there too, holding very still. My hand doesn't feel like it's hurting so much any more. A bubble is growing in my chest. I think I will be adding a knight to my paper joust.

We walk along a bit further. Carmen is taking us up Hanna's road, I realise.

'Do you live here?' I ask warily, looking at the familiar front doors as we pass.

'Not far from here,' she tells me. 'Solomon, thank you for rescuing me tonight. No one has ever done anything like that for me before.'

She pulls her hand from my hand, places both palms on my cheeks and kisses me. She actually kisses me right there, in the street.

Wow.

She tastes of warm honey. Her tongue is soft, her mouth is pliant. Her hair is thick in the fingers of my uninjured hand. I haven't kissed anyone since Lucy Shapiro, not even a melon. But I discover that it's not something you forget how to do.

Hanna

I don't think I have ever felt this low. Not when Dad left, not when Dan dumped me, not when I missed half that GCSE paper because I didn't turn it over. This is the bottom of the pit.

On FaceTime, Sol looked pretty good in his beanie and white tuxedo. He might even get with someone tonight, seeing how he's without me round his neck for once. If he does, I hope it's just a party thing and not a girl who he wants to date. The way I feel right now, I don't think I could handle him dating anyone.

I turn off the overhead light, sit on my bed, lower my head to my pillow and gaze at the paper solar system hanging from the ceiling. Sol and I made it at primary school. I've never taken it down, even though the planets are wonky and Sol's little Sharpie-d ping-pong moon is hanging on by a thread and the polystyrene Sun is so big that I bang my head on it if I ever jump up from the bed without thinking. Saturn is twirling in the breeze from my half-open window, its badly cut-out paper ring listing heavily to one side. Outside I can hear a normal Saturday night in full flow without me. I could drop off the world and no one would realise. They'd all be like, 'Oh Hanna, yeah, self-absorbed cow wasn't she, no great loss.' It's depressing to think that Sol's the only one who might miss me. Why don't I have more friends? Could it be – I don't know – *because I'm the most horrible person in the entire world?*

I should call Mum. Get all this off my chest. Only, she's out with James on one of their monthly evenings together, in a dress I haven't cut up yet. She won't want to hear from me tonight. She probably never wants to hear from me again.

I head downstairs. Raz is on the sofa with his nose in *Crime and Punishment*, a bottle of beer clamped firmly in his hand. He looks washed out.

'I'm going to clean the fridge,' I announce as I pass through the living room on my way to the kitchen.

'Why?'

'Because it needs cleaning.'

It does. The shelves are thick with grime. The cheese needs rewrapping, the ketchup and mayo bottles need wiping. The salad drawer is swimming in old lettuce leaves and there are a couple of yoghurts practically walking out the door by themselves.

I meticulously arrange the edible foodstuffs on the kitchen table, dispatch the rest, slide out the greasy shelves and put them in the sink with a hefty squirt of washing-up liquid. I snap on a pair of Marigolds. I might clean out the cutlery drawer next. It's not like I have anything else to do tonight.

Raz drops his book on the kitchen table beside an assortment of crusty condiment bottles, where it makes a sizeable bang. 'I'm reading *Crime and Punishment*,' he says, taking a swig from his beer. 'I know guilt when I see it. This is about Mum's dress.'

'It's about the *fridge*,' I say.

Raz sits at the kitchen table and glares at me as I scrub the shelves and condiment bottles in silence. What is with his mood at the moment? Outside, I can hear bangs and crackles. Dan's birthday fireworks, just a few streets away.

'Raz,' I ask at last as I arrange the freshly polished jars and condiments in the fridge in order of size, 'what's the worst thing you've ever done?'

Raz examines his beer bottle. 'Dumping Leah by text is probably up there,' he says. 'Although it seemed appropriate in the circumstances.'

I pause with a pickle jar poised in mid-air. 'What do you mean, you dumped Leah?'

Raz gives a thin smile. 'Not sure I can say it any clearer than that, Hanna.'

'Why did you dump her?'

'I caught her sexting someone else.'

I sit down. 'OMG, Raz. Who?'

'Oh, this is the good part,' says Rasmus. 'Jono.'

'As in, your best friend, Jono?'

Raz gives a humourless laugh. 'Not my best friend any more,' he says. He flicks at the pages of his book with the ridge of his fingernail. *Brrp.*

Rasmus without Jono is like chips without salt; Rasmus without Leah, sky without sea. The balance of the known universe is gone.

'I never liked either of them,' I say feebly.

Rasmus dips his head at my lie. 'I'd better not get back together with them then, had I?'

I think about Dan. About Lizzie. About best friends, and how, when they betray you, it hurts worse than anything.

'Would you?' I ask. 'Get back with Leah if you could?'

Raz looks tired and sad. 'I hope I wouldn't be so stupid. But the heart and the head have different rules.'

I replace all the fridge shelves, make myself a cup of tea and trail upstairs to my room again. I desperately want to call Sol for an update on the party, but at the same time I can't face it.

My curtains are still open on to the street. I set my tea on my desk and, reaching up to draw them, I see two figures outside curled around each other like cats' paws. She has a scorching red dress on. He's wearing a beanie and a white tux. There's nothing gentle about their kissing at all.

I yank the curtains together. The sudden movement proves the death knell for Sol's ping-pong moon, which drops off its little thread with a tiny *plink* and rolls under my bed. I close my eyes and slide down the wall and bury my head in my knees. Hope the sudden, sweeping sense of nausea will pass before I puke on the carpet.

31 MARCH

Are we watching a movie tonight?

Han?

Earth to Han *taps mic*

Sure

Rein in your excitement.

We don't have to do the movie if you don't want to?

Stuff on my mind

Got a better offer?

What?

Its OK if U dont want 2

Have you been eating cheese again? You know it screws with your mood.

WHEN HARRY MET
SALLY (1989)

DIRECTOR   ROB REINER

WRITER   NORA EPHRON

In 1977, college graduates Harry Burns (Billy Crystal) and Sally Albright (Meg Ryan) share a car ride from university in Chicago to New York, during which they argue about whether men and women can ever truly be strictly platonic friends. Harry and Sally meet several times over the next ten years, and attempt to stay friends without sex becoming an issue between them.

The songs performed for the film by Harry Connick Jr brought him his first Grammy award for Best Jazz Male Performance.

SOL

Hanna must know I punched Dan. As she would say, *everyone* knows, judging from the social media storm of the past couple of days. Why hasn't she told me she knows? I wish she'd just come out and say that she's mad at me. Then we can clear the air and get back to normal. But I am apparently supposed to work it out by myself from her snippy texts. So, I decked the man of your dreams the other night, Hanna. I'm sorry, OK?

If she keeps this up, tonight is going to be a blast.

As if this wasn't enough to worry about, I have also spent most of the past forty-eight hours wondering when Dan Dukas is going to lay assault charges on me. It's not his style to forgive beta males who punch him on his eighteenth birthday. He's obviously got other plans. This is giving me a tension headache like you wouldn't believe.

And then there's Carmen. Beautiful Carmen Mendoza. Who is unaccountably into me. We've spent most of the weekend together. Half of me is as taut as a kite string in a gale thanks to Han's weirdness and my imminent arrest and imprisonment, while the rest is soft and loose and relaxed. It's an unsettling combination.

Hanna's brother answers the door on the second ring.

'Well, if it isn't Mohammed Ali,' he says. 'Didn't think you had it in you, bro.'

I wonder whether to take my beanie off, and decide to keep it in place. I feel the need for armour tonight. 'Sorry to hear about Leah,' I say.

'Shit happens,' Raz tells the beer bottle in his hand. 'My sister is in the living room.'

My stomach twists uncomfortably. Why am I here? Hanna made it clear in her texts earlier that she wasn't bothered either way. I'm suddenly feeling glad I haven't dressed up.

Hanna hasn't dressed up either. She is punching a cushion into submission on the sofa as I enter the living room.

'Sit,' she says. 'I'll fetch snacks.'

I sit as instructed. I'm feeling quite scared, to be honest, as she clatters around in the kitchen. The opening of crisp packets and the pouring of snacks into ceramic bowls has never sounded so loud.

'You thought better of *The Fisher King*, then?' I say into the silence when Hanna comes back and plunks the snacks hard on the coffee table.

'Guess I did,' she says.

We sit and watch two old people talking about love, straight to camera. I wonder if it's a real couple with a real story or just actors, and take out my phone to check. Reading movie facts has to be more comfortable than sitting motionless beside someone who hates my guts.

'Texting someone?' Hanna asks.

I put my phone away. We watch another half an hour of the American Film Institute's twenty-third funniest film in the history of American cinema in silence. Around the point where Harry meets Sally in the New York bookstore, I can't stand it any longer.

'I'm sorry I hit him,' I say.

Hanna takes a handful of snacks and crunches them.

'When I saw him dumping so publicly on Carmen, something snapped.' A police car whirls down the road, blue lights going. I feel myself going rigid until the woo-woos fade away into the night. 'I really am sorry.'

Hanna says nothing until we get to the paprikash scene at the museum.

'Lucky Carmen's dad is who he is,' she says eventually.

As Carmen's non-ex boyfriend, I know exactly what Hanna means. As a confused person in the real world, I have absolutely no idea.

'Mmm,' I say.

'Mmm,' Hanna repeats. 'A useful word that, isn't it, Sol? A word that means nothing and says even less.'

'Mmm,' I say again.

'That's it?' Hanna asks.

What else does she want?

The atmosphere hasn't lightened at all. If anything, Hanna has become even more glacial. We keep watching the film with grim determination. Even the soundtrack, which can usually be depended upon to cheer anyone up, isn't helping. I wonder if I can make my excuses and leave before the final credits roll.

We get the final New Year's Eve party at full volume: the music, the razzmatazz. Harry running into the building, ready for the rest of his life to start as soon as possible.

'Call her if you want,' Hanna says. 'Don't let me stop you.'

I look at her warily. 'Call who?'

Hanna's blue eyes don't blink. 'Carmen.'

The world might know about me punching Dan, but I haven't told a soul about Carmen. I certainly haven't told Hanna. How does Hanna know about Carmen? *I* barely know about Carmen.

'Why would I call Carmen?' I say weakly.

Hanna's gaze is withering. 'I saw you snogging outside my front door.'

I feel myself flushing bright red, like I've just been caught with my pants round my ankles. Hanna *saw* us? That feels – weird.

'Friends call each other.' Hanna brushes hard at some invisible dust on her jeans. 'They tell each other things like this.'

'I *do* tell you things!' I protest.

I don't tell her things. I never, I suddenly realise, tell her things. She tells *me* things. She tells me things all the time.

103

I feel myself blundering around like a bear in the dark. I am not enjoying this conversation.

Hanna snaps off the TV with a flick of her wrist as Sally tells Harry just how much she really, really hates him.

'I guess we'll never know how it ends,' I say into the silence.

An ill-timed joke, even by my own standards.

Hanna

5 APRIL

I've been having that dream a lot lately. The one where Dad's leaving. He turns round at the front door with his suitcase and I scream because he has the head of a fish and his round alien mouth is blowing bubbles instead of words. I only have it when I'm really down, when everything in my life is complete crap. I haven't had it since Lizzie and Jake last summer.

I refuse to be sorry that I stuck with my original choice of film last week. It was a film about friendship, after all. It made a point. An *important* point. But I can't make the evening go away. The whole thing just keeps playing over and over in my head like a crazed weasel with a mousetrap on its tail. I gave him so many chances to tell me about Carmen and he didn't say anything until I put him on the spot. That's not friendship. That's just rude.

I feel more betrayed than when Dan kissed Lizzie. I'm not exactly swimming in friends. Sol is the only decent one I have. Vashti and Laura only tolerate me because I hang around with Trixie, the way Lizzie and I tolerated Trix when we were all at school. I don't like this change of dynamic much. When did I lose the power? Now, with no boyfriend and no Sol, I am getting the strangest feeling that there's no one in my life but me. I guess that fits neatly with the self-absorbed thing Mum and Sol and everyone else think I've got going on.

I take out my phone and scroll down my list of contacts. There's not a single name on here who I want to talk to. Not one. Is that a reflection of me or them?

I scroll back a bit and press a number.

You're through to Lizzie. Leave a message if you want.

'Um, hi Lizzie, it's Hanna here. Hanna Bergdahl.' I pause, wondering why I've called and what I want. 'Just checking that you're OK,' I say before the pause gets too long. 'Call me maybe? Only if you want.'

One weird message to someone I haven't spoken to in months. The sum total of my social life right now.

I could kill Sol.

Beep.

Do you want me to sing like Harry sings to Sally in the film? I'll sing if you want. I don't recommend it though.

I smile. Just a bit.

I'm sorry. Please talk to me.

106

Just because I'm furious at him, doesn't mean I can't text him.

> Your apology is a start.

What else?

> Go to hell.

calls cab *pays extra to cover melted tyres*

I'm not prepared to defrost just yet. I'm about to switch my phone off so I'm not tempted into one of our ping-pong text marathons when it rings.

'Hi Hanna.'

'Lizzie?' I say, stupidly. I wasn't expecting her to call back so fast. To tell the truth, I wasn't expecting her to call at all.

'I got your message.'

Her voice sounds thick and congested. I am taken straight back to when we were fourteen and she was crying in the toilets over Hugo Jackson.

'Um, how are you?' I say, groping my way into the conversation.

'How do you think I am?'

'Feeling a bit shit?' I venture.

'Give the girl a prize.'

'Is it, um . . .' This is a tough question but I ask it anyway because, apparently, I like putting my own fingers through a paper shredder. 'Is it because of Dan and, you know, Carmen, and . . . everything?'

'Are you asking me that to be nice?' Lizzie enquires. 'Or is this going to turn into one of those conversations that will screw me over?'

'I wouldn't do that,' I say.

I hear her blowing her nose on the other end. 'Hanna, I don't know what you would do nowadays. We haven't spoken since the summer.'

Dan and Jake hang between us like ghosts.

'Dan made the move on me, by the way,' she says into the space left by our thoughts. 'Not the other way round, like everyone seems to think.'

I think I know this. I think I have known it for a while.

'I'm guessing he made the move on Carmen and Vashti too,' I say.

'You don't say.'

'So,' I say after a moment. 'Apart from that, is college going OK for you?'

'Fabulous. You?'

'Couldn't be better,' I say.

We both laugh thinly because I think we know we're talking out of our backsides.

'How's your brother?' Lizzie asks.

'Acting a bit weird, to be honest. He dumped his girlfriend for cheating on him with his best friend a couple of weeks ago.'

'Nice,' says Lizzie.

I crush the urge to say something pointed about best friends getting off with boyfriends. It's way too late to get into that now.

'He's too hot to stay single for long,' Lizzie says. 'Half the girls in college are in love with Rasmus.'

'Are you still going to be an architect?' I ask.

'Ask my maths tutor after the exams. You?'

'I don't know,' I say. 'It's starting to worry me.'

'You're clever. You'll figure it out.'

'Glad someone's confident,' I say.

There's a pause.

'I know Dan started it,' says Lizzie awkwardly, 'but guess I should apologise about it anyway. I didn't think we were friends any more, so it didn't seem that much of a deal at the time. But maybe it was. So – sorry.'

I swallow the lump in my throat and wait for her to mention Jake and the summer party thing.

'Tell me about the guy you're always with,' Lizzie says instead. 'Are you seeing him?'

No apology for Jake then. I guess it was a long time ago. It had seemed so important at the time, but now Jake was just Jake, someone I can't believe I ever went out with.

It's weird trying to explain Sol to Lizzie, but I give it my best shot.

'So you're just friends and you don't fancy each other,' Lizzie says eventually, 'but you're mad that he's dating Carmen?'

'I'm mad that he didn't *tell* me he was dating Carmen,' I correct. 'They've dated before, and he didn't tell me about that either. I'm surprised Carmen's dad permits it. Do you remember how she was never allowed out at weekends?'

'That was because of her horse. She was always eventing and mucking out and whatever else you do with horses.'

'Handy, don't you think?'

'Are you're saying that Chief Constable Mendoza gave his daughter a horse to stop her going out at weekends?'

'That's exactly what I'm saying.'

'I'm glad my parents didn't think of that,' says Lizzie, with feeling.

'That's the trouble with having a police officer for a dad,' I say. 'No one is better placed to know what teenagers really do at weekends.'

I am feeling more relaxed than I have in ages. How have we left this conversation so long?

'So if the chief of police is prepared to buy his daughter a horse in order to stop her going out with boys,' Lizzie says, 'you're wondering how Carmen has been allowed to date Dan and Sol?'

'Oh, Dan's easy,' I say. 'Mr Dukas and Chief Constable Mendoza are friends. Who better to date his daughter than his golf buddy's son? Sol is . . . just Sol.'

'I don't imagine Mr Dukas and Chief Constable Mendoza are still golf buddies,' says Lizzie. 'Would you stay friends with a guy whose son so publicly dumped on your daughter? Parents have feelings too.'

I get an ugly flashback to Mum and the dress.

'And with Vashti bitch-face Wong of all people,' Lizzie adds.

I don't say anything.

'Sorry,' says Lizzie after a moment. 'I know she's a friend of yours.'

'Not a friend exactly,' I say. 'More a political ally.'

'Probably sensible having her on your side. Take it from someone who isn't.'

'Are you angry with me?' I ask, bracing myself.

Lizzie exhales in a long whistle of air. 'I'm bloody furious. You dumped me like an old dog by the side of the road. One minute we're best friends, the next you're blanking me in favour of a shiny new gang.'

I clutch the phone very tightly. 'I'm sorry,' I say. 'Trixie was saying things, and that first week in college was really confusing—'

'Trixie was saying what?'

I might as well say it. Clear the air.

'You know,' I say. 'About you and Jake in the summer.'

There is a deathly silence on the other end of the phone. And I know what I should have known all along, that Lizzie and Jake never did anything at all.

'Lizzie?' I say, worried. 'Are you still there?'

'Don't bother calling again,' she says.

And I'm left with the dialling tone and six months of Trixie Logan's lie booming in my ears.

SOL

She hasn't replied. I thought it was quite funny too, the bit about the tyres.

I shouldn't be thinking about Hanna, seeing how I'm about to meet Carmen. She hasn't found me out as a boring loser yet, but if I keep this up she soon will. I bring her thick, dark, incredible-smelling hair to mind, to help me focus.

The moment my phone rings, I snatch it up. I knew that tyres joke would pay off.

'Solomon?' says Carmen.

'Hi,' I say, surprised.

'Can we change the plan? My father wants to meet you.'

'Your father?' I repeat.

She sounds embarrassed. 'I'm sorry, he is very protective.'

I'm suddenly picturing Mr Mendoza as one of those Victorian boxers in a tight vest with a huge waxed moustache.

'Is he scary?' I enquire, hoping that Carmen will laugh.

'Yes,' she answers, simply.

It only takes fifteen minutes to walk to Carmen's house. It felt like about three the night of Dan's party, but I think I was flying on adrenalin and astonishment. Now I need some extra time to gather my thoughts. I'm already in just the place.

'Give me half an hour,' I say, eyeing the station footbridge steps. There's nothing like diving into other people's lives for a while, to get your own into some perspective.

'Thank you,' she says. 'He's at the station.'

I freeze, one foot on the bottom step. 'The *railway* station?'

'The police station.'

'And he wants to see me?'

'Yes. By yourself. Sorry. Text me when it's over, OK?'

The footbridge is windblown, but I lean my forearms on the railings as usual and rest my chin on my joined hands and attempt to calm myself down. The platform below is busy, the train to London just pulling in. There are couples kissing, old ladies squabbling, a guy wrestling with a fold-down bike that refuses to fold down. There's even a flash of black as a cat flies across the platform. It looks a bit like Nigel. I try to clear my mind and think about stories and angles. I pull out my phone and film for a while, zooming in on interesting faces and hats. There is a seed of an idea in my head for a storyline that would combine real footage with my usual stop-animation. I hope I stay alive long enough to make it happen.

'Mendoza,' I instruct Siri, holding my phone close to my mouth to cut out the wind. 'Police.'

'*Alex Mendoza was appointed Surrey's chief constable in February 2012. He began his career in the Metropolitan Police Service before moving to the National Criminal Intelligence Service as a detective superintendent. In 2002, he transferred with an unblemished record to Surrey, where he oversaw several countrywide initiatives before a brief transfer back to the Metropolitan Police in 2009. He was awarded the Queen's Police Medal for distinguished service in the New Year Honours 2010.*'

Oh my God. Carmen's dad is RoboCop.

Chief Constable Mendoza regards me from behind his large brown desk. His hands are massive. Seriously enormous. They could wipe out continents.

'So you are the boy who defended my daughter last week,' he says.

'I guess,' I say. 'Sir,' I add, as an afterthought.

He seems to like this. 'My daughter is very taken with you,' he says. 'I am sure you won't take advantage of her gratitude.'

'I would never do that,' I say, affronted.

The chief of police leans forward. 'I am not a man to trifle with,' he says.

For a wild moment I imagine his desk covered in jelly and custard.

'I'm not a guy who takes advantage of girls.' I do my best to hold his gaze. 'Sir.'

'*Dead or alive, you're coming with me.*' Han would know

that quote. *Don't think of Han,* I instruct myself. *This guy can probably read minds.*

Chief Mendoza studies me in silence for what feels like eighteen months, but is only three seconds according to the clock on the wall behind his enormous head. 'These are the rules,' he says at last. 'No dates on weeknights. You do not take my daughter anywhere in a car. You do not take my daughter to a pub. You do not drink alcohol in my daughter's presence.'

'I'm don't drink, sir,' I say. 'I'm only seventeen.'

'You do not endanger her,' he continues as if I haven't spoken, 'humiliate her, or put her into any situation which will reflect badly on me. Are we clear?'

I think about the assault charge I've been expecting from Dan Dukas. Something tells me Carmen's dad won't be processing it any time soon. I try to feel comforted, which is an improvement on terrified.

'Clear as glass, sir,' I say.

He gives a nod. 'Carmen's expecting you at Costa,' he says, looking back down at a pile of stuff on his desk. 'Don't be late.'

I think I'm dismissed. *Serve the public trust, protect the innocent, uphold the law.* Back outside, I text Carmen as instructed. My phone rings. I pick up with shaky fingers.

'You were right about your dad,' I say.

'What about my dad?'

I really need to get these calls in the right order. 'Sorry Hanna, I thought you were Carmen.'

The airwaves drip with icicles. 'Sorry to disappoint,' Hanna says stiffly.

115

'Can we start again?' I say quickly before she hangs up. 'I'm sorry for not telling you about Carmen sooner. But it had only just happened and—'

'Whatever. Sol, I really need to talk to you. Something bad has happened. Well, something bad happened months ago actually and I need to sort it out. Can we meet?'

Right. Awkward.

'I'm kind of on my way to meet Carmen at Costa now,' I say.

'Oh,' says Hanna. It's an 'Oh' that cuts me like a blade.

'But we can meet later if—'

'Forget it.'

She's gone. Should I call her back? I ought to call her back. I will call her back. No, wait – I'm still too close to the police station. I can't call another girl when I'm on my way to a date with the chief of police's daughter. He would *know*. He's *police*. There'd be this . . . cheaty smell on the wind, blowing through his office window. I think of his huge hands again.

But Hanna sounded worried. Not 'I don't know what to wear' worried. Not even 'Dan is kissing Lizzie Banks' worried. Properly disturbed.

I call her back as I turn on to the high street. There's no answer. Part of me feels a tiny bit relieved. She can't accuse me of not trying. I attempt to convince myself that it's just one of Hanna's standard emotional crises. For once, she's going to have to sort it out on her own, because I have a DATE.

I'm so deep in thought that I find I have been staring at a waving Carmen in the window of Costa for a full three seconds before I remember to wave back.

Hanna

'Nice phone.'

I bring my gaze back into focus. 'What?'

Vashti taps my Android with a long red fingernail. 'I said,' she repeats, 'nice phone.'

I weigh up the correct answer. 'Thanks' is probably fine, but I'm not entirely sure Vashti means 'nice phone' when she says 'nice phone'. 'It's a piece of crap but it'll do' is risky because she might actually mean 'nice phone' when she says 'nice phone'. 'I wish Mum had bought me an iPhone' is probably what Laura would say, so maybe I should say that, except I do genuinely like my phone and it was quite expensive. 'Nice phone yourself' could cut both ways: Vashti might think I'm taking the mick, or she might appreciate the matey approach.

I haven't settled on an answer when Vashti turns to Laura. They talk about mutual schoolfriends for a while over their skinny lattes and I am forgotten. And that's OK. I have a lot on my mind right now.

Trixie appears, clacking through the canteen in a pair of sparkly flats that I saw in a shop window in town over the weekend and wanted for myself. My heart squeezes into a tight little stone in my chest. I tried to call Trixie on my nice/not-nice phone straight after that awful conversation with Lizzie yesterday – well, straight after my almost-as-awful conversation with Sol – but she didn't pick up and I never worked up the courage to call a second time because, to be honest, I hadn't figured out what I was going to say. 'Trixie, did you lie to me about Lizzie and Jake in the summer?' sounded too blunt in my head. Sol would have known what to say, but he was obviously too busy snogging Carmen over blondies and gingerbread lattes to call me back.

'Hi babes,' says Vashti. 'Nice shoes.'

'Thanks,' says Trixie, looking pleased.

'I almost got them myself,' says Vashti sleekly. 'Only there was a better pair in The Courtyard so I got those instead.'

She twists one slim ankle for us to admire her very classy silver flats with diamante straps. I'm now glad I didn't use the 'Thanks' response to Vashti's phone statement.

'Move up, Hanna,' says Trixie after a moment. 'God, I can hardly move this morning. This weekend was *insane*.'

Laura laughs at something Vashti is saying. Both girls fail to pick up on Trixie's conversational cue.

'What's the joke?' I ask as Trixie takes a long sip from her skinny latte cup.

Vashti waves a hand. 'Just something Dan told me yesterday in the woods.'

She and Laura smirk and giggle, and Trixie shoots me one of her sympathetic looks. I look down at my coffee. I really hate skinny lattes.

'Trix, your hair is awesome today,' Vashti says.

Trixie puts her hand to her tonged black curls and smiles non-committally. I can tell she's not going to make the same mistake twice.

'Han,' she says to me, 'did I miss your call yesterday? I would have answered only I was doing this *totally* insane thing and I *totally* forgot to call you back.'

I'm in no mood to step into the gap left by Vashti and ask about Trixie's weekend insanity.

'Trix,' I begin. 'You know Lizzie?'

Trixie looks surprised. 'Lizzie Banks? God, I don't know why you're asking about *her* after what she did to you.'

An image of Lizzie kissing Dan – Dan kissing Lizzie – flashes into my brain.

'You remember in the summer?' I go on.

Trixie throws a sideways glance at Vashti and Laura. 'The summer was *awesome*, wasn't it? We had *so* much fun. Remember Stevie's pool party?'

'Well, you know how you said about Jake and—'

Lizzie's familiar gait shambling down the corridor catches my eye and I stop. Her gypsy skirt is so long it's trailing the ground. Her boots peep out from underneath the ragged red hem like two large black beetles. She doesn't look in my direction, even though I know she knows I'm sitting here. I feel upset and angry all at once.

119

'God,' says Vashti. 'What is Lizzie Banks *wearing*?'

'Halloween was six months ago,' says Trixie.

'Five, actually,' says Laura, glancing at Vashti.

I try again with Trixie. 'You know how you said in the summer—'

'Trix?' says Vashti, resting her hand on Trixie's bony wrist. 'Do you want to come to the woods tonight? Dan's on the track.'

Trixie colours with pleasure. 'God, I'd *love* to!' she says, as if watching Dan Dukas blast around the woods, slobbering over Vashti between laps, is her ultimate delight.

The look Vashti gives me next feels less like an invitation and more like a challenge. 'You can come too, Hanna babes,' she says. 'But only if you want. I'd hate it to be awkward for you.'

I imagine Steve McQueen flying through the Alps on his Triumph 6 in *The Great Escape*. Dan's dirt biking would be more fun if they threw in some barbed wire and a selection of angry German soldiers. I look again at Lizzie's back.

'Love to,' I say, forcing myself to take a sip of my latte. It's thinner than Laura's freckled arms.

SOL

Han looks half frozen to death, standing on my front step in the dark.

'Can I come in?' she says through chattering teeth.

I shut the door in her face and run up the stairs three at a time. My latest batch of paper figures are all over my room: on my desk, on the floor, on the bookshelf. I'm not making a film for her this time, but Hanna wouldn't have to be Einstein to see the figures and work backwards a couple of months.

Frank is on my desk, in a manner of speaking.

'What's the rush?' he asks, leaning closer to his webcam. 'Hey, are those your new pieces? Can I see? Mine always turn out more praying mantis than human. I've gotten so frustrated that Mr Yamauchi has put me back on rabbits.'

I throw my figures into their box with more haste and less care than normal. 'Don't you have a life of your own?' I say as I shove the incriminating box to the back of my wardrobe and grab my phone off its tripod.

'Lucy Shapiro has it in this little glass snowglobe, like the ones you get from London with the Towers of Parliament.'

'Your love scheme is never going to happen, Frank,' I say. 'The sooner you accept that, the sooner we can all move on with our lives.'

I shut Frank down, fold up the tripod and charge back down the stairs. Hanna is halfway down the road by the time I open the door again. Maybe shutting the door in her face just now was unwise, but what else was I supposed to do? She'd have seen *everything*.

'Hanna!' I bellow.

I chase her down the road despite the fact that I don't have any shoes on. The pavement's cold and the neighbours two doors down have a very large dog who craps out here of an evening, which might give some indication of how strongly I feel that Hanna mustn't leave. Then Nigel springs at me halfway down the road and clamps his teeth around my bare ankle, before flying away again like a vampire in the dark.

At least she stops walking at my wail of pain and looks back. Her face crumples. She comes towards me and I pull her into my arms and hold her. Her hair is ice cold against my face. Damn, my ankle hurts.

'Did I come at a bad time? Is Carmen with you? I wondered if . . .' She looks up into my face and blushes. 'You looked so shocked and you ran up the stairs . . . I thought maybe Carmen was . . . you know. In your room.'

I picture Carmen on my bed. I picture Chief Constable Mendoza's face.

'Her dad would kill me,' I say.

Hanna looks relieved. 'She was really lovely at school,' she says. 'I'm glad you're back with her. I'm sorry I've been so weird about it. I think it's the fact that you kept it a secret from me. Promise you'll never keep secrets from me again?'

I imagine my films and my figures burning a small hole in the side of my wardrobe.

'I'll try,' I say.

I take her cold fingers and pull her back down the road towards the warm yellow light of my hallway. Why the hell isn't she wearing a coat?

As soon as we get inside, Hanna cries for a solid five minutes. I stand there and wait, feeling terrible. How much can happen in the space of one week?

'Tea?' I suggest when she stops.

She sniffs gratefully. 'Do you have proper fat milk?'

We take the tea up to my speed-blitzed bedroom, where Hanna tells me everything. I do my best to keep up, but she loses me somewhere around Trixie's flats.

'So,' I say, backtracking to the last bit that made sense, 'you called Lizzie?'

'And it was so nice, you know? We were just talking like we always used to, and then I said what Trixie said about her and Jake in the summer.' Hanna sighs and takes the tissue I'm handing her. 'And it was completely obvious that she never did what Trixie said she'd done with Jake, and what kind of friend was I to think for a minute that she had? Because she knew I was going out with him and she would never have done that. As soon as I said it I knew I was wrong, but she'd hung up on me by then and—'

'Take me back to these flats you said Trixie had,' I say. 'Is she renting them out or something?'

Hanna stares at me, and then starts laughing. It takes about five minutes for her to get herself back under control, during which she bangs the table with her fist and repeats the word 'flats' a lot.

'God,' she says, wiping her eyes with the tissue and taking a sip of her milky tea. 'You're such an idiot.'

'I know,' I say. I'm no clearer on the flats thing.

'Do you think Carmen will find this weird?' she asks when the tea has been drunk and we're lolling on my bed. 'You and me?'

I take a piece of her hair and wind it round my finger. It slips away like water. Carmen's is thicker and springier – something to do with being curly, I guess.

'Carmen will be fine,' I say. 'I don't know about her dad.'

This last is a joke, but Hanna looks worried. 'Don't tell me I can't see you like this any more, Sol, I think it would kill me,' she says earnestly. 'You have no idea what it's been like without you.'

It's nice to feel wanted. I allow myself to luxuriate in the feeling. 'Honestly, Han,' I say, 'it's fine.'

'Have you told her about me? What has she said? Does she remember me? She's so pretty and nice.'

'So are you,' I tell her.

Hanna shakes her head.

'Han, you're perfect,' I say patiently. 'You have amazing hair, and you're kind, and you have straight teeth, and you're funny, and your eyes are like sapphires held up to the light, and you have a fully functioning body. These are all things to be proud of.'

'I'm not perfect,' Hanna moans. 'I'm self-obsessed. I'm a bad friend.'

'Well, yes, but—'

'You're not actually supposed to *agree* with me on that!'

'What do you want me to say?' I protest. '"You're none of those things, babes"? You and I both know that's not true.'

She looks oddly stricken. 'Don't call me babes,' she says.

'I thought it was the way girls talked to each other.'

'You're not a girl.'

'You noticed, babes?'

'Please don't joke about it.'

It looks as if she might cry again, so I stop. It's so nice having her here, and not feeling my usual urgent need to jump on her and lick her face. Finally, friendship without any lurking subtext. Hanna can thank Carmen for that.

She gets off the bed. 'I'd better go,' she says.

If she goes, I'll be able to get my figures back into position and maybe even get a few seconds of film in the can before dinner. There's a backlog of college work I need to focus on as well. It's getting harder and harder to care about that aspect of my life at the moment.

'Sure,' I say, getting up too.

'Fine,' she says. 'I'll go then.'

'Isn't that the general idea of "I'd better go"?' I say.

She is still hovering in the doorway of my room. To my horror, I realise there's a little paper figure lying on the carpet just behind the door.

'I should call Lizzie again, shouldn't I?' she says.

If I do more than glance at the incriminating paper figure, Hanna will follow my gaze and see it too.

'I apologised to Mum about the dress. And I make a point of asking Mum, James and Raz how they are every time I see them now. They thought it was suspicious at first but they've got used to it,' she said. 'So that just leaves Lizzie. I'm really trying not to think about myself all the time like you told me.'

I have no memory of telling her that.

'Great,' I say, while thinking: *Please don't look at the floor. Please don't open the door any further either, because you will crush that little guy and I'll have to make another one and they take bloody* ages.

'Thanks, Sol. For everything.'

She steps forward, missing the little figure by inches, and hugs me.

'Film night at mine in a couple of weeks,' I remind her, detaching myself.

'What's it going to be?'

'A classic,' I promise.

24 APRIL

> But isnt it really old?

I said it would be a classic.
Classic usually means old.

> Is it sad?

Devastating.

> Does any1 die?

They all die inside.

> Will wear waterproof mascara!

Wear jaunty hat. Posh accent
essential. Got to go, sorry.

> CU on Sat?

Out Sat.

> Sun?

Talk tomorrow.

> OK! Pip pip & tally bongo!!

> (Talking to myself I see!!)

BRIEF ENCOUNTER (1945)

DIRECTOR DAVID LEAN

WRITER NOEL COWARD

Returning home from a shopping trip to a nearby town, married housewife Laura Jesson (Celia Johnson) meets virtuous doctor Alec Harvey (Trevor Howard) at the train station. During their weekly visits, their casual friendship soon develops into something more emotionally fulfilling, and they must face the potential havoc their deepening relationship would have on the lives of those they love.

The screenplay is based on Noel Coward's 1936 one-act play *Still Life*, and the film heavily features Sergei Rachmaninov's Piano Concerto no 2.

Hanna

4 MAY

Once again, I am standing at Devil's Turn getting covered in sand. At least it's a nice evening and the coat thing isn't an issue. The sun is striping through the tall pines, buttery fingers linking through twiggy ones.

'Trixie,' I say. 'Have you ever seen *Brief Encounter*?'

Trixie adjusts her enormous, bug-like sunglasses. She's standing in a shady bit of the woods so I'm not sure why she needs sunglasses on at all. 'What's that, hon, a *YouTube* show?'

'It's a film,' I say. 'It's really sad. And really famous. I watched it with Sol the other day. It's about these two people who are married to other people but fall in love at a train station.'

'Do they wear anoraks like those weirdos with binoculars and notebooks?'

I think about Celia Johnson's perfectly positioned hat and the awful grief on her face as her friend prattles on and Trevor Howard leaves her for ever with a silent hand squeeze on her shoulder.

'No,' I say.

Vashti is standing alone beside us in sunglasses even bigger than Trixie's.

'Are you OK, Vash?' Trixie asks sympathetically.

'Why wouldn't I be?' Vashti says.

Trixie cocks her head. 'It must be really hard for you, seeing Dan and Laura. You're doing really well. I can't believe you came tonight, actually. Some of the things people were saying online, I can't believe how nasty people can be.'

'I was getting bored of him, to be honest,' says Vashti.

'Course you were, hon,' says Trixie, and pats Vashti's arm.

Jake Molino screeches up the hill towards us. He stands up in the seat for our benefit and revs his engine. Vashti pulls down her own sunnies and shoots him an X-rated look over the top. This spot on the dirt-bike track isn't called the Devil's Turn for nothing. Jake almost hits a tree.

'Dan Dukas is history,' Vashti says, sounding satisfied.

Steve blunders up the slope behind Jake.

'Go Stevie!' Trixie screams. As Stevie roars past us with a wave, she fiddles with the scarf around her neck. 'Stevie bought me this yesterday,' she confides to me, just loud enough for Vashti to hear. 'It's really nice that he's still so crazy about me after five months, isn't it? Oops, sorry Vashti,' she adds, making a face. 'Like you needed to hear *that* right now!'

Trixie's enjoying her moment of power, I realise. Just like she did when Dan and I broke up. Her moment of triumph, her chance to be top of the heap. I feel a bit sick.

'Trixie,' I say. 'Why did you lie to me about Lizzie?'

'What do you mean?' Trixie asks, turning back to the action on the track. 'You saw her snogging Dan for yourself.'

'I'm not talking about Dan. I'm talking about Jake and Lizzie in the summer.'

Trixie glances at Vashti, then back at me. 'I told you about Jake and Lizzie Banks for your own good, babes.'

'No you didn't.' I'm certain of this.

'Believe me, it *was* for your own good. Lizzie Banks was never going to make the cut at college with her weird clothes and attitude problem.'

'Lizzie was your *friend* when we were at school,' I say, appalled. How can Trixie say these things? 'Same as she was mine. Why would you say that about her?'

'Let's talk about this later, Hanna,' Trixie says.

I can feel the heat of Vashti's gaze.

'I don't want to talk about it later, I want to talk about it now,' I say stubbornly. 'Why did you have it in for Lizzie in the summer? Why did you lie about her and Jake? She and Jake never did anything, did they?'

Trixie's face works like one of those stretchy rubber puppets you buy in joke shops.

'Did they?' I press, relentless as the Terminator in *Terminator 2*. Everyone knows that liquid-metal guy was way better at the relentless thing than Arnie in *Terminator 1*.

131

Trixie seizes my arm and drags me a short distance away among the pines, where there's a strong smell of resin and dog poo.

'You should be thanking me,' she says. Her eyes seem drawn to Vashti like magnets. 'I made you *acceptable* this year, Hanna. Everyone watches us at college, everyone has an opinion about us. Our mistakes, our clothes, our phones, who we hang out with – it all *matters*, so much more than it mattered at school. Don't you want to matter? Because I do.' She takes out her lipgloss and applies it with quick, jerky movements. 'People talk about us for the right reasons, not the wrong ones. We get the party invitations, we get the boyfriends.'

'You mean, you get *my* boyfriends.' I hardly recognise my own voice. 'You'd have Dan in a heartbeat too, wouldn't you? If he ever showed an interest. Poor, dedicated Stevie.'

Trixie's face twitches some more.

'Not everyone's as effortlessly pretty and popular as you. Some of us have to work at it.'

I almost laugh. I don't feel pretty and certainly don't feel popular. Not with the people who count.

'Anyway,' Trixie continues, 'don't come over all innocent with me. You know this is how it works. If you were so keen to stay friends with Lizzie Banks, why did you dump her the minute we started college, just because of some rumour that I may or may not have started?'

I can't think of anything to say. On a deep and truly awful level, Trixie is right.

Trixie caps her lipgloss with a *pop*.

'Now,' she says, 'I have a boyfriend to watch and a life to live. Follow me back to Vashti and we'll pretend this conversation never happened.'

'You were always on the edge, weren't you?' I say, recovering. 'You followed me and Lizzie around at school like a little flea, jumping from skin to skin, sucking where you could.'

'Don't be *gross*.'

'And this summer, you saw your chance to be the dog.' It's all, suddenly, so horribly clear.

'I am the dog?'

That's a direct quote from *When Harry Met Sally*. Trixie wouldn't know that. Sol would.

Lizzie would.

'I'd do it with Jake,' Lizzie says as we loll beneath the big tree with drooping, rain-starved leaves. 'What are you waiting for?'

Jake and I have been going out for three weeks. We're at a stage where he's making noises about taking things further. I can't decide what to do about it. This conversation with Lizzie isn't helping.

'Back off,' I say jokingly, only not jokingly. I adjust my bikini. It's properly teeny weeny, and white. I feel a bit exposed, if I'm honest, but I need to build my tan for Sweden this summer because all the girls there are beautiful and brown like conkers, and it's worth it for the looks I'm getting from the other side of the pool.

'I would though.' Lizzie lies back on her towel, adjusting the straps on her swimsuit. 'What are you scared of? Sex is just bodies fitting together.'

'I'm not scared,' I protest.

A ball splashes into the pool, and covers me and Lizzie with water. I squeal and leap up, yanking furiously at my bikini bottoms. Lizzie just laughs and picks up her book.

'Nice moves there, Han,' calls Stevie.

'Stevie fancies you,' Trixie says. She's on the lounger on my opposite side, in a bikini that's even tinier than mine and sits uncomfortably on her birdlike frame. 'He keeps looking at you. If you can't decide about Jake, maybe you should give Stevie a try. He's lovely.'

'How do you know he's looking at me?' I say, feeling a bit better. 'He could be looking at you.'

Trixie fiddles with her tube of sun lotion. 'He isn't.'

'He could be looking at Lizzie then.'

Trixie eyes Lizzie's swimming costume. She has a point.

'Did you have to wear that thing, Lizzie?' I ask, reaching down to twang one of Lizzie's fuzzy cozzie straps. 'This isn't a Year Eight swimming gala.'

'Get over it, Goldilocks,' says Lizzie. She puts her book on her face.

I haven't done any swimming yet. I'm worried my bikini will come off if I dive in. The humiliation doesn't bear thinking about. Still, I am really warm.

I get off the lounger, aware that everyone is watching, and slide into the deep end with as much grace as I can. The water is cold but I try not to show it.

Stevie leaps in, practically drowning me. When I have finished spluttering and whacking him, he grins, his freckled face creasing like a friendly paper bag.

'What happens if I pull here?' he says, reaching for one of the strings tying my bikini bottoms on.

We have a big, splashy chase around the pool's perimeter.

'Don't you dare,' I say, breathless as he catches up to me.

'Some other time, Bergdahl,' he whispers in my ear, flipping my plaited swimming braid back over my shoulder.

Getting out of the pool is another problem. Stevie's efforts have definitely loosened the strings on my bottom half, and I have to manoeuvre really carefully up the steps to avoid disaster.

Lizzie and Trixie aren't on the loungers any more. I wander around the garden for a bit, enjoying the sun on my damp skin, climbing over snogging couples and trying to suck in my tummy. I can't see Lizzie anywhere.

Trixie comes hurrying round the side of the house, her towel clamped around her body.

'Hey Trix,' I say. 'You seen Lizzie?'

Trixie stares at me. 'Yes,' she says after a moment.

'Is she in the house?'

Trixie's eyes are very wide. 'Yes.'

'I'll just—'

Trixie catches me round the elbow. 'Don't,' she says.

The weird look on her face makes me feel as if Stevie O'Shea has just splashed me all over again.

'What's going on?' I ask.

'It's Lizzie,' she says. 'Lizzie and Jake.'

'What?' I say, when I can breathe.

Trixie squeezes my arm. Her eyes are bigger than I've ever seen them.

'I'm so sorry, babes,' she says. 'So unbelievably sorry.'

'I'm the *dog*?' Trixie repeats, staring at me. 'Well, you're the ungrateful *bitch*, Hanna. Screw up your own life if you want, but you're not screwing up mine.'

She readjusts her sunglasses despite the fact the sun has now gone down over the ridge, and rejoins Vashti. She's just in time to see Dan making big air over the ridge and roaring like he's the King of the Jungle, not the Dirt Bike Dork of Surrey. Trixie claps like a crazed groupie and Vashti glares and, somewhere down by the finishing line, Laura Hamilton waits with baited breath, racing heart and parted lips for Dan's sweaty, temporary attentions.

I bend down, scoop up a palmful of damp sand by my feet, mould it in both hands and hurl it at Dan mid-flight. It smacks against his helmet with a skittering *thunk*, and showers his shoulders with golden crumbs.

'TWAT,' I shout.

Vashti looks round. Trixie sets her glossy lips tight. Dan glances at me curiously through the flipped-up visor on his spattered helmet as he hits the ground. He screams away round the Devil's Turn, coating Trixie in sand from head to toe.

136

SOL

I adjust my camera and settle down for a good, long session on the footbridge. It's evening now, and the light is incredible. Two trains are due at any minute.

I'm meeting Carmen at Costa later. I'm getting a bit bored of their frappé selection, but she's worth it. Carmen says she likes me because I don't pretend to be someone I'm not, so now I'm toying with the idea of telling her that I make films. I might even make her one. It would be nice to make a film for a girl who actually knew I'd made it.

On Platform 1, there's a fight breaking out by the toilets between two businessmen. I lean over the edge of the footbridge and focus my phone. When it starts ringing right up by my eye, I almost leap out of my skin.

'Hey, it's me. You won't *believe* what just happened, you would be so proud of me. Are you around? Can we meet?'

'Now?'

'Yes, now. Are you free?'

One of the trains is pulling into the station, sending up a loud squealing sound of brakes.

'God, what was that?' Hanna says.

'Train,' I say. I wonder how to hang up politely.

'How funny, I've been thinking about *Brief Encounter* loads today. I've decided that Celia Johnson and Trevor Howard should have just run away together on that train, even though they were both married and had kids and everything. And before you say it, I know Dad ran away even though he was married and had kids and everything and it was awful at the time, but Mum and James are really happy together and Raz and I wouldn't have Linus if Dad hadn't run away, would we?'

The train on Platform 2 is due any minute. 'Your dad chose one way,' I say. 'The characters in *Brief Encounter* chose another. Maybe there's no right or wrong, just decisions that take you in different directions.'

The fight on Platform 1 is escalating. Someone needs to invent a camera phone where you can talk and film at the same time.

'That's *such* an appropriate analogy, you have no idea. This thing I have to tell you, it's about a decision I made that took me in the wrong direction. I'm walking into town right now, so are you free or not?'

I can see the train for Platform 2 approaching in the distance, its headlight gleaming. I should probably buy a camera that isn't a phone, but I like the reportage-y thing a phone camera gives the footage. Maybe a second phone is the answer.

'Are you still there?' Hanna says.

'No,' I say. 'I'll call you later.'

I hang up just in time to catch the big bloke in the suit taking a swing at the little bloke in the suit. He misjudges the guy's height and his fist smashes into a curly wrought-iron platform pillar over his head. The guard's weighing in now, and people are looking out the windows. To add to the excitement, the Platform 2 train is arriving. I see the cat that looks like Nigel again, lurking near the steps at the bottom of the footbridge.

I zoom in on my phone.

It *is* Nigel.

My phone rings again.

'What are you doing?' asks Hanna in a funny voice. 'Right this minute?'

I am wondering if I will reach my cat before he starts a full-scale attack on the commuters about to pile out of their train.

'Hanna, I really can't talk,' I say as I break into a run.

I clock her standing in the street below the footbridge, watching me with narrowed eyes, her phone pressed to her ear.

'I can explain,' I say hurriedly, taking the footbridge steps two at a time, the iron treads clanging beneath my feet. 'But not now.'

The train doors are opening. I can see Nigel's tail lashing with its usual rattlesnake venom, right underneath the bottom tread. I have seconds before some poor sod has a heart attack.

'You promised you wouldn't keep secrets any more! Sol, you *did*, don't pretend you didn't!'

The first commuters are striding way too fast towards the footbridge steps. 'I didn't promise not to keep secrets any more,' I say, speeding up. 'I just said I'd *try*.'

'You're arguing this? You don't answer my calls, you don't answer my texts. You lie about your girlfriend, and now it seems you've been hiding a train hobby. I've got enough crap friends in my life at the moment without you, thanks. Movie night at mine this month, in case you were wondering? Movie night is OFF.'

I fling myself down the last two steps, reaching for Nigel, praying that my cat won't leap on to the electrified train tracks barely a metre to my right and explode in a mess of black fur and teeth. I'm also trying very hard not to crash into the commuters coming the other way. By the time I have gathered Nigel into my arms, been savaged by his claws, and apologised a hundred times to everyone, Hanna has marched away and out of sight.

I'm going to be late for Carmen too.

ANNIE HALL
(1977)

DIRECTOR WOODY ALLEN

WRITERS WOODY ALLEN and
MARSHALL BRICKMAN

Comedian Alvy Singer (Woody Allen) examines the rise and fall of his relationship with struggling nightclub singer Annie Hall (Diane Keaton). Alvy reflects on his childhood and his early adult years before telling the story of how he and Annie met, fell in love, and struggled with the obstacles of modern romance, mixing surreal fantasy sequences with small moments of emotional drama.

Film critic Roger Ebert called it 'just about everybody's favorite Woody Allen movie'. It features the song 'It Had to Be You': something it shares with *When Harry Met Sally*. The movie won the Oscar for Best Picture in 1977.

Hanna

31 MAY

'I'm still so furious with him, you have no idea.'

Lizzie picks up the crisp bowl and tips the crumbs down her throat. 'Are you sure about that?'

I pick at the throw Mum keeps on the back of the snug sofa. Lizzie always knew how to make me squirm. I've missed the multicoloured Indian harem pants she's wearing. They're ridiculous, yet cute.

'Coke?' I say, keen to change the subject.

'As long as it's not the diet one the skinny girls drink. That stuff kills your kidneys.'

I go downstairs to the kitchen, take the Diet Coke bottle out of the fridge and pour it down the sink.

'Sorry, thought we had some,' I lie up the stairs. 'Coffee?'

'Fat milk?'

'Practically obese,' I say gratefully.

'I can't believe you called Dan a twat,' Lizzie says when I come back with two coffees so milky they are almost mooing.

142

'I can't either.' I beam at the memory. 'You'd have been proud. I went for it. I didn't care what anyone thought.'

'For that, if nothing else in the past ten months, I salute you.'

My old best friend clinks mugs with me. And I think I am happy – truly happy – for the first time in ages.

'What are we watching again?' Lizzie says as I cue up the screen.

'*Annie Hall.*'

Lizzie nods in approval. I know she loves this film. It's one of the reasons I chose it. I don't know if Sol likes it or hates it, and I don't care.

'I caught him trainspotting, can you believe it?' I say.

'Trainspotting is less harmful to the environment than blasting through the woods on a souped-up scooter. Except of course . . .' Lizzie lifts a finger in the air. 'Vashti and Trixie and Laura wouldn't approve.'

'I don't care what Vashti and Trixie and Laura think,' I say, blushing.

'So it's fine that Sol trainspots. The world is a better and more varied place for it. Now shut up and watch the movie.'

We watch Alvy and Annie battling through their doomed relationship. I always hope they'll work it out, even though I know they don't. I find myself wondering why we must always want the impossible.

The front door slams.

'Hi girls,' says Mum, passing the snug door with Linus.

I don't think Mum ever realised that Lizzie and I fell out. For her, seeing Lizzie in the snug is entirely normal. The last ten months of my life: a blip.

My little brother is a bit sharper. He runs into the snug.

'Hi stinkypants,' says Lizzie.

'Hi smellybum,' says Linus. 'I ate a brownie just now.'

'Half a brownie,' Lizzie says. 'The rest is on your face.'

Linus squashes Lizzie's nose. Lizzie squashes his nose back. Linus flicks his eyes to me, then back to Lizzie again.

'Will you come back soon?' he asks. 'Can we do Lego?'

'That depends on whether your big sister goes back to Stupidtown.'

'I won't go back to Stupidtown,' I say as Linus runs out again.

'Tell me again about calling Dan a twat,' says Lizzie when he's gone. 'And really spin it out this time.'

'Can I ask you something?' I say when I've finished. I clasp my hands together nervously. 'Did you sleep with Dan? Everyone says that you did but – well. You can't trust rumours.'

'Didn't stop you believing the one about me and Jake.'

'I know,' I say, taking the hit. 'That's why I'm asking you now, not the grapevine. It doesn't matter, but I just – want to know.'

Lizzie lifts her chin. 'I did sleep with Dan, yes. You?'

'I nearly did,' I say. I remember our conversations about Jake all those months ago: Lizzie, the voice of experience, urging me on. 'Story of my sexual history in three words,' I add apologetically.

Lizzie gives me a half smile. 'When you finally decide to have sex with someone, make sure it's someone nice. Not someone who dumps you shortly after telling you that you're the worst shag he's ever had.'

'Someone did that to you?' I say, appalled.

Lizzie studies the bottom of her coffee cup. Understanding blooms like a bloodstain across my heart. Lizzie and Dan.

Dan.

'Dan was your first?' I say, aghast. 'You . . . At school, you said . . .'

Lizzie waves a hand. 'I talked the talk at school, but that was it. Starting college was tough. And then I did it with Dan because you and I weren't friends any more and it seemed like the thing to do and I got burned. No big deal.'

I think about the things Trixie and Vashti have said about Lizzie this year. The things I've said too. About how I wasn't there for her when she needed me. I wish I could take it all back. I wish I could go back to that summer, that poolside, and push past Trixie and see Lizzie and talk to her for myself. But I can't.

'I'm so sorry,' I say inadequately. 'You'll meet someone nicer, I promise. Someone who understands you and laughs at your jokes and doesn't say horrible things about you behind your back.'

'Talking of someone nicer,' Lizzie says, 'how's Raz doing in his Leah-free world?'

'He's not looking for a new relationship any time soon. Besides, you can't date my brother, it would be too weird.

145

Sol might know someone.' I remember I'm still mad at Sol and frown. 'Forget I said that. Sol doesn't know his own bum from the ten-fifteen to Basingstoke.'

'Sol is adorable,' Lizzie says. 'He looks like a fox, all whip-thin and pointy. You know, he was pulling off his hoodie at the lockers the other day and his T-shirt was riding up and every girl in the corridor forgot where they were supposed to be.'

'You fancy Sol?' I say disbelievingly.

'Are you telling me you've never been tempted?'

I stare at my hand, at the fading scar where Sol bandaged me up the day I fell through Dan's garage roof. 'Never,' I say. 'It would be completely wrong.'

'You know what they say about forbidden fruit.'

'Forbidden fruit juice?' I say.

'Han,' Lizzie says, suddenly serious, 'don't cut me dead on Monday.'

'I wouldn't do that,' I say.

'Trixie would.'

'I'm not Trixie.'

'For a while there,' says Lizzie, 'I wondered.'

SOL

I click listlessly through Netflix, wondering what Hanna would have chosen to watch with me tonight. *Leap Year*, probably. I have had a lucky escape.

I stopped calling about two weeks ago. I finally worked out that there was no point ringing and ringing, leaving message after message and getting nothing back. I have thrown myself into life with Carmen instead, like any normal boyfriend would. We have had three more dates at Costa and two trips to the cinema. I have been to her house for tea and shaken Chief Constable Mendoza's immense hand four times. I have been escorted firmly but politely off the Mendoza premises by six o'clock two Sundays in a row, with Carmen waving at me as she heads up the stairs on her way to finish her revision for the week ahead. I have not achieved as much kissing as I would have liked in the circumstances. And I have done more revision myself in the last three weeks than possibly in the entirety of my life, because there has been literally *nothing* else to do.

I cue up *Annie Hall* and reach for the Twiglets. I have decided to lose myself in Woody Allen's genius for a while and try to forget about Hanna Bergdahl. I will relish the surreal parts, and laugh at Jeff Goldblum's cameo, and fancy Diane Keaton, and I will enjoy every moment.

'Sol,' Gareth bellows. 'How many times have I told you not to leave your shoes where I can trip over them? It's a bloody accident waiting to happen. There is a shoe rack, otherwise known as a RACK FOR SHOES.'

It's Gareth's mother's birthday today. As usual, there has been no phone call. As usual, he is moving around the house in a large, black weather front, best avoided.

'I have enough going on without adding a trip to A and E to my schedule!'

There is a yowl and a shriek from the kitchen.

'FOR GOD'S SAKE, ANDREW, I AM GOING TO CASTRATE YOUR CAT WITH MY BARE HANDS AND SAVE US ALL A VET'S BILL.'

Andrew marches into the living room with Nigel struggling in his arms and drops on to the sofa beside me. I offer him a Twiglet.

'That bloody woman still causes trouble and we haven't heard from her in twenty years,' says Andrew. Nigel is hanging on to his wrist like some kind of four-legged Grim Reaper. 'Stop eating me, Nigel. I am not tuna.'

'Want to watch the film with me?' I ask.

'I thought you did this movie night thing with Hanna.' Andrew switches Nigel round so the cat is free to savage his right wrist instead. I get the full benefit of Nigel's wildest glare.

'We aren't talking,' I say.

'What about the girlfriend you haven't let us meet?'

'I haven't not let you meet her. I just haven't had her round here yet. And I don't date Carmen on weeknights. Revision. We're about to start exams.'

'I spent more hours getting beaten up for looking at the football team in what constituted a "poofy" manner than I ever did on revision,' Andrew says. 'Happy days.' He releases Nigel, who streaks towards the kitchen in an enraged blur.

My phone beeps.

Hi Solomon. I miss you. C xxx

I don't know how you're supposed to respond to messages like that from girls. When Hanna texts me, it's usually part of some running joke or half of a quote. That's easy. When Carmen texts me, she's just being . . . nice.

'Girlfriend?' Andrew asks.

'Just a phone credits sale thing.'

What is this compulsion in me to lie about private things? Now Hanna isn't around distracting me from myself, I notice that I do it all the time.

Andrew puts an arm round me. His bracelets jingle by my ear.

'Everything OK?'

'Um, yeah,' I say. 'It's good.'

'Bloody better be,' says Gareth, clomping into the living room. 'We worked hard enough on your personal statement to impress those accountancy courses. You're ahead of the game. You can't fail now, Sol, it's too important.'

'I know,' I say.

'You know how many kids take their eye off the ball at this stage? Year Twelve is easy, they say. AS levels don't matter, they say. Balls to that.'

'Gareth,' Andrew says gently. 'Sol knows what we expect. Give him a little credit.'

I feel a bit sick. 'The exams I've done so far haven't been too bad,' I say to fill the space. 'My revision for the rest seems to be on target.'

'Keep it that way,' Gareth advises. 'I don't mean to be a pushy parent . . .'

Andrew clears his throat loudly. Risky, given Gareth's mood. But Gareth is away on his pet topic now, and there's no stopping him.

' . . . job market these days isn't how it was when Andrew and I were young . . .'

Rebellious thoughts of snipping through the racks of pinstriped suits at Marks and Spencers swim through my head. *We had our pick of the jobs . . .*

'We had our pick of the jobs just because we'd been to university, but everyone's at university now and with the market changing the way it is . . .'

'The tech revolution,' Andrew supplies.

'The tech revolution . . .' Gareth realizes Andrew is taking the mick and stops. 'Well,' he says, gathering himself. 'You get the gist. You're still dropping Geography?'

This is a conversation about private things, right? It's not so hard.

'I guess,' I say.

Andrew joins in. 'At the risk of sounding like your dad which – oh! – I am, good accountancy firms won't be interested in Geography.'

I picture a room full of accountants urgently debating oxbow lakes. I think Andrew's doing the same thing.

'Who'd have thought,' Andrew says. 'An accountant in the family! I don't know whether to be proud or to cut you out of my will.'

'It's the most secure career out there,' says Gareth. 'Was it auditing or tax you're thinking about long-term?'

I'm thinking about leaving the room, actually. I can feel the sweat prickling around my neckline. 'I'm keeping my options open,' I say.

'Not too open, I hope. A decent career needs focus.'

'I get it,' I say, squirming.

'You have a head for numbers. Just like me. Your birth mother was good with figures too.'

I'm not you. I'm not her either.

'It's a gift in this merciless world. You're going to make the most of that talent.'

This feels like an order rather than the compliment my dad intends. I'm glad one of us is sure.

'You must get your common sense from Gareth, because it's certainly not from me,' says Andrew brightly. 'If you want any help with arranging uni visits, let me know. But three hours is probably my taxi limit, so if it's Edinburgh or Harvard, you're on your own.'

'Great,' I say. 'Thanks.'

Gareth makes an effort to smile. He claps me on the back. 'I'd better check on Nigel's whereabouts,' he says. 'If he shreds any more of that cat flap, our heating bills will go through the roof.'

I go upstairs and turn on my computer. For once, Frank isn't there to talk to. Is it sad that the only friend I have is five thousand miles away and available only in two dimensions? And is also an idiot? I can't decide. I can't decide anything at the moment. I am adrift, bobbing alone on a swell that could be just a swell, or could be the rumblings of a giant tsunami out to drown me.

I turn to my latest paper tableau. I have recreated the fighting businessmen as best I can, but my heart isn't in it. Seeing them poised and for ever beating the crap out of each other only reminds me of the mess I have made with Hanna. I don't want to look at them right now.

My phone beeps again.

Tomorrow at Costa usual
time? Dad says it's OK
if I'm back by 6. C xxx

8 JUNE

College feels different with the exams on. There's a quiet in the corridors that makes me think of the hotel in *The Shining*. The sooner this weirdness is over, the better.

I have taken to waiting for Lizzie near her bus stop so we can walk in together. Having her beside me gives me back the courage I'd forgotten I once had. It's clear to me these days that my whole thing with Sol was a comfort blanket in a Lizzie-free, yoghurt-coated environment.

Given that we attend the same college, it's amazing how infrequently Sol and I bump into each other now we're not talking. We were running into each other all over the place before. I think we have both thrown up some kind of repulsive shield. It's the only explanation. I don't even know his exam timetable. He did the Maths papers same as Lizzie, and Lizzie says he didn't look upset when the papers were over. So that's good, I guess.

People are starting to come out of the exam rooms. Some are high as kids on a sugar rush, a paper over. Some are pale as death for the same reason. Lizzie and I lean against the walls and watch the multitudes moving through the steps of the dance, ebbing in one direction and flowing in the other.

'Teaspoon game,' says Lizzie.

'Who?'

She nods at a guy fixing the laces on his trainers in the middle of the hubbub. 'Him.'

'I can't see his face.'

'That's a risk you'll have to take. The question is as it ever was. Would you rather kiss him, or saw your own head off with a blunt teaspoon?'

'I can't see him!'

'Choose.'

I focus on the guy with the laces. His shoulders are good, and he's wearing what *might* be a bad hat if seen face-on, but from above seems OK.

'Kiss him,' I say.

The guy straightens up. The hat is awful.

'Your turn,' I say when we've recovered. 'The one over there with the suede backpack.'

'Blunt teaspoon,' says Lizzie.

'How do you always know?' I ask when the guy turns round.

She waggles her fingers and smiles mysteriously. 'I have the sex sense.'

'That's not a thing.'

'It totally is a thing.'

'Fine. Him.' I point.

'Hanna, he just closed the door on that classroom. I saw him for half a second.'

'Choose.'

'Kiss.'

'You really are good,' I say with admiration.

'Why, who was he?'

'Alistair McDonald. Does Media Studies with Trixie and Vashti. Really hot.'

'Don't tell me,' says Lizzie. 'The Plastics have been sniffing around him since the start of the year.'

I flinch at the *Mean Girls* reference.

'Before you apologise yet again,' she says, seeing my expression, 'let's just assume you're sorry for the whole of the future, foreseeable and otherwise, and play the game. I am due in Physics in five minutes.'

I try to calm my flustered brain – *I've been hanging out with the Plastics* – as a guy's backside comes poking out of a door, reversing into the corridor traffic. Skinny jeans that fit. Good trainers too. New, but scuffed up like he doesn't care too much.

'Him,' I say.

'I have to make a judgement call on his butt?'

'It's a good one,' I point out.

'It is,' she agrees. 'Kiss.'

We wait for Door Guy to fully emerge. He does.

'Told you he was hot,' says Lizzie in satisfaction.

Unaware of our gaze, Sol heads on down the corridor

with his arms full of books, a moss-green beanie perched on the back of his head. My whole body feels like it's on fire. I can't believe I just ogled Sol's bum.

'You look like I just caught you fancying your own brother,' says Lizzie, laughing.

I press my hands to my face. My cheeks are hot.

'Hanna, it's OK to fancy Sol,' says Lizzie in amusement. 'A lot of girls do.'

'I *don't* fancy him,' I say.

'It's OK to fancy just his bum, then.'

'I *don't* fancy his bum,' I say loudly.

Two girls glance and giggle as they press past on their way to whatever exam they are taking.

'I don't fancy his bum,' I say a little more quietly. 'I don't fancy any part of him, Lizzie.'

'Whatever you say. What have you got now? English?'

I am feeling very strange. Not quite in my own skin.

'Yes,' I say after a moment, when I realise that Lizzie is waiting for an answer. 'In about fifteen minutes.'

'Good luck,' she says. 'Meet you after.'

The exams are getting to me. I am mad to be fancying Sol's bum. *Sol's* bum. Of all bums.

'Hey.'

Dan has materialised in front of me like an evil but hot genie. The animal part of me – the part that is plainly tired and emotional today – registers that he is looking gorgeous. He's got a bit of stubble, and his hair is pulled back into a knot on the back of his neck which suits his jawline. His eyes are a bit bloodshot, but that's about the only fault I can pick right now.

'Um,' I say. 'Hey yourself.'

Dan hitches up the side of his mouth in a half-smile. I am reminded of Farmor's dog Pippi in Sweden, who does the same thing when you tickle her tummy.

'You're going to English,' he says. He smells as lovely and lemony as he did in November. It's such a familiar smell that I'm confused into thinking maybe the last six months never happened.

I do my best to gather myself together. 'Last time I looked.'

'Haven't seen you since the woods,' he says, falling into step beside me.

'Nope.'

'We haven't spoken much since December.'

'Funny that,' I say. 'How's it going with Laura?'

He looks blank.

'Your girlfriend?' I prompt.

His face clears. 'Oh, *Laura*. That ended last weekend.'

My stomach goes *boing*. Just a little. I can't help it. He is too good-looking.

'She couldn't stand getting sand in her face any more?' I say.

Dan laughs. 'You're funny,' he says.

'Oh I'm hilarious.' I rummage in my pockets to check that I have everything I need: pen, pencil, mascot, stress ball. I squeeze the stress ball silently. *I'm talking to Dan again.*

157

And he's talking to me. Even though I called him a twat in public.
'I'm headlining at the London Variety Show next Christmas.'

'Listen,' he says, sliding his hands into his back pockets. 'Let's go out on Saturday.'

'What?' I say, my hand paused on the stress ball mid-squeeze, in possibly not the most intelligent voice I have ever used.

Dan flicks the air with his fingers. 'Out,' he repeats. 'We could go to that Chinese we never went to in November.'

Dan is asking me out? Again? After everything? Dan Dukas doesn't ask a girl out twice. Have I slid into a parallel *Donnie Darko* world?

We reach the room where we will be taking our English exam. Hundreds of people are obsessively checking pens and pencils. Over by the doors, Trixie, Laura and Vashti are huddled together. They glance briefly in our direction. Laura looks wan and thinner than ever. Vashti looks furious. Trixie's eyebrows rise like two caterpillars perched on a pair of forklift trucks.

I need to play this cool. I need to *think*. What would Lizzie do? No, wait – Lizzie caved with this guy. I'm by myself. Writing my own script.

'Sure,' I tell him.

'Great. I'll meet you at—'

'Jeez, Dan,' I interrupt. 'Do you really think I meant that?'

An expression appears on Dan's face that I've never seen before. Shock.

'What?' he says, in a fair imitation of me a few moments earlier.

'I'm not going out with you on Saturday,' I say clearly.

He looks puzzled. 'But you said that you were up for it.'

'I was kidding.' I spread my hands. 'Sorry.'

I don't know where this reckless approach is coming from, but I like the feeling of power it's giving me. Maybe it's tied up with my recovered sense of loyalty to Lizzie, or the sudden, scattered order of the universe that descended on me the moment I clocked Sol's tush. Or the fear I always feel just before I enter an exam room, which drives reason out of the window for a few short hours.

'So we're not going out on Saturday?' Dan says. 'Or we are? You know, just so I'm clear?'

I don't think I've ever heard Dan Dukas ask a question before. I can't help laughing. He looks so confused.

'Good luck in there,' I say as the room doors open. I pat him on the arm. 'I have a feeling you'll need it.'

SOL

I stare at the question about flooding in the Sundarbans and picture tigers swimming through the mangroves, their stripes blending with the light-marked ripples in the rising waters.

Using Figure 2 only, comment on the relative importance of physical and human causes of flooding.

I write at length about Kolkata depending on the fast disappearing mangroves to protect them from the increasing storms and floods affecting the Ganges-Brahmaputra Delta. I can't get the image of the tigers out of my head. Their wet heads gleaming, their whiskers loaded with water and drooping like Nigel's after that incident with the neighbours' Koi carp pond.

I finish the paper. Cold polar regions, tundra, the fishing industry in Newfoundland, coastal deposition in Suffolk. Places I'll never go to, people I'll never see from behind my sensible desk in my sensible accountants' office, in my sensible tie and sensible shoes.

'How did it go?'

I gaze at Stevie O'Shea's freckly face as we shuffle out of the hall and back to real life.

'OK,' I hedge. 'You?'

He pulls a face. 'I don't suppose I'll need to know where the Sundarbans are in my future life.'

'That depends on the future life you want,' I say.

Stevie aims a kick at an invisible football, blasts it into the top corner of the corridor. 'Nothing involving coastal erosion, that's for sure. Coming out tonight? A bunch of us are going to Dan's.'

'I don't think the invitation includes me,' I say. 'Do you?'

Steve guffaws, mimes a punching action. 'You hit him hard, man,' he says. 'Where did you learn to do that? You don't strike me as the type to have a punchball in the garage.'

'I don't have a garage,' I say.

'We should hang out more,' Stevie says, prodding me in the chest. I don't think I imagine the tiny pause before he adds, 'You know, as mates.'

Don't panic Stevie, I think. *You're not my type.*

A blond head is moving up the corridor ahead of us, making for the main doors and the sunshine outside. I'm pretty sure it's Hanna, but the light slides off her like it did on the tigers and she's gone in a blink.

'So hot,' Stevie mutters. He glances sideways at me. 'Did I say that out loud? Sorry.'

'Nothing to apologise for.' Does he think I'll tell Trixie?

Stevie waves a hand. 'I know she's kind of yours now.'

There's a double-edged sword right there. Especially as Hanna's further from being *kind of mine* than she's been at any point in this process.

'I'm not the gay best friend, Stevie,' I say.

Stevie's still watching the place where Hanna slipped from view.

'I'm not gay.' I open my mouth and shape my lips and tongue and actually say this. Out loud. 'I'm not even the best friend at the moment, to tell you the truth. But primarily I am. Not. Gay.'

Stevie switches his gaze back to me. 'Mate,' he says. 'I know.'

'I'm sick of everyone assuming I'm gay just be—' I stop, rewind. 'You *don't* think I'm gay?'

'No.'

'Oh,' I say, a little inadequately. 'But you thought I was gay at the start?'

Stevie looks puzzled. 'No,' he repeats.

'Because of my parents,' I press on. 'Everyone thinks I'm gay because of my two dads. It's obvious.'

'What's obvious,' Stevie says, 'is that you are crazy about Hanna and have been since the first day of college.'

This is not the conversation I was expecting to have.

'Dan thinks I'm gay,' I bleat.

'Yes, but Dan's a dick.'

I find that I'm pointing at him now, willing him to confess. 'At Dan's party, you said Vashti was on to a winner in this sarcastic voice.'

162

'Because you only have eyes for Hanna,' Stevie says.

'That thing about not being the type to have a punchbag . . .' I say weakly.

'No one as skinny and laid back as you whales on a bag of sand at weekends. Jesus, man, how many times? No one thinks you're gay.' Stevie considers. 'Well, maybe a couple of the girls do.'

'Because of my two dads,' I say, feeling faintly vindicated.

'Because you spend your days with Hanna Bergdahl and have never been seen to make a move on her,' says Stevie.

No one thinks I'm gay. Everyone thinks I'm in love with Hanna. I don't know which is worse.

'You need to sort it out,' says Stevie. 'With Hanna.'

'Yeah, well,' I say after a moment. 'About that.'

'You got yourself into the Friend Zone,' Stevie says, nodding. 'I can tell. Rookie error, mate. Listen, we're going down to the lake at the weekend. Me, Jake, some of the others. Want to join us?'

I clear my throat. 'Sure,' I say.

'I'll text you.' Stevie raises his arms and heads down the corridor towards the daylight. *'Blue is the colour . . .'* he sings as he goes. *'Football is the game, we're all together, and winning is our aim . . .'*

The corridor pings to life with a hundred different notification sounds as phones are switched back on. I take out my own.

> **How was your exam? C xxx**

Good. You?

> **Awful! Dad's going to kill me!! Costa tonight? C xxx**

Sure. See you there.

My finger hovers on the x button but I can't do it. I press send, feeling like a coward, then slip my phone into my pocket.

One more exam tomorrow. Then I'm going to spend some time getting my thoughts straight. It's only in the last month that I've realised how off-centre I really am.

Hey

Hi!

Im back *jazz hands*

How are you? How
were your exams?

Fine. U?

Can we be friends again?

Listen, want to b friends
again but on 1 condition

Think our messages crossed.

msgs xd?

I'm really sorry about
everything

UR an idiot

What's the condition?

U dont lie any more ever

It was an omission, not a lie.

U saying u never lied
2 me about anything?

I saw you with Lizzie . . .?

Friends again. Hows
Carmen?

Good.

Dan asked me out again

What did you say?

No!!! Not that stupid. Want
2 do movie night this mth?

Whose turn?

10 THINGS I HATE ABOUT YOU (1999)

DIRECTOR   GIL JUNGER

WRITERS KAREN McCULLAH
and KIRSTEN SMITH

Kat Stratford (Julia Stiles) is beautiful, clever and unpleasant to most of her fellow teens, especially the guys. Unfortunately, her younger sister, Bianca (Larisa Oleynik), can't date anyone until Kat has a boyfriend, so plans are hatched to set Kat up with handsome new high-school arrival Patrick Verona (Heath Ledger). Will Kat let her guard down in time to save Bianca from a life alone?

Gil Junger's movie was based on Shakespeare's play *The Taming of the Shrew*.

SOL

12 JULY

Stevie passes me a can with a comfortable belch.

'You got a girlfriend how?' I enquire.

Stevie flexes a large, tanned bicep. 'Luckily for all concerned, Trixie didn't look any further than these guns.'

I glance at my own upper arms. They are muscular but as pale as the undersides of two snails, even after several hours in the afternoon sun.

'No pressure,' says Stevie with a smirk.

'Some of us work the intellectual side of our personalities a little more than others,' I tell him, pulling on my shirt.

Stevie plucks the can he just gave me from my hand. 'Better have that back then, hadn't I?' he says. 'Everyone knows alcohol rots the brain. Oi, JAKE you twat! The goal's *that* way!'

Stevie hurls himself back into the football game on the lake shore like a large, freckled salmon at a waterfall. Feeling warm and comfortable in the sun, I scroll through today's cache of film, bringing the phone up under my brim to throw some shadow on the screen. The light at this time of the day is long and rich and yellow, like cream. I wonder if I can blend some stop-animation against the footage. A Sundarban tiger made of paper, prowling through the lakeside reeds.

A hand reaches over my shoulder, plucking the phone from my hand.

'Any nudey pics on here, gay boy? Got to love a well-oiled, muscular guy on a beach.'

Dan has been wary of me since I punched him, and we generally manage to avoid each other. But, like a scab he can't quite stop picking, he still seems to enjoy these little games.

'Glad to hear your tastes are wide-ranging,' I say.

There is a whistling sound as the remark sails over Dan's head and lands with a gentle *plff* in the sand. He pushes his glossy black hair away from his face and drops down beside me.

'Want a feel of this?' he says, thrusting one of his biceps under my nose. It gleams with oil and smells of coconut. 'I bet it makes you hot.'

I eye the football game and wonder if it's worth joining in.

'Are you propositioning me?' I ask.

Dan pulls his arm away. 'Perv.'

'You're the one waving bits of yourself around,' I point out.

Dan glances down the lake beach to where a group of girls are eyeing him. He stretches his arms over his head to maximise his musculature for their benefit, then leans over and punches me. It's gentle, and on my upper arm, and I think perhaps it's his attempt at a friendly gesture.

'Listen,' he says. 'You know Hanna.'

I haven't seen Hanna since our last movie night. It was a weird night, if I'm honest. Both of us on our best behaviour and neither of us enjoying it. We didn't hug hello or goodbye. I don't think we touched each other once. I couldn't tell if Hanna had chosen the movie because she liked it, or because she was trying to tell me something about loyalty and lying. Our post-movie chat about Heath Ledger's death put a downer on things too.

'She's still into me,' Dan states.

I wonder what it must be like to be so confident of your own sex appeal that you know you're irresistible. No ifs, no buts.

'She's into me but acting like she's not,' Dan continues. 'It's getting boring. I mean, come on.'

He is studying his body as he says this. Seriously, he is. I am tempted to say that Hanna thinks he's an idiot, but what do I know? Maybe Hanna *is* into him and is pretending she's not, like he says. God knows, she was mad enough for the guy earlier in the year. So mad for him she practically killed herself falling through his garage roof.

'You should probably ask her yourself,' I say.

'That's where you come in, gay boy.' Dan brushes a clump of sand from his chest. 'Tell her to call me.' He glances at the girls further down the beach again. 'I'm never on the market for long.'

'That's good to know,' I say as he gets up. 'Really heartening. I'll make sure to tell her.'

Dan nods. He flicks through several bursts of video on my phone before tossing it back to me. 'Nice footage,' he says. 'No shots of me though.'

His oily, coconut fingerprints are all over the screen. I wipe it irritably with the hem of my shirt, making the images zoom up and down and side to side like crazed bees in a jar. The Sundarban tiger idea has just developed a new angle, involving a stealth attack on Dan Dukas. Put together with all the other stuff I've been amassing these past few weeks I've got almost enough film for a twenty-minute piece.

I realise with a sudden, weird jolt that Dan Dukas is the first person ever to have seen something that I have filmed. The person I like least in the whole world, with the possible exception of Chet Langdale, has drunk my heart blood through his eyes and, with what there is of his brain, passed judgement. None of it was edited, but the ideas, the angles – they were all there, as exposed as a kitten's belly. I feel sick.

Then I don't. He didn't laugh. If anyone was going to laugh it would have been him. He would have told me right off if it was bad, and he didn't. And that's not because he likes me – we have established that loud and clear – and it's not because he feels sorry for me, because Dan Dukas never feels sorry for anyone. He didn't tell me it was shit because, maybe . . .

It isn't?

Hanna

14 JULY

'Read it and weep, sister,' says Raz, scrolling through his phone.

'Seriously,' I protest, glaring at the Scrabble board, '"unshared" is taking the mick.'

'You're just mad because I finished my letters.' Scroll, scroll, scroll. 'Fifty-point bonus, get IN.'

'Be good, Han,' says Linus unexpectedly from the corner of the living room, where he has been building something robot-ish with his new Lego.

'You heard the man,' Raz says as I splutter.

'Ten minutes till the barbecue's done,' James calls from the back garden. 'Can someone bring out the salad?'

'Fetch it, will you, Hanna?' Raz says. 'I have to send a message.'

'It's my *birthday*,' I say irritably, but his head is bent over his phone and he doesn't answer.

Mum has done one of her nice tables outside on the patio, all checked napkins and lanterns with candles in

172

them. Linus's cake sits in the middle, a perfect Lego creation of red, blue and yellow fondant blocks with seven candles. Mine is a neat shiny penny of chocolate with seventeen candles ranged around the sides. Today, I am ten years and one day older than my little brother.

'Happy birthday, Linus and Hanna,' says James.

We all raise our glasses. Linus raises his tin of Sprite and bashes it so hard into Mum's glass that she almost spills the contents down her crisp white shirt.

'May your Lego last as long as your imagination, Linus.' James tips his glass to me and Raz next. 'And here's to the fun-filled, sun-soaked Swedish summer that lies ahead for you two. We'll miss you.'

Dad may have left us, but Farmor – Granny Bergdahl – never did. I think of all the aunts, uncles and cousins, of the red-stained porch of the summerhouse at Singö with its wooden deck and its pots of sweet-scented herbs, the sound of the water on the sand and the old bicycles we ride along the shore, the boathouses and jetties and the lonely cry of the birds. *Next week*, I think. *Next week we'll be there.*

The dusk is slow and warm as we finish our meal. Moths are taking a fancy to Mum's candle jars, and the whine of mosquitoes brings me so close to Singö I can smell it.

The doorbell goes shortly after we have sung 'Happy Birthday' and the cake has been parcelled out.

The last time I saw Carmen Mendoza, she was wrapped around Sol like tinsel round a Christmas lamp post. The time before that, she was hand in hand with my ex-boyfriend in the supermarket. Now she's standing shyly in my garden, clasping her hands in front of her tiny waist.

'Hello,' I say in surprise.

'I'm sorry to disturb you.' Carmen looks at us all anxiously with her huge, dark-brown eyes.

'Cake?' James offers. 'You can't move for birthdays in this house today. Did you want to see Hanna?'

I take Carmen into the kitchen, my mind whirring. I don't know when I last talked to her. The only reason I can think of her being here is—

'It's Sol,' says Carmen.

Accident. Broken leg. Broken neck. Death. I should have called him, I could have texted him. But – well. I haven't. Our last movie night wasn't exactly a success. Around halfway through I started stressing over what kind of message I was giving out by putting him through *10 Things I Hate About You*, whether I was saying I hated him or the opposite, like with Kat's poem. I also kept thinking about the way Heath tucks Julia's hair behind her ear when he kisses her at the end, and how it would feel for a guy to do that to me. Sol maybe. It made for awkward conversation.

'I don't know what to do,' Carmen says. 'You're his best friend, so I thought maybe you could help me.'

You're a little out of touch on that one, I think sadly. 'Have you argued?'

'We never argue. He's always so nice when I see him. The perfect boyfriend, really.'

'So why is there a problem?'

174

She clasps her hands together. 'The only way I can explain it is that there is a distance that I can't cross. Like he's on the other side of the river and there's no bridge. Do you know what I mean?'

Crapping cat, right there. I nod.

Carmen looks like she's going to cry with relief. 'I knew that you'd understand! I feel like I've been going mad, that this is something I've been doing wrong . . . I'm so glad that I came to see you. So what I wanted to ask you is this.' She leans forward. 'How do I cross the river?'

She's looking at me like I'm some kind of Sol Wiki.

'I'm really sorry,' I say, feeling like a fraud. 'I don't know.'

Carmen's face falls. 'But you are so close to Sol, I thought if anyone knew, you would—'

'I don't think anyone knows Sol very well,' I say. 'Least of all me.'

Carmen bites her lip. Her brown eyes are filling.

'You probably know him better than you think,' I say, hoping to ward off the overspill. 'After all, you've been out with him twice.'

Carmen sniffs. 'No. Just once.'

'I don't know if you were keeping it a secret or something before,' I say, 'but Sol told me at New Year.'

'I have only been dating Sol since March,' says Carmen, her forehead creasing.

Confusion covers me in a big, tangly blanket. 'You *haven't* been out with him twice?'

'No. Did he say we had?'

175

I rewind my head. I could *swear* Sol said he'd split up with Carmen at New Year.

'Maybe I misunderstood,' I say uncertainly. 'Anyway, this kind of proves what we've been saying. Sol is a mystery. I think you have to accept that about him, or give up.'

'Your cake is going cold, Han,' says Raz, putting his head round the kitchen door.

Carmen blushes and stands up from the table. 'I've taken up too much of your time. Thank you, Hanna. Please let me know if you think of something I can do to get closer to Sol. Happy Birthday.'

'How the hell did Solzhenitsyn get *her*?' says Raz as Carmen closes the front door behind her.

31 JULY

How's Sweden?

V Swedish. Hows Venice?

Hot, damp and smelly. Like a very beautiful armpit.

Lovely image, thx

Seen any movies?

Loads. They do this free open-air cinema thing here

They do it here too. Not free though.

Shame about movie night

Shame about movie night

Jinx!!! August if U want? Your pick

Message failed to send

SOL

3 AUGUST

The light here is just like it is in the old paintings you see,
peachy and soft and glowing. It makes every other kind of light
I've ever seen look flat and dull. I want to bathe in it, suck it
into my pores and keep it for ever. I've been returning to the
hotel about ten times a day to download the images I'm getting.
I'm pretty sure the hotel manager thinks I've got the runs.

Of all the bridges in Venice, this one is my favourite. The
life washing beneath me makes our train station look like
the dark side of the moon. Lovers in a slim and beautiful
gondola, more bird than boat, embracing inches away from
their impassive *gondoliere's* bum. A raucous fire barge; a
vaporetto full of tourists hanging off its sides like camera-
clad baubles; an electric-blue funeral boat flying along
unbothered by its serious cargo. I observe it all in the
company of five cats who sit on the parapet beside me as
still as the lions carved at either end. The cats make me
think about Nigel. I wonder if he's killed any dogs or
pedestrians in our absence.

There are a lot of girls who look like Hanna here. I catch endless glimpses of blond ponytails swishing down alleys and round corners. You'd think I'd see more Carmens, but I don't.

My FaceTime button is winking, confusing my eye as I try to photograph a passing ambulance boat.

'Those canals don't look as British as I was expecting,' Frank says.

'Probably because I'm in Venice,' I respond.

'The Vegas one or the other one?'

'The real one.'

'They're both real, man.'

'The one in Italy,' I say patiently. 'Where have you been?'

'Sorting out my love life, like you said.'

I sit down by the parapet. One of the cats jumps lightly off its perch and rubs its mangy coat against my knee. 'Has Lucy dumped Chet yet?'

'Yup,' Frank says. 'I told you this would work out.'

'Don't get too excited,' I advise. 'Lucy dumps people all the time.'

'She never dumped you.'

'I conveniently left the country so she didn't have to. Stage One was always going to be the easy part, Frank. Stage Two is where you are going to come massively unstuck. You are truly deluded if you think—'

Chet Langdale walks past behind Frank's shoulder. I'm so horrified that I almost hurl my phone over the bridge and into the canal. He can't hit me from California, can he?

No one's invented an app where a fist can explode through a touchscreen?

'Frank,' I say quietly. 'Chet's in your room.'

Frank gives a beatific smile. 'I know.'

My throat is as dry as the canal isn't. 'He appears to have no shirt on. Frank, *Chet Langdale is half-naked in your room.*'

'Yes he is,' says Frank.

I put my phone face-down on the hot stones by my feet and cover my eyes with my hands. The parapet cat nudges me again. I give it twenty seconds, then pick the thing up again.

'He was in denial,' Frank says. 'He's not any more.'

'If I'd thought any of this might get real, I would never have encouraged you,' I say when I can speak. 'The guy is a psychopath. Have you forgotten all the stuff he did? The beatings, the torture? Dangling you by the ankles from the fourth-floor window?'

'He was just frustrated and confused. It's always the true closets who hit hardest. Sexually fluid individuals like myself just go with the flow.'

'Just so I'm clear, who moved on who?'

'You have to ask?'

'You are certified,' I say, aghast. 'If you'd been wrong, he might actually have killed you.'

Frank considers this. 'Well,' he says at last, 'he didn't.'

Chet looms on the screen. His face is as dented and furious as ever. 'You tell anybody about this, Adams, and I'll gut you like a jack rabbit,' he says.

'So cute,' says Frank fondly. 'Lucy was a bit freaked when she caught us making out, but she's already dating Preston Lubitz so I guess she's over it. How's things with Hanna?'

Another Hanna-like swishes past, down by the side of the canal below and under the bridge. 'I have no idea,' I say. 'I'm dating Carmen.'

'I can't keep up. Is she hot?'

'She's lovely.'

'Lovely is how you describe old people,' says Frank, unimpressed. 'Is Carmen someone's grandma?'

Chet walks past Frank's phone again, pecs rippling. I hold the screen at arm's length.

'I'm going now, Frank,' I say. 'You can have too much of a good thing.'

I gaze at the canal for a while after I hang up, but don't see much. All I can think about is Frank making a move on the scariest guy in high school. He knew that his teeth could have ended up down his throat if he was wrong, but he still did it. How can any good outcome outweigh that kind of risk? I can't imagine ever being like that.

A green garbage boat clanks towards the bridge. *I am that boat*, I think glumly, as I pick myself up from the cobbles and lean on the parapet of the bridge again. *Full of crap, hidden deep in the dark recesses of my hull*. The garbage boat's slim white arm picks up the shiny dustcarts beside the canal and places them on the deck dumpsters so that their silver bottoms open like music boxes. It's mesmerising, a grubby but rhythmic dance. I film it for a while, until I am calmer.

Hanna

14 AUGUST

I dabble lightly over the side of the diving platform. The water is cold and soft, and drags gently at my fingers. I'd like to stay out here for ever, but that would mean missing Farmor's meatballs, which is not an option.

Raz is still for the first time in hours, sunglasses on his nose, fingers threaded together and resting on his chest. This reclining Buddha thing feels like the quiet before a storm. I'm trying to ignore the feeling that something's up, and am talking to him instead about the plans I've been cooking since we got here. I think he's listening but I'm not a hundred per cent sure.

'There aren't many places in the UK that offer Scandinavian studies but I've found a few online. The one at UCL offers it combined with film studies, which would be completely amazing, don't you think? And you spend a year somewhere like Uppsala or Gothenburg.'

'Mm,' says Raz.

I prod him. 'Don't say that. Sol says that when he doesn't want to talk about something, which basically means that he says it all the time. Do you think it's soft, wanting to do Swedish?'

'Those courses are never just Swedish,' says Raz. 'You'll look at the other Nordic languages as well. Nothing soft about them. What's the time?'

'You asked me that five minutes ago,' I say. 'I said twenty-five minutes to meatballs then. So we can safely assume it's now twenty minutes to meatballs. So, you think it's a good idea?'

'What?'

'Scandinavian studies,' I persist. 'For me.'

'A course like that would suit you.'

'Is that good or bad?'

'I don't know, do I?' he says irritably. 'I'm not you.'

The stillness has gone and he is twitchy again, his foot tapping on the platform and his fingers drumming on his chest. We're at that stage where in films like *A Perfect Storm* or *Life of Pi*, the water begins to rock and grow.

'Are we waiting for something?' I ask.

Raz shades his eyes and stares at the shore. He seems to tense.

'Race you back,' he says.

He reaches across the platform and shoves me in the shoulder. I topple into the chilled satin lake with a squeal. By the time I surface, Raz is halfway towards the shore. I tread water furiously as I adjust my cozzie, then power after him. I haven't done this much exercise since Miss Salter's gym class back at Gordon Lane. I make it to the shore only a couple of seconds after my brother does.

'You cheated,' I gasp, as I haul myself out of the water.

Raz helps me to my feet by putting his arm around my shoulder. Heavy and cold from the lake water, it feels like a dead thing.

'Han,' he says. 'Don't be angry at me, OK?'

I push my waterlogged hair out of my eyes. 'Angry about what?'

A car is idling beside the lake, its engine puttering in the quiet air. A blond woman sits behind the wheel. Walking towards us from the open passenger door is a man who is familiar but not. His sunglasses look like the ones Raz is wearing.

'Him,' Raz says.

It's Dad's snaggly front tooth that catches me, like a shin on the furniture. Isn't it weird, the things you remember? I look at Raz, seeking some kind of cue for how I'm supposed to react.

When Dad reaches us, we all gaze at each other like animals in separate enclosures at the zoo. Someone should sell ice creams, I think.

'You're both very like your mother,' Dad says at last. 'Strange how genes work out.' He glances towards the idling car, the woman behind the wheel. Two small, blond-haired children peep out of the rear window, watching us like a movie.

I want to say something but I have no idea what. Everything I can think of sounds completely stupid in my head. How are you? Is that her? Are they yours? Would 'I carried a watermelon' work in this context?

'I can't stay long,' Dad says.

'The shorter, the better,' says Raz.

Dad slides his sunnies up and I see his eyes for the first time in eight years. They shift uncomfortably in their sockets. 'Making contact was your idea, Rasmus,' he says.

Raz looks exhilarated. 'I said I wanted to see you. I didn't say I wanted to talk to you. You can go back to your other family now.'

'You pulled me twenty minutes off my route just to tell me this?'

'Off you go now.' Raz flicks at the air with the tips of his fingers. 'Shoo.'

'Don't, Raz,' I say uncomfortably.

'I'm sorry, Hanna,' Dad says, looking at me. 'I thought you both wanted to talk to me. But it looks like I have been summoned just to make a point.'

The woman at the wheel of the car is mouthing something at Dad and beckoning. One of the kids in the back has started crying, his wails dimly drifting on the warm summer air.

There is the bang of a screen door and I see Farmor running from the summerhouse, legging it down the lawn with her yellow kaftan billowing and her fingers twisting her old wooden beads tightly in her fist.

'If there's nothing else,' Dad says, 'I'll go. We still have a long drive ahead of us.'

'Where are you going?' It occurs to me that I asked the same question the last time we saw each other.

'North. Else's family has a summerhouse in Juniskär. Four hours from here, give or take. The kids need lunch.'

'Can't disappoint the kids, can we?' says Rasmus.

'I'm sorry,' Dad says. 'I shouldn't have come.'

He walks back to the car. The passenger door has barely shut before the woman has put the car into drive, swinging away from the lake with a crunch of gravel. Farmor reaches us, gasping, her hands pressed to her chest as the car drives away.

'It's OK, Farmor.' Raz finds my hand and squeezes it. His palm is sweaty and his fingers are trembling. 'He was never going to stay for meatballs.'

24 AUGUST

Fancy a Danish?

Eaten already thx

A Danish film set in Italy. Saw it in Venice. A-MA-ZING.

Never heard U so enthusiastic but Swedish not the same as Danish . . .?

You want to do Scandinavian Studies with Film Studies? Preparation right here.

Will I have 2 concentr8?

Bit more than normal maybe. Completely worth it.

Fine coz need sth 2 stop me THINKING

Seen Trixie lately?

Haha NOT

ITALIAN FOR
BEGINNERS (2000)

WRITER &
DIRECTOR   LONE SCHERFIG

Based on the novel by Maeve Binchy

This gentle romantic comedy follows the stories of six people whose lives interweave one dreary Copenhagen winter. Soon after arriving in town, Andreas (Anders W. Berthelsen), a young sensitive church minister, is persuaded to sign up for Italian lessons along with five other lonely singletons. Upon his arrival in the class, each of the characters makes a major decision that will change the course of their lives.

Italian for Beginners is shot according to the austere rules of the 'Dogme 95' movement, which requires the use of natural lighting and hand-held cameras with no special effects. In May 2010, Scherfig admitted to having borrowed the story idea from Irish author Maeve Binchy's book, *Evening Class*.

SOL

31 AUGUST

My hands are shaking as I cue up the movie.

'Why are you nervous?' Hanna's long brown legs are wound up in some kind of knot that looks as if it'll need a blast of WD40 to straighten them out again.

I wipe my hands on my jeans and attempt to steady my fingers. It's ridiculous that a movie has made me feel this way. I must have seen it twenty times since we got back from Venice, and every time I watch it I'm amazed all over again. I will probably always associate it with the smell of the garbage boat making its rusty way down the canal below our hotel window as I watched, transfixed, late into the night on my hotel-room telly.

'I just really want you to like it,' I say.

'Will I fancy anyone in it?'

'Han, you have to start thinking more seriously about movies if you want to study them,' I say. 'This is art, not pornography.'

'No need to be so bloody serious, Professor.'

'Sorry,' I say. 'I don't mean to be heavy-handed. It's just . . . I love this film.'

I settle beside her and drench myself in the hand-held camera work and the grey and dreary light of a Copenhagen winter. The staccato sounds of Danish blast around the room, raw and unattractive and hypnotic. All the editing work that I do with my films seems so fake by comparison. At last, something *real*.

After about twenty minutes, Hanna speaks.

'It's easier to understand than I thought it would be. Danes understand Swedish but it doesn't always work the other way round.'

'That's what the subtitles are for,' I point out.

'The subtitles aren't right though. They aren't translating it properly.'

'It's fine,' I say, concentrating.

'His hair is *awful*, isn't it?' Hanna says a few minutes later. 'Like a greasy pair of curtains.'

She peppers the next ten minutes of the film with similar observations. Everyone is ugly. Doesn't it ever stop raining?

'Are we watching this or not?' I say.

'You want me to stop talking?' says Hannah. 'Fine. I'll stop talking.'

For the next forty-five minutes, I am permitted to lose myself in the story without interruptions. The hapless characters unfold like the paper figures in Mr Yamauchi's classes, all stiff limbs and issues. No tricks, no props. No stage sets. Everything painfully, wonderfully true.

As the evening class makes it to a Venice so cold and rainy that it looks like Manchester, Nigel smashes into the room and hurls himself at the curtains. I leap out of myself, spilling what's left of my stone-cold tea down my front.

I pull off my T-shirt as Gareth appears in the door with a cat box, wearing gardening gloves and a fencing helmet. 'We're down to the last vet in the area prepared to worm him.' His voice is muffled by the helmet. 'I hope this one has stronger nerves than the last. Hanna gone, has she?'

I realise for the first time that Hanna isn't on the sofa.

'Bathroom?' I hazard.

Gareth pulls a chair close to the curtains and climbs up. 'There's no one in the bathroom,' he says, grabbing for Nigel and almost bringing down the curtain pole. 'I heard the back door shut about ten minutes ago though. Come here you bloody cat.'

Hanna is sitting at the garden table, staring at the hedge.

'I wondered when you'd notice,' she says as I join her on the bench. Her legs are knotted up again, tied around each other like pick-and-mix licorice laces.

I wait.

'Dad doesn't want to know us,' she tells the hedge. 'He left. After two minutes.'

'You said Rasmus told him to leave.'

'He'd have stayed if he wanted to. Whatever Raz said.' She wipes at her eyes with the heels of her hands. 'Everything's weird at home now. Farmor rang Mum and told her what happened. Now Mum and James are both creeping around Raz like he's ill and me like I'm made of glass and they keep asking: how do you feel? How do you feel? *All the bloody time*. I don't know how I feel. I don't think you can summarise this in a handy little parcel of "upset" or "angry" or whatever one-word answer they're looking for.'

I put my hand on hers. The heat of her skin soaks upwards into mine. It's the first time I've touched her in months.

'Raz had been building up to those two minutes since March, just after Leah screwed him over. He says it made him think about the last person to hurt him like that. He got in touch with Dad to stop him thinking about Leah. Now he needs something to stop him thinking about Dad. It's a mess.'

The snake that eats its tail, I think.

Hanna pulls her hand free and wipes her nose with the sleeve of her jumper. 'Was Dad leaving why I started expecting the worst of people? The worst of Lizzie over the Jake thing last summer?'

'Only you can answer that.'

'How can a person not want to know their kids?'

'Gareth's mum doesn't want to know Gareth. He told her he was gay when he was twenty and she turned him out of the house.'

'God,' says Hanna, staring at her hands.

'She's my real grandmother, by the way,' I feel compelled to add. 'Gareth's my birth father. She's never met Andrew, despite the fact that my parents have been together for twenty-four years. Gareth sends her a Christmas card every year, and every year she doesn't send one back. I wouldn't know her if I saw her.'

Hanna stops staring at the hedge and looks at me. Unaccountably, she turns bright red.

'Why aren't you wearing a T-shirt?' she says.

'Tea.' I gesture at my chest, for reasons unknown as it's clear she can see it for herself. 'Nigel made me spill it.'

'Put something on, for God's sake!'

She sounds genuinely horrified. And there's me thinking my chest was one of my few decent features. It's even gone a little browner than normal. Shows what I know. I go inside and fish a T-shirt out of the cupboard above the boiler, where Andrew puts the laundry when he can't be bothered to carry it upstairs.

'Better?' I say, going back outside. 'Look, this has only just happened, it's going to take time for you both to absorb it. Don't expect too much of yourselves for a while.'

My phone beeps. I have an awful feeling that it's Carmen. I've been avoiding her since I got back from Venice, hoping that she'll think I'm still away and have no reception.

Hanna stands up. 'I'd better go. You've probably got things to do and I've got things to do and there are, you know, things to do.'

'Did you like the film?' I ask, feeling anxious.

'Yes! I mean, I wasn't really watching it, but yes. It was good, what I saw.'

'Can we watch it again some other time?'

Hanna seems nervous all of a sudden. 'That breaks the rules of movie night a bit, don't you think?'

'Promise me you'll watch it, though? You don't have to watch it with me, but – just watch it, OK? If you want to do Scandinavian film studies, you could do worse than dazzle the director of studies in an interview with stuff about the Dogme 95 movement.'

Nigel rockets down the garden with the cat-box grille attached to his back legs. It makes the most horrific clanking sound you've ever heard.

'Right,' says Hanna. 'Bye.'

She goes one way for a kiss and I go the other and we sort of bang noses. We've never done that before. She retreats, blushes, stretches out a hand and pats me on the shoulder before heading into the kitchen almost as fast as Nigel left it.

'Do you want to meet at the lake tomorrow?' I say, following her to the front door. 'There's a whole load of people going.'

'Better not. College starts next week and I have to be ready.' She makes these little boxing movements, then stares at her fists like she's never seen them before. 'What subject are you dropping this year by the way?' she says, looking at me in a way that suggests this is a very important question.

I'm a little bewildered by the sudden change of subject. Last time I looked, we were talking about life, not textbooks. 'Geography. I did OK in the AS but I don't need it for what I want to do next. You?'

'History. I love it and everything but I think I need Media Studies and English and, particularly, French because French is a language and I ought to show that I can speak a language.' She says all of this very quickly. 'See you.'

'Uh, yes,' I tell the door as it closes behind her. 'Sure. Next week.'

'Have you seen Nigel?' asks Gareth breathlessly from the landing. What remains of the cat box dangles from his hand.

Still staring at the front door, I gesture over my shoulder with my thumb. Muttering, Gareth comes down. The fencing helmet cannons off the kitchen door frame as he goes outside.

Hanna

1 SEPTEMBER

Lizzie looks at me lurking behind a pine tree from over the top of her sunglasses.

'You can come out now,' she says. 'The Gruffalo's gone.'

'I told Sol I wouldn't be coming today,' I say anxiously. 'I really, I don't think I should be here. I think I'll just . . .' I point back in the direction of the bus stop. The exhaust from the last bus is still hanging in the air under the trees.

'Is this about the Sol-baring-his-chest thing?'

It was only yesterday but I've relived it for what feels like about six months. 'It was so awful, Lizzie,' I plead. 'He must think I'm completely insane.'

'Tell me again,' Lizzie asks, grinning. 'His *whole* T-shirt was off?'

'Explain to me how it was ever going to be half a T-shirt?'

Lizzie hefts her beach bag over her shoulder. 'You can see what I mean about him stopping traffic that time by the lockers now,' she says. 'Come on, you idiot. We're here, so you're going to make the best of it before I have to go.'

First I notice his bum. Now I will never be able to unnotice his chest with accompanying six-pack rippling down to his tummy button and these muscly bits leading into the waistband of his jeans. I'm going to see it again today, if he's here like he said he was going to be. I'll probably see most of the rest of him too. He's hardly going to be hanging out by the lake fully clothed in temperatures like this. Where am I going to look? Steadily into his eyes? People only look steadily into your eyes when they are trying *not* to look steadily everywhere else.

I *like* how it's always been with Sol. Well, apart from the secrets and the trainspotting thing. Now that I've noticed I'm holding a soap bubble, I can guarantee that my fingers will twitch and – POP. What we have will vanish in a spray of rainbows. With everything else feeling so shaky in my life at present, this level of confusion is the last thing that I need.

More people are walking this way from the bus stop. I look like a fool or a flasher standing here. I peel myself reluctantly away from the tree and follow Lizzie over the pine cones and needles and tree roots to where the sand begins.

It's like the seaside today. Little kids digging channels to flood muddy sandcastle moats, girls in bikinis, barbecue smoke hanging in a haze. Brightly coloured towels are scattered around the scrubby sand like slicks of poster paint.

Down by the water's edge, Stevie has started a football game, with all the usual suspects running around in dodgy beach shorts. Sol isn't with them, unsurprisingly. Lying close to the action like a row of spray-tanned sausages are Vashti, Laura and Trixie. Every now and again, they squeal as the ball showers them with sand. Like they don't get enough of that at the dirt track.

I can't see Sol. Maybe he's not—

'Over there,' says Lizzie, pointing. 'With Carmen. God! Doesn't she look amazing?'

Sol and Carmen are sitting in what look like matching deckchairs set a little way back from the shore. In a red swimsuit that is both demure and spectacularly sexy, Carmen is oiling her slim brown arms with something. A battered straw hat is tilted forward over Sol's face, shading him from the sun. He's wearing a shirt, although it's unbuttoned.

Lizzie dumps her bag in a sandy space partially shaded by the lake reeds. It's not in Sol and Carmen's direct eyeline. Nor is it within range of Trixie, Vashti or Laura. It'll do.

'Down to business,' Lizzie says when we have finished putting sun cream on each other. 'Worst swimming costume?'

I stop staring at Sol and Carmen. 'Him,' I say, pointing at a gentleman carrying an ice cream down the beach in a long blue and yellow Hawaiian pair. 'Worst eyewear?'

Lizzie points at Vashti's bug-eyed numbers. We continue down the list we have always compiled on the past occasions we have visited the lake on hot summer days: worst footwear (sparkly heels), best hat (huge floppy white number on a girl by the café), worst towel (brown scrag barely large enough for its owner's bum), most inappropriate beach make up. With their drawn-on eyebrows, red lips and glittery cheekbones, Vashti, Laura and Trixie tie for that one. I laugh at Lizzie's imitation of Vashti trying to cope with sand embedding itself in her lipgloss, and I feel . . . almost normal.

'Raz is over there,' Lizzie says presently.

I prop myself up. 'Where?'

'Where half the girls on this beach are looking.'

With his Swedish tan, aviators and the moody expression he's taken to wearing recently, Raz is getting more than his fair share of attention as he lies sprawled on his towel with half his face in *War and Peace*. He looks up as I wave. He looks down again without waving back.

'Do you think he needs oiling?' Lizzie asks hopefully.

'That's my brother you're talking about,' I say. 'Oil him at your peril. He's been awful since . . . Well. Since.'

'So have you,' Lizzie says. 'I still covered you in sun cream.'

Raz's sour expression together with the glimmer and gleam of the lake are bringing back something I don't want to deal with this afternoon. Naturally, it comes into sharp focus. Mainly the bit where Dad walks away. It makes me think about what Sol said about his grandmother. It makes me feel angry.

'Bitch,' I say under my breath.

It feels good, saying that. Like when there's someone really horrible in a movie and you're allowed to shout and yell at them because none of it is real.

'Bitch,' I say again, more loudly. I snatch up my beach bag and bury my face in it. 'GODDAMN BITCH,' I say very loudly indeed.

'Charmed,' says Lizzie, from somewhere underneath the multicoloured straw sombrero she's had since we were fourteen.

I lower the beach bag.

'Hello, my name is Mr Lewis,' I say evenly. 'I am very angry with my father.'

'*Pretty Woman*,' says Lizzie. 'Good work, Han. Keep it up.'

I flop back on my towel. 'Sol told me something about his grandmother yesterday,' I tell the sky.

'Before or after he removed his shirt?'

And – the chest is back. Broad. Warm. Sitting beside me. 'He said his grandmother kicked his dad out of the house because he was gay.' It's the first properly private thing Sol's ever told me, I realise.

'How does a parent do that to a child?'

'My question exactly.'

Who's wrong? I think with a sudden jolt of clarity. *The parent or the child?* It's obvious, isn't it? Why should the answer I'm looking for be any different?

Dan suddenly looms over us both in skimpy bathers. He has a leather string around his neck, complete with shark tooth.

'Hey, Hanna,' he says.

'There are two of us here, Dan,' I say as Lizzie silently pulls her sombrero over her face.

'Right,' says Dan. 'Hi, Lizzie.'

Lizzie raises her arm from the towel and offers him a middle finger. Dan scratches himself under one powerful, coconut-scented armpit. He's still unbelievably hot, I think sadly. Unbelievably, spectacularly hot.

'You know where I am,' he says.

'Indeed we do,' says Lizzie from under her hat as he saunters away. 'We can smell you from here.'

I drag my eyes from Dan's perfectly formed butt and tip up the edge of Lizzie's sombrero. 'I won't go out with him again,' I say.

She arches her eyebrows at me.

'Lizzie, I mean it. There is no way on earth that I would go out with him again. Not after everything. Not after you.'

I glance at Sol and Carmen's deckchairs and feel a moment of panic. Sol isn't there any more. I twist around like a fish on a line, scoping out the crowds. Preparing myself to be entirely and completely normal.

He's seen me. He's coming to talk to me.

He wants to know why I acted so weirdly yesterday.

What am I going to say?

A wet hat flies up from the water and lands beside me in the sand. The most godawful commotion starts up in the reeds next to us. And as Lizzie and I both get to our feet, we are confronted with a sight that I won't get out of my head for all eternity.

SOL

I push back my hat and squint down at the reeds beside the lake, to the place where my girlfriend is pointing. She's right. Hanna's here. I try not to stare at her long brown legs stretched out on her towel. All that Swedish sun and emotion has turned her the most unbelievable colour.

'She said she wasn't coming,' I say.

Carmen slathers one last bit of sun cream into her ankles. 'When did you last see her?'

I feel a surge of guilt. Why? All I did was touch her hand, repulse her with my body and make her run away. That hardly constitutes adultery.

'Yesterday. Movie night.'

'I saw her last month,' Carmen says. 'Did she tell you?'

I feel a rush of panic. 'You saw her?'

'There's no need to look so worried. You're not in trouble. I just went to talk to her about something.'

'What did you talk about?' I ask uneasily.

Carmen taps her nose. 'Girl things.'

Do 'girl things' include weird lies your boyfriend has told about dating you twice? Carmen would have said something. Hanna too. Or was that why she ran off? These thoughts chase around my head like scared rabbits. Sweat prickles under my arms.

'I need a swim,' I say. 'Do you want to come?'

Carmen settles back in her chair. 'No thanks. But you can swim if you want. Don't worry about me.'

I drop my shirt on the chair and pick through the sunbathing crowds, weaving through the little kids with their buckets and spades. A swan watches from the reeds, nodding its ice-white head in disdain as I wade into the water and sink into its green depths. It's not hard to see why water is a thing in so many religions. It really can feel as if you're washing something away. I lie back in the chill, float for a bit, paddling gently with my hands, feeling the water turning me round in lazy circles.

I have a sense after a while that someone is watching me. Lowering my feet to the silty mud, I stand up. Vashti Wong is in front of me. She is eyeing my chest.

'You do keep yourself under wraps,' she says.

I have an absurd urge to cover myself with my hands. 'Hey,' I say, casting around for help.

She dips down, smiling, and swims a little closer. 'I know you find me attractive,' she states.

I swallow. 'You – how do you know that?'

She lifts one water-spangled shoulder. Dips down into the water and swims closer still. 'Boys do.'

She is backing me into the reeds. Water trembles on her oddly long eyelashes.

'Vashti, look, I'm really flattered and everything,' I begin, 'but I'm here with my girlfriend and—'

She is close enough now for me to feel her against my chest.

'No one can see us here,' Vashti says. 'Stop worrying so much.'

She lifts my hat off my head and tosses it over the reeds. Then she grabs my head between her hands and lunges at my mouth. Her lips taste sweet and sticky. She's – her body is—

The swan explodes out of the reeds, its mean little eyes glaring and its wings battering the water. Vashti screams. I get a noseful of green lake water. All I can see are white feathers, hard black feet and the odd flash of bikini.

Vashti screams again and puts her hands over her head as the swan grimly batters away. A multicoloured sombrero appears over the top of the reeds directly behind the action. Like something in a bad movie, Hanna's head pops up beside it. I attempt to shoo the swan away, shielding myself from the blows of its wings. With one last lunge, the swan ruffles its feathers and slopes back into the long grasses fringing the lake shore, hissing under its breath. Vashti is still shrieking like a rocket balloon.

'I thought he was one of the good ones,' says the sombrero. It's Lizzie.

204

The look on Hanna's face would kill that swan stone-dead if it looked in her direction. 'Turns out all boys are the same. Nice lipgloss, Sol.'

I attempt to wipe the lipgloss off my mouth. There's sand in it. Why do girls wear this stuff? 'This isn't how it looks,' I say.

Hanna stares wordlessly at the top half of Vashti's bikini, which has come off in the fight and is now floating towards the shore. Vashti is splashing after it, trying to catch it before one of the grinning little kids with buckets can scoop it up and fly it from the top of their sandcastle.

'Nice, Sol,' Hanna says. 'Really classy behaviour.'

This really isn't fair.

'She came at me!' I shout.

'And I suppose the swan took Vashti's bikini top off for her?' Lizzie asks.

'That'll be its opposable thumbs,' Hanna says.

'This isn't my fault!'

Hanna throws my hat at me. It hits my shoulder with a soggy thump.

'Course it's not,' she says. 'And I'm sure Carmen will see it that way too.'

RoboCop will kill me. 'Don't tell her,' I say in horror. 'Hanna, don't you dare . . . This . . . I'm—'

Hanna drops out of view. Swearing violently under my breath, I wade all the way round the reeds and back to the shore, where Vashti is huddled on her towel with Trixie and Laura, all three of them shrieking in unison and peering at me. Hanna wouldn't tell Carmen, would she?

'Han!' I bellow, shortly before collapsing on the sand, thanks to a football bouncing off my stomach.

'Golden rule of beach football, man.' Stevie helps me, wheezing, to my feet. 'Never run between a man and his goal. What's going on with you and Vashti?'

'Vashti jumped me just now and Hanna saw,' I say in frustration. 'I have to tell her it wasn't my fault.'

Stevie shakes his head. 'Nine months dating Trixie has taught me a few things about women,' he says. 'They believe what they want to believe.'

'Well, Hanna believes I'm a complete lowlife!'

'Better than believing you have no balls at all.' Stevie replaces the ball on the sand. 'Incoming!' he roars at Jake in goal.

I move a little more thoughtfully up the beach to where Carmen is waving at me, all red swimsuit and long black hair.

'What was that noise?' she asks.

I replace my wet hat and sit down. 'Swan attack,' I say from under the brim.

Hanna

I am still trembling from the shock as I stand in line for ice creams. Twice now I've had to watch Sol with his tongue down a girl's throat. Friendships rarely survive this level of graphic oversharing. I rub my eyes. I don't think I'll ever erase the picture of him in the reeds with his arms round Vashti Wong, water running down the muscled indentation of his spine.

I get a waft of lemon and coconut as I reach the counter. Detaching himself from a nearby pine tree, Dan sidles over again.

'Waiting for an ice cream?' he says.

'No,' I say irritably. 'I'm just standing in the queue enjoying the wasps.'

Dan runs his hands through his hair, throwing the muscles on his arms into fine relief. 'I'm sorry about everything in December,' he says, looking at me from under his thick black eyebrows. 'I'll buy you an ice cream to make up for it.'

Dan Dukas, apologising? I don't know how many more shocks I can take today. 'Ice cream doesn't really cover it,' I say. 'But – thanks.'

He nods at the café guy, who seems to produce a coffee and chocolate ice cream in double-quick time. I'm astonished all over again.

Dan gives me one of his mega-watt smiles. 'Favourite flavours, right? I haven't forgotten anything about you, Birdgal.'

I give an instinctive snort through the ice cream. He never could say Bergdahl.

'Let's go for a walk.' Dan clears his throat. 'I mean, do you want to go for a walk?'

I'm enjoying Dan-who-asks-questions. It won't last, but it's amusing.

'A walk?' I check. 'Or a "walk"?'

'You ask the dumbest questions sometimes, Birdgal.'

OK. So now I'm walking towards the trees that fringe the lake, with Dan's arm round my shoulders. This is weird. And also wrong. But very nice. But very bad. Lizzie will kill me.

'I've missed you,' Dan says.

I have a mouthful of coffee and chocolate ice cream and a case of brain freeze, so I don't answer this incredible statement.

'You've missed me too,' he supplies, giving me that sidelong look that always slays me. *Used* to slay me. 'Have you missed me too?'

I've certainly missed this, I think. Attention from a hot guy with tar-black eyes. A genuine distraction from all the recent crap.

'Not much,' I say.

'You're not like the other girls.'

'I hate to be the one to break the news, but girls aren't all the same,' I say, sinking down by the root of a shady tree.

'You were for a while. Then you weren't.' He frowns. 'You threw sand at me in the woods.'

I colour. 'I was mad at you.'

'Girls don't do that stuff to me. I can't stop thinking about it. About you. I've been waiting for you to come back, Hanna. I've been waiting to make it right.'

The ice cream is gone, gobbled down embarrassingly fast. I bet Vashti would still be nibbling at it in a fetching manner. I lean my head against the tree and close my eyes and try not to belch. What am I doing here?

'I'm not back, Dan,' I say. 'I'm just—'

I feel a hot mouth on my ice-creamy lips. I open my eyes wide in shock to find that Dan has put his arms round me and is properly, full-on, *snogging* me. His tongue is bucking in and out of my mouth. His chest is warm and fragrant against me. His hands are – busy.

I'd forgotten how good he is at this.

I haven't kissed anyone in such a long time. I've missed it. Even Sol's done this a hundred times more than I have in the last nine months. With two girls. More, for all I know. I've missed how fantastically uncomplicated it is when you're doing it and how you don't have to think about anything else. I've had so much stuff running around my head for weeks, months, and now it's all flooding out of me in a great big whoosh of heat and energy. I can't seem to stop it.

'You're so hot,' he mumbles against my mouth. 'You taste amazing.'

That'll be the coffee and chocolate ice cream, I want to say, but lust is raging through me and I can't seem to talk. *I'm melting . . . MELLLTIING . . .* as the Wicked Witch of the West would say in a similar situation. Someone needs to save me from myself—

'Hanna?'

I push Dan off at the horrifying sight of Trixie boggling at us through the trees. There is too much blood in my head right now for me to formulate a sentence. Trixie squeals and vanishes. Somehow I get to my feet. It's not entirely clear whether my legs are going to hold me up.

'Don't try that again,' I say when I'm upright, wiping my mouth with one trembling hand.

Dan pouts like a sprawling Greek god at my feet. He wraps a hand around one of my ankles. 'Why not? Birdgal, we're so hot together.'

Does he really not know? Is he really so stupid? I shake him off my ankle, turn my back and walk unsteadily out of the trees. If I don't play this carefully, things with Lizzie could go as pear-shaped as they did in the summer.

Trixie is waiting for me on the fringes of the beach. There's an expression on her face that makes me nervous.

210

'It's not what it looks like,' I begin. A bad start because it puts me on the defensive. I may have seen *Rocky* four times (*Keep hittin' them in the ribs, ya see? Don't let that bastard breathe!*) but clearly it's taught me nothing.

'Come on, Hanna. You weren't exactly collecting pine cones.'

'Dan surprised me,' I say weakly.

'You walked in to the trees with him. He had his arm round you. What happened next was a "surprise"? And with Lizzie being so heartbroken over Dan too.' Trixie catches my expression. 'Not as stupid as you think, am I?'

Plan A is out of the window. Whatever Plan A was going to be. Plan B is basically to beg.

'Please Trixie, for the sake of our friendship—'

'Babes,' Trixie points out, 'you haven't said two words to me since your embarrassing little outburst in the woods in May in front of Vashti and Laura. I don't think friendship comes into it any more. Do you?'

Trixie isn't Trixie any more, I realise. She's Michael Corleone, she's Clint Eastwood in *Unforgiven*. She's every revenge movie I have ever seen, minus the blood.

'Don't look so worried, Hanna,' Trixie adds. 'I might not tell her at all.'

4 SEPTEMBER

> U seen Lizzie @ college this wk? Is she OK? I cant find her

Is there a problem?

> Have you heard stuff?

What stuff?

> Forget it. I didnt tell Carmen by the way even tho U deserved it

Looked worse than it was.

> U were kissing V tho

You ever been in a situation which looks bad but isn't your fault?

> Ask Lizzie 2 call me? If U C her?

Hanna

'The trouble with beer,' Raz informs me, 'is that you have to pee *all* the time. Someone needs to distil—' He breaks off here to hiccup, 'the essence of beer into a neat, small mouthful, like a cup of espresso.'

When Rasmus is drunk, he's all words. He's been drunk since we got back two weeks ago. That's a *lot* of words.

'I'm thinking of trying absinthe. The stuff of poets and artists. I bet Dostoyevsky drank it. It comes in smaller portions than beer and drives you mad.'

I try Lizzie's number again. Still nothing. I don't know what she's heard, what she knows or thinks she knows. All I have to go on is a text message sent after she vanished from the beach, saying she had to leave because she was too hot and she'd talk to me later. But we haven't talked later. We haven't talked at all. The uncertainty of what Trixie's said or not said is *killing* me.

'Going to order some absinthe online,' Raz says, trailing up the stairs.

He shuts his bedroom door with that extra-careful clunk he does when he's off his face, in the hope that Mum and James won't notice.

The phone has barely squeaked when I'm snatching it up.

'Lizzie, it's true but it's totally not my fault and I still mean it when I say I wouldn't go out with him again. It's—'

'I'll stop you there,' says Sol. 'I think I know why you haven't heard from Lizzie.'

My hands are suddenly so clammy that it's a challenge to hold the phone. 'What's Trixie told you?'

'I never speak to Trixie.'

'You're friends with Stevie though. And since Stevie is going out with Trixie, I assume he talks to her.' If I grip this phone any harder, it's going to shoot out of my hand like a bar of soap. 'Tell me the worst.'

'Hanna, you're being weird. I've just worked out that Lizzie is probably in Scotland visiting universities. There are a couple with open days this week, a few people in our maths class were heading up there.'

Sweet baby badgers gambolling in sunsets. Architecture at Strathclyde and Dundee. Lizzie even told me she was going. I've been so caught up in this whole thing that I completely forgot. If Lizzie's in Scotland, it's likely that she still hasn't spoken to Trixie. She won't know about me and Dan. She's still talking to me. In an abstract kind of way at least. She might not have phone reception.

'That is the best piece of news I have had all week,' I say in relief. 'I could kiss your face right off for telling me that.'

214

Not appropriate. I need to get a grip.

'I'm going to Sheffield next week,' Sol says. 'Thought I'd check out a course there. Are you doing any open days?'

'Haven't made any plans.'

'I thought you wanted to check out Scandinavian film studies.'

Upstairs, Raz has turned on what I call his Angry Music. It's loud and is rattling the light fitting above my head. I think of Singö and the sound of tyres on gravel.

'I did,' I say. 'I don't any more.'

'Because of your dad?'

I wish Sol wasn't so perceptive.

'Don't let him stop you exploring ideas for your future, Hanna. If I overthought half the things my family does, I'd never leave my bedroom.'

My eyes fill with tears. They've been doing that a lot lately. 'Which feels worse, do you think? Your mum not wanting to know you, or your dad?'

'Depends on the relationship you have with them.'

I ponder this. 'I never had much of a relationship with Dad. Even when he lived with us. It's a horrible thing to say, but it's true. He was always travelling. Business. I didn't even know why he left. None of us knew. He never said a thing. If he'd told us, we might have been more prepared, and maybe none of this Rasmus stuff would be going down right now.'

'I think I only met him once.'

I nod even though Sol can't see me. 'My birthday party in the town hall with a magician. The magician had a real rabbit, and when he pulled it out of the hat I cried because I wanted to keep it but Dad said I couldn't.'

'How do you remember that?'

'Easy,' I say. 'He didn't come to any of the others.'

'Did he go to any of Raz's?'

I stare at the wall. 'Don't know. Don't remember.'

The Angry Music upstairs gets louder.

'Raz will be OK,' Sol says. 'In a couple of weeks, he'll have university to distract him.'

'I hope so,' I say.

We're quiet for a bit. I don't mind. It's nice. I get more comfy on my sofa and imagine Sol getting comfy on his. Maybe without his shirt on.

'Sol,' I say presently, 'can I ask you something? It's a big question.'

'Should I be worried?'

'I know you don't like personal questions, but after you told me about Gareth's mum and everything I wondered if maybe you were ready for some more questions, like—'

'Hanna, just ask it.'

'How often do you think about your mother?'

I wonder if I've crossed the line. But amazingly, Sol answers without a beat.

'I don't. But she's never been in my life, which brings us back to what I said about relationships. The rest is just biology.'

'You're so *together*,' I say.

'I'm the opposite of together, Han. I'm—'

216

He stops.

'You're what?' I ask.

'Curious,' he says slowly. 'What did you mean when you said it was true but not your fault? When you thought I was Lizzie?'

'Nothing,' I say, blenching. 'Forget you heard it. Bye.'

As I hang up, I think about his back again, the water droplets on his shoulder blades and Vashti's arms round his neck. I hope for Carmen's sake he's telling the truth about that snog not being his fault. Although I'm hardly in a position to judge him for it, am I?

SOL

13 SEPTEMBER

Gareth storms out of the bedroom and slams the door so hard the glass jumps in the window frame.

'I thought he'd at least *listen*,' I say at last.

Putting Nigel down – who has been strangely docile throughout this drama – Andrew gets off the bed and dusts down his trousers. 'Based on what?' he enquires, rubbing his forehead. 'Your shared interest in *The Godfather Part II*? You've just dropped this on us like a very heavy rock! There should be *gradients* with these things, Sol. Hints, discussions. We were only talking about accountancy a couple of months ago, or is my memory full of holes?'

I shake my head. His memory works just fine.

'You shouldn't have gone skulking off to check out this Sheffield film course like some kind of Navy SEAL with a camera, you should have talked to us about it. Is it any wonder Gareth is upset?'

Anger has started spreading through me like a hot red

218

mist, like the time I punched Dan. *I'm allowed a life*, I think. *I'm allowed that.*

'He should have listened,' I repeat stubbornly.

'And you should have been honest about your plans sooner.'

Well, that's rich. 'And we all know where honesty got Gareth,' I say before I can stop myself.

Andrew looks astonished. 'What did you say?'

I grab my phone and shove it in my pocket. I'm down the stairs, two or three steps at a time.

'Where are you going?' asks Andrew. 'Sol, tell me where you're—'

But I have already slammed the front door. Every part of me is blazing like a furnace. I could rip up the shrubs that crouch beneath the windows all along this road. I could leap into the traffic, arms windmilling, to smash windscreens and crunch car bonnets beneath my mighty feet. I am not my mother, my father, my bloody grandmother. I am not an accountant, I'm not the gay best friend. I'm ME.

Somehow I'm on the footbridge already. Feelings are surging through me that I can't contain. I have to focus, and the only way to focus is through the little screen in my shaking hand, to contain this uncontainable world, reduce it to pixels and stop it from hurting me. Right now, it's hurting me a lot.

My phone slides from my trembling grasp through the lattice ironwork of the footbridge and clatters to the tracks below. I can't breathe for the horror. I have lost the only anchor I have.

Incredibly, my phone lands on its back, its screen intact and glinting up at me, swearing blind that it's alive and well and isn't it clever for falling so far, so fast? Without thinking, I'm taking the steps back down four at a time, flying as I go, vaulting over the handrail and landing with a crunch on the slim segment of the platform between the steps and the tracks.

I jump down further. I have lost all sense of time and timetable. I need my phone, my films. Without my viewfinder, I am nothing and nowhere.

A cry goes up along the platform.

'Man on the track! MAN ON THE TRACK!'

Stupid guy, I think, scrambling down to the tangle and hum of steel. I hear the DING DING DING of the crossing, the great white arms swinging down from their lofty heights to prevent idiot drivers from killing themselves in the race to be first at the school gates or the hairdressers, or wherever they think is more important than the imminent splintering of blood and bone. Four express trains hurtle through this place, Cyclops eyes unblinking, passing through on the half hour, twice on their way to London and twice on their way back, carrying broken hearts and bicycles, worlds within worlds, families, lovers, mothers with their sons.

Everybody knows that.

Hanna

I still haven't told Lizzie about me and Dan. I am telling myself that this is because there *is* no me and Dan, so there's really nothing to tell. I'm not going out with him again. I haven't even spoken to him since the beach. He's tried calling a few times but I always let it go to voicemail. Every time I struggle, I make myself remember Lizzie's face over her coffee cup in my bedroom in May. When I look at it like that, it's really not so hard.

It helps that Lizzie can talk about nothing but the incredible architecture course at Strathclyde. How it's everything she's ever wanted, how amazing the tutors are, how much practical experience she'll get on the course, how she can't wait for it all to happen. If the conversation ever feels like it's drifting into dangerous waters, I say, 'Tell me again about those urban context projects you'll be doing in your third year', and she's off, happily boring me to death.

Do I trust Trixie? No. Can I see what Trixie would get out of telling Lizzie any of this stuff? No. Round and round it goes, through my head, as rhythmic as the clatter of this train, weaving through today's jumbled impressions of lecture theatres, film equipment, library facilities.

There is a sudden squee of air brakes and a lot of shouting as we pull into the station. The train stops more suddenly than it normally does, and throws several people off balance as they reach for their coats and bags.

Sliding the fat UCL brochure into my bag, I gather my things together and peer out of the window, down the length of the train, up to the front where the platform slopes away to the road and the level crossing arms. People are clustering around something on the ground. There seems to be a lot of noise beyond the slamming train doors, whistles and announcements.

I hear the tapping sound of fingers on the train window. Dan is thrusting a bunch of flowers up against the pitted glass, crushing their stamens in a pitiful smear of yellow.

'Birdgal!' he mouths. Behind him, I see a girl cannon off one of the station concourse pillars because she's staring at him. 'I've been waiting for you! I got you flowers!' he says, as if I can't see them for myself.

I get off the train, trying to see past the heads and bodies walking and running towards whatever is going on.

'I got you flowers,' Dan repeats.

My stomach clenches. It's a person lying on the platform. I take the flowers and stuff them into my bag and duck Dan's kiss.

'What's going on? Down there, what's happened?'

Dan reluctantly winds his lips back in. 'Someone jumped in front of the train. I never got a girl flowers before,' he adds. 'I got them from the garage over the road.'

Someone jumped. Someone actually chose to run and jump in front of my train. I picture *Brief Encounter*, Celia Johnson running towards the express, anguish all over her elegant, black and white face. 'How awful,' I say, when I can speak.

Dan frowns. 'The girl in the garage said you'd like them.'

Is he serious?

'Was the person hit?' I ask, pushing him aside. 'Are they dead?'

'Do you like them? Or should I have got the roses?' Dan asks, trotting after me like a glossy, rather stupid horse.

He really needs to shut up. Right now. Close his mouth and hide his shiny teeth. Because as the person on the ground struggles to their feet, I realise with the purest horror that it's Sol.

The world reduces to one small grey patch of station platform as Sol dusts himself down and leans against a station pillar and rubs his face. His beanie hat is lying several metres down the track. I break into a full run, leaving Dan for dust, my bag whistling away behind me like one of those windsocks at an airfield. My UCL brochure falls out and hits the platform with a loud flopping sound.

People mutter and pulse around me. The only point of stillness is a stern-looking lady with a large black handbag and eyes as green and hard as marbles. I push through them, grab my best friend's shoulders and shake him. My tongue struggles to make its way around my heart, which has jumped up between my teeth.

'What the fuck?' I shout, over and over.

'There is no need for that language,' says the marble-eyed lady. I think I've seen her before somewhere.

'Well *excuse* me for not giving a shit,' I snarl. 'Sol, are you in there? It's me, it's Hanna!'

Sol's cheeks are very pale and his eyes seem too large for his face. There is a smattering of freckles across the bridge of his nose which I don't think I've ever noticed before. His pupils adjust and he takes me in.

'My phone,' he says. 'I dropped it.'

The marble-eyed lady with the black handbag looks even more disapproving. The words 'youth of today' flit around us like invisible birds.

'You jumped in front of a moving train because you broke your phone?' I say disbelievingly. 'I know it can be a nightmare, but there are places where you can fix phones, Sol. You can't fix your head back on to your shoulders if a train has just removed it!'

'It didn't break,' he says. 'It was on the tracks. I had to get it.'

He sways suddenly, and the crowd leap back as if afraid he will send them flying. Steadying himself, he puts his arms round my waist and leans his forehead against mine and closes his eyes.

'I had to get it,' he repeats.

I put my arms round him too, to balance us out, and I feel the hard muscles under his T-shirt quilting and spasming under my hands.

'It's just a phone,' I say, leading him over to one of the platform benches.

As we sit down, he rests his head on my shoulder and slides his cold hand into mine. His breathing slows and steadies, warm against the sensitive skin on my neck. I feel goose pimples over my entire scalp.

'Just a phone,' I repeat.

'I love you,' Sol whispers into my neck. 'I love you, Hanna.'

'Only the roses were more expensive than the daisies,' says Dan, jogging up. 'Get your hands off my girlfriend, gay boy.'

A little colour has returned to Sol's cheeks. He rubs his eyes like a little kid and sits up, and the air cools the little patch of my neck where his breath had been warm.

'Dan,' I say evenly. 'Sol almost got hit by the train.'

'Might have known. Are you coming or what, Birdgal?'

I take the flowers out of my bag, tear off their heads one by one and scatter them around the bench like confetti.

'Is that a no then?'

Two new figures skid on to the platform. Their eyes are wild and their faces a little bit lost. The marble-eyed lady with the black handbag draws back as Andrew hauls Sol from the bench and hugs him. Gareth makes a sort of moaning kangaroo leap and flings his arms around them both.

'It was an accident, I swear,' I hear Sol say, though his words are muffled in his parents' jumpers.

To add to the fun, Dan now shrieks like an airhorn.

Sol's cat Nigel has appeared from nowhere, flashing out from under the footbridge stairs, sinking his claws into Dan's leg, shinning up Dan's body like a murderous four-legged ninja and wrapping himself around Dan's head. Arms flailing, Dan cannons off a station pillar, and off Gareth and Andrew and Sol, and off me, and off the marble-eyed lady with the handbag.

Nigel springs for the lady on impact. He lands on her shoulder. Hissing like a busted gas canister in her ear, he makes her scream and spin in circles, and for a while it's impossible to tell which flash of black is handbag and which is cat.

'Christ,' says Gareth, lifting his head. 'Mum?'

Everyone watches, transfixed, at the way Nigel is riding Gareth's mum's head like Bernard Smith on the sinking *Titanic*. When she finally hits the ground with the side of her skull and lies flat out on the cold stones with the contents of her handbag spread around her, Nigel jumps off and starts delicately licking his balls.

It's pandemonium all over again. There are paramedics now, and flashing blue lights. Dan leaves, limping and cursing. Trains arrive. And through it all, the only thing I can hear is Sol's voice.

I love you, he is still whispering into my neck. *I love you, Hanna.*

29 SEPTEMBER

UR going 2 like
the film tomoro

Is that an order?

Telling that wld be . . .

No way.

WAY!!!!

You hate that film!

Never seen it. Any more
news on UR granny?

She's not dead yet if
that's what you mean.

STAR WARS:
A NEW HOPE (1977)

WRITER & DIRECTOR GEORGE LUCAS

Luke Skywalker (Mark Hamill), Obi Wan Kenobi (Alec Guinness), Han Solo (Harrison Ford), Princess Leia (Carrie Fisher), Wookiee Chewbacca and robots C-3PO and R2-D2 joins forces to save the galaxy from the Empire, its great battle station the Death Star, and the evil Darth Vader.

Stars Wars is one of the most successful films of all time, earning over $775 million at the box office at the time of its release and $4.38 billion from the franchise as a whole. A prequel trilogy was released between 1999 and 2005, and a sequel trilogy starring many of the original actors began with the release of *Star Wars: The Force Awakens* in December 2015.

SOL

30 SEPTEMBER

'But if you had to,' Hanna says as the titles roll.

'I don't have to.'

'But if you *had* to kiss Jabba the Hutt or saw your head off with a blunt teaspoon, which would you do?'

'Jabba shouldn't even be in the movie,' I say. 'He only gets a name-check in the original.'

'Sorry for being unauthentic, but he's in the version I downloaded, OK?'

I don't want to fight about a fat alien. Hanna has done a noble thing tonight and invited me to hers to watch one of the greatest films ever made, and without complaining or observing or gossiping for the entire movie. I'm feeling a relaxed Jedi calm which isn't a particularly normal feeling for me, particularly given current circumstances, and I'm loath to lose it. I pick up the ping-pong moon that's sitting on the table and roll it between my fingers, remembering how pleased I was with the authenticity of my Sea of Tranquility. I'm glad Han's still got it.

229

'I'd saw my head off,' I concede, and she nods, and we're OK again.

It might be because of the whole station thing, or the business with her dad in the summer, or Dan and those tragic flowers (or a combination of all three), but Hanna isn't herself at the moment. She still hasn't asked about that day, to begin with, which for a girl like Hanna – who has to know every detail about everything – is unusual. I mean, she's asked about the ongoing health and wellbeing of my grandmother in the ICU at the Royal Surrey, but anyone who'd seen Nigel fell Gareth's mum like a tree on that platform would ask that. She hasn't asked anything else. Not a thing. I appreciate her efforts and everything, but perversely it's making me feel . . .

'I told Gareth I wanted to do film studies not accountancy,' I say as the rebel forces assemble. 'I've been thinking about it for a while, and after I saw that film in Venice, the one I showed you last month, *Italian for Beginners*, which was everything I ever wanted, suddenly the thoughts became more urgent and I couldn't stop wondering if I could do it and if anyone in the film world would want or value my stuff. There was an open day in Sheffield and I told Gareth and Andrew I was checking out the accountancy course there but I was going for the film one. According to the website it's one of the best film courses in the country and if you're looking at options you want the best, don't you?'

I wonder if perhaps Hanna's not actually that interested, but I've started talking now and I want to see where I end up.

'I went to it and there were all these people just like me, talking about bridging shots and depth of field, showing all this amazing work in these tech-loaded studios. I got talking to this one guy about the work I do and it was incredible.'

Han hasn't interrupted yet.

'I have to go there, I can't be an accountant,' I say desperately. 'I like and understand numbers but I like stories more. Telling them, framing them, imagining them. And I thought about what you said about your dad, about maybe being more prepared for what happened if he'd talked to you about leaving before he actually left, and I knew I had to tell Gareth and Andrew before it was too late to apply.' I rub my eyes. 'It was the most terrifying moment of my life, telling them. Gareth completely freaked. He had my future laid out in his head, all lovely and logical and safe: getting ahead, finding security, buying a house, supporting a family. He raved on about how those things may not sound very romantic but are important and I was crazy if I thought he'd pay the fees for an airy-fairy filmic future. And I stuck it out somehow and Gareth flipped and the world went red. So I went to the station to do the thing that calms me down.'

'Photograph the trains,' says Hanna.

I stare at her in surprise. 'You think I photograph the trains?'

'You *don't* photograph the trains?'

'Trains are inanimate vehicles,' I say, bewildered. 'Why would I photograph them?'

Hanna sounds defensive suddenly. 'I don't know, do I? It's not like you've told me any of this before.'

'It's not about the trains,' I say. 'It's never been about the trains. It's about who they carry and what they mean. Journeys. Beginnings, endings. *Stories.*'

Five minutes from the end of the movie, the crashing sound of the front door flying back on its hinges makes us both jump. Raz peers into the living room. His jacket looks like he fell in a puddle on his way here.

'You look and smell like a tramp,' says Hanna in disgust. 'Mum will be back from work in about twenty minutes, she'll go *berserk*—'

'George Orwell was a tramp once,' Raz interrupts. 'Hey, Solzhenitsyn, I hear railway tracks are the place to be. Very *Anna Karenina.*' He squints at the titles still rolling on the TV. 'You want to watch out for that whole thing Luke and Leah have going on in this movie by the way. Very unsavoury.'

'Leia,' Hanna says. 'Not Leah.'

'Luke wants to get into Leia's pants,' Raz says. 'Leah wants to get into everyone's pants, or maybe just Jono's pants. Dad wants to get into Else's pants but not my pants. Wait, I don't want Dad in my pants, that's obscene.' He sways lightly like a birch tree in a breeze. 'Han Solo,' he says, looking hazily at me. 'Han 'n' Solomon. You kissed my sister yet, Solzhenitsyn? She knows you want to.'

'Shut up, Rasmus,' Hanna squeaks.

I suddenly have the most appalling recollection of something I told Hanna at the station, when the shock wiped out all the usual caution that stakes out my lizard brain and I smelled the salty skin of her neck pressed against my face and I held her hand and . . .

'Excuse me,' Raz says, 'I have to go and be sick now.'

. . . I told her I loved her.

'Oh God,' Hanna says, biting her lip as Raz lurches off towards the downstairs bathroom. 'I'm so sorry. He shouldn't . . . I shouldn't . . .'

The ground is warping beneath me. If I stand up, I will fall.

'It was the shock.' She can't look at me. 'I didn't mean to tell Raz what you said, but I needed a sounding board for one of the strangest days of my life and he was there. I'm sorry he twisted it to sound like – well. Like I wanted you to kiss me. Or something.'

My phone beeps.

> Dad asks if you want to
> come for dinner? C xxx

'I know you didn't mean it like I *love you* love you or anything,' Hanna rushes on as I raise my eyes from Carmen's message. 'Please don't feel stressed about it. You have enough to worry about with your granny in a coma.'

Two pink spots have flared in the centre of her cheeks. It's awful that I've put them there. That Jedi calm I was talking about? It's gone.

233

'Are we OK? You don't hate me for telling Raz what you said?'

'I'd better go,' I manage, putting the ping-pong moon down before I crush it. 'Carmen's invited me to hers for dinner.'

She makes a big fuss of finding my coat and bringing it to me as I stand by the front door, lost in the tragedy of my situation.

'It's so sad when summer's over,' she babbles. 'Although to be honest, I don't mind putting this summer behind me because it's been pretty awful, what with everything. But at least it's your birthday next month. Even if you have to cancel the party because of your grandmother, we can still celebrate, can't we?'

I make myself look at her. 'Why would we cancel the party because of her? My grandmother has never been in my life until now.'

'I thought maybe Gareth wouldn't want a party—'

'We're having the party,' I say loudly. 'And for your information, even if Nigel *had* killed her, we still wouldn't be cancelling anything.'

Hanna tries to smile. 'Even Luke Skywalker and Darth Vader make up in the end,' she says. 'I mean, I haven't seen the next film so I don't . . . I'm not completely sure—'

I put my hand on the door handle.

'Life isn't a movie, Hanna.' I've told her this before, but it feels particularly, horribly true today. 'In life, dads walk out on their kids without looking back, and coincidences

234

happen with no major consequences, and mothers continue hating their sons after being half-murdered by their cats.'

'I won't lose hope,' Hanna says very quietly.

I won't either, I think, as she shuts the door behind me.

You can't lose something you never had to begin with.

31 OCTOBER

And he said what, that you *weren't* OK?

> He didnt say ANYTHING Lizzie!!!! Well he said he had 2 C Carmen mayB 2 tell her what an idiot I am

He's probably embarrassed

> Raz made out that I was into him!!!! I feel wretched

Clueless

> Not in the mood for quotes

Well excuse me for living

> Officer and a Gentleman

Bing!

> Groundhog Day CAN U STOP NOW THIS IS SERIOUS

BRIDE OF
FRANKENSTEIN
(1935)

DIRECTOR   JAMES WHALE

Victor Frankenstein (Colin Clive) is persuaded to create a mate for his Monster (Boris Karloff). The Bride of Frankenstein (Elsa Lanchester) comes to life when she is hit by lightning at the top of Frankenstein's laboratory tower. But contrary to Frankenstein's hopes, the Bride screams on sight of the Monster, and the Monster destroys Frankenstein's laboratory in rage when his love is not returned.

In 1998, the film was added to the United States National Film Registry for being 'culturally, historically or aesthetically significant'. It is described as James Whale's masterpiece, and often credited as the best horror movie ever made.

Hanna

'He's right, you know,' I say, pausing glumly to admire the black polish I'm applying to my toenails. I found the most fantastic pair of shoes covered in spidery black straps, which I'm wearing tonight. They are going some way towards helping how shit I feel. 'About life not being a movie. If life was a movie, his grandmother would have woken up by now and the family would have been reunited with tears and apologies.'

And more besides. My heart constricts as I feel his breath against my neck again. *I love you. I love you Hanna.*

'Life is more like theatre, really,' I go on. 'A live performance.'

'Life isn't *like* a live performance, Hanna,' says Lizzie. 'It *is* a live performance.'

'But a really *weird* live performance,' I continue, 'where nothing makes sense and people drift on and off the stage for no reason and there are all these loose ends flapping around, like when Mum pegs out her tights on a windy day.'

'Why didn't Shakespeare think of that?' Lizzie asks. 'Shall I compare thee to fifty denier, thou art more lovely but prone to laddering . . .'

I slide the brush back into the bottle. 'You know what I mean. Nothing happens like it's supposed to. There's no proper narrative arc like they always talk about in English. Dad hasn't got in touch to tell me what a mistake he made, Raz is still bombed half the week, Sol's granny is still unconscious with added cat hairs. There's no rewind button or subtitles or out-takes.'

'My whole life feels like an out-take,' Lizzie sighs.

I consider her from my position on her bedroom floor. I can only see the blue half of her face from down here. 'Isn't the theme Gothic?' I ask.

Lizzie turns her face so I can see the green half. 'And?'

'I think the idea was emo,' I say. 'Not stained-glass window.'

'Sol won't care, he's not that kind of guy. I know originality is a crime around here, and that Vashti and Trixie and Laura will all come as Lena from *Beautiful Creatures* or some shit like that, but so what? I can only be me.' She regards my outfit. 'What are you, anyway?'

'Lena from *Beautiful Creatures*,' I say.

Lizzie waves a blue and green hand at me. 'You get away with it because you're my friend. They don't because they're not. Do you think Dan's going tonight?'

I'm almost used to the squeeze of guilt I get whenever Dan's name is mentioned. It'll always be there, I know. But I tell myself it's better than the void we'd have if I ever told Lizzie what happened that day at the beach.

'Unlikely,' I say. 'He and Sol aren't friends.'

'You and Sol aren't friends either, and you're going.'

'We ARE friends!' I say, cut to the heart. 'We just – we haven't spoken much recently.'

'You haven't spoken since *Star Wars* night.'

'Not on purpose,' I protest. 'It's just . . . That night was really awkward with Raz completely dropping me in it like that, and I'm pretty sure Sol didn't want to speak to me anyway, not for the first week, and I didn't know what I was going to say to him the second week, and then with his granny still not waking up and everything—'

'Best friends one minute, not speaking the next. What does that remind me of?' Lizzie raises a finger to her red stained lips. 'Oh yes. You and me! Although there is, I concede, a crucial difference between you and Sol now and you and me last year.'

'Yes,' I say. I start applying the second coat with irritable vigour. 'He doesn't talk bollocks.'

'You *love* him,' Lizzie says with satisfaction.

I silently thumb off the large blob of black varnish which has fallen on to my toe. They say you don't notice cumulative things. My feelings for Sol have been coming so slowly that I almost missed them. Probably would have kept right on missing them if he hadn't said what he said that day and brought it all into focus.

But how do you get past something like *Star Wars* night? If this were a movie, I'd face down the humiliation and be rewarded somehow. But it's not a movie, as we've already established, and so I'm planning not to face it at all. This is allowed in the real world. It's one of the few perks.

'Are you worried about Dan being there?' I ask.

'If he came at me for a snog then I might not be able to resist because I'm female and he's hot. But he won't because he doesn't tend to repeat himself.'

I blush as I slide my feet into the spider sandals.

'Beyond that,' Lizzie concludes, 'I don't feel much, really.'

'He won't be there.' I smooth down my Lena corset. 'Sol won't have invited him.'

'The guest list is out of Sol's hands,' Lizzie points out. 'Half of college knows about it and his address isn't exactly a secret.'

I sit down a little abruptly on the end of Lizzie's bed.

'Oh God,' I say. 'Then he *will* be there.'

'Yes,' says my friend. 'He will. Yippee.'

What are the chances, I wonder, of Sol's grandmother dying in the next couple of hours and the party being cancelled after all? I don't mean to be horrible, but you can only live in hope.

SOL

I peer through the hallway curtains at the flood of people in fancy dress making their way with worrying determination up the road. Nigel growls from behind the special barred-off area under the stairs that Andrew's made for him, complete with dangling spiders on elastic and DON'T FEED THE FAMILIAR hanging on the bars. Already I'm sweating in the burgundy velvet smoking jacket Andrew persuaded me to wear, and the party hasn't even started.

I smooth my greased hair back in an attempt to relax. *I can be in the same room with her at the same party*, I tell myself, *and it won't matter a bit that I told her I loved her and she didn't want to know.* It's been a month since that particular horror story unfolded. Tonight is going to be about other horror stories, celluloid ones. At least my parents and I agree on that.

'How many people have you invited?' I ask.

'You're eighteen,' says Andrew. 'It was never going to be small.'

'And God knows,' Gareth adds, 'I need a bit of fun after your little bombshell, not to mention spending most of my afternoons sitting with a person in a coma who hates me.' He hasn't mastered his vampire teeth yet, so this comes out a bit lispy.

The doorbell goes, making me rear like a startled horse. I'm on the verge of bolting upstairs and burying myself in my latest edit, until I remember that my laptop is positioned on top of the fridge so that Frank can feel a part of proceedings.

'We've invited some of our friends,' Andrew says, heading for the door as I attempt to still my frantic heart. 'To keep the lid on things. You know how these parties can disintegrate into chaos if the entire guestlist is under twenty.'

'The last lid your friends kept on anything was on the dustbin they blew up on bonfire night last year,' I hiss.

'That was just a small firework mishap. Could have happened to anyone. Don't mind us, we'll stay out of your way.'

I rub my eyes. 'Where are you going to be?'

'In the study,' says Andrew. He glances at Gareth. 'By the phone.'

In case my grandmother dies tonight, I think. A suitably gothic notion.

Suddenly there seems to be more noise in this house than is possible. My parents' friends come trooping through the door, waving at me from underneath an assortment of cloaks and wigs, and all I can think is: thank God there's a theme tonight that goes half-way to explaining them. The sound of creepy organ music starts roaring from the speakers in the living room, mingling with Nigel's growls.

'Happy birthday, gay boy,' says Dan Dukas, edging through the door with his arm round a very thin girl with an enormous Afro who I vaguely recognise from Geography. At least six other people are coming up the path behind him, all staring and pointing at the skeleton arrangement in the front garden. 'This house looks practically normal for a gay house, apart from the dead stuff.'

I peer over his shoulder at the incoming crowds, paralysed with anxiety about Hanna. I haven't seen her in four weeks; I haven't spoken to her or heard anything about her. For all I know, she's started seeing someone. How am I going to feel about that? I pray to God that Carmen gets here before Hanna and her date. Poor Carmen. She deserves better than me.

'Who are you supposed to be?' Dan asks.

'Gregory Anton.'

'Who?'

'The murderer in *Gaslight*. One of the greatest Gothic movies ever made.'

'Has it got Jake Gyllenhaal in it?'

'Jake Gyllenhaal wasn't born in 1944.'

'Not what I asked, but whatever.' Dan assesses my smoking jacket. 'That looks kind of hot.'

I try to loosen my sweaty collar. 'It is,' I agree unhappily.

'Where did you get it?'

'My dad's wardrobe. Who are you?'

Dan looks taken aback. 'I'm Dan Dukas, you twat,' he says.

'Solzhenitsyn!' roars Raz, crashing through the door in a sort of turban. 'Love will find a way through paths where wolves fear to prey' is written on his form-hugging white T-shirt, below a picture of a guy I recognise as Lord Byron.

My heart feels as if it's about to leap out of my mouth and make a spectacle of itself. 'Hey Raz,' I say, my throat suddenly dry. 'Hanna with you?'

'She's coming with Lizzie. Is this the granny-killing cat?'

Nigel fires a razor-sharp claw through the bars of his prison, missing Raz's eye by millimetres.

'She's not dead yet,' I say as Raz hurriedly straightens up. 'Just unconscious. How's uni?'

'Between you and me, I have no idea. I've only been to two lectures.'

A dozen girls in heavy eye make-up and short glittery dresses follow Raz, giggling together and looking curiously at the candles flickering on every surface, the red curtains hanging heavily in the windows, the candelabras and the endless cobwebs. The creepy organ music is getting louder, with a new electronic beat weaving through it. Did I invite any of these people or did my parents just post an ad on Twitter?

I feel myself relax at the sight of Stevie, bandage ends trailing out of the neck and sleeves of his jacket and more bandages wrapped around his large, freckled head. Standing beside him in a tiny Cleopatra outfit is Trixie. She flashes a non-smile at me, on and off like semaphore, her heavily kohled eyes darting all over the heaving hallway as she assesses the other guests.

'How's it going, mate?' Stevie pumps my hand vigorously with his own bandage-wrapped paw. 'Happy Birthday and all that.'

'You should have come as Julius Caesar, Stevie,' Trixie complains. 'There are three other mummies here, and they all look a lot more realistic than you.'

'I'm too overfed,' Stevie tells me as Trixie detaches herself from his side and squeals across the room to join Vashti and Laura, who have come as Victorian-looking witches. 'Couldn't look dead if I tried. Hanna here yet?'

'I think I saw her outside,' says Carmen, appearing behind Stevie. Her gorgeous, full-length dress, in a sort of cobwebby material, doesn't leave much to the imagination, and she gives me such a warm just-for-my-boyfriend smile that I feel half-blinded with a combination of guilt and desire. How can I still be so confused about Hanna with a girlfriend who looks like this?

'You look incredible,' I say. 'How did you get that outfit past your dad?'

'That's why I'm late,' Carmen giggles. 'I changed in the Costa toilets. I'm so sorry, have you been waiting? Hello Stevie, how are you?'

Stevie looks like someone genuinely pulled out his organs and filled at least five canopics jars with them.

246

Carmen smiles happily at him, takes my hand and tugs me deeper in to the party. 'The house looks so beautiful,' she says. 'I feel as if I'm in a gothic movie for real! How do you know all these people?'

'I don't,' I tell her. 'Do you want a drink? We've got some guys mixing cocktails in the kitchen.'

'Alcoholic ones? My father doesn't like me to drink.'

'You're eighteen now,' I point out.

'He still doesn't like it,' she says, looking worried.

The cocktail guys have set up a bar at the kitchen island, with tubs of ice and lemon slices, glacé cherries and olives, spirits and mixers all lined up in glittering rows as they pour and shake. Everything in here is lit as dimly as the rest of the house, so the drinks look blood-red. I get the bartenders to fix a Virgin Mary and head back to where I left Carmen.

'Loving the party, man! Thank you so much for inviting me!'

I look up to see Frank's face looming large on the top of the fridge.

'Good of you to join us,' I shout back. 'How's Chet?'

'Still adorable, with issues. How's Hanna?'

'I don't even know if she's here,' I yell, waving at the heaving kitchen.

'The thing with being on top of your refrigerator is that I'm approximately seven feet tall,' Frank shouts back. 'She came in about ten minutes ago with a girl looking like a cathedral window!'

'Hanna looks like a cathedral window?'

'Not Hanna, her friend!'

I put the Virgin Mary down and hurry back through the kitchen, my heart pounding uncomfortably. All I can think is that I have to get this first meeting over with. I have to get past the whole 'I love you' debacle and remind myself that she thinks it was the shock, that's all, that there's no reason why we can't still be friends.

Hanna and Lizzie are both by the fireplace in the living room. Lizzie has painted her face and is wearing a strange mixture of red, green and blue which is drawing narrowed glances from Trixie, Laura and Vashti across the room. Hanna has her head thrown back in laughter, her thick blond hair shining down her bare back, her throat exposed, a Gothic virgin in a house of wolves.

Hanna . . .

Just Hanna, really.

Hanna

'Keep laughing,' Lizzie advises. 'He's coming over.'

Being told to keep laughing is a guarantee that you stop laughing – or at least start looking like you're having a seizure. I have been dreading this moment since we came through the door fifteen minutes ago. The blood rushes to my face as I keep my lips in a kind of rictus snarl.

'Hi,' says Sol behind me.

He looks almost otherworldly in a vintage jacket of burgundy velvet, white shirt and black tie. His eyelids are shadowed, his eyes almost luminous, his face deathly pale. The jacket clashes magnificently with his hair, which lies darkened and smoothed to his head.

'You look like a red setter that's just come out a pond,' I say.

Lizzie chokes into her drink. Good, I think. Yes. When paralysed about talking to someone, compare them to a wet dog.

'Not quite the look I was going for.' He puts his hands in the two big pockets at the front of his jacket. 'You look beautiful.'

Not having pockets, I find that I don't know what to do with my hands. Should I keep them by my side? Together's too prayer-like. Behind my back? Too Prince Charles. I extend them awkwardly and somehow get them around his velvety shoulders and plant a kiss somewhere near his ear. He smells nice. Woody. Hopeful. He smells of Sol.

'Happy birthday,' I manage to say, before casting around like an amateur fisherman for a suitable bit of chit-chat. 'Any more news on your grandmother?'

'No.'

'Is Carmen here?'

Something snaps into focus in his green eyes. 'Shit,' he says. 'I got her a drink and I forgot to give it to her.'

'A red setter?' snorts Lizzie, as he threads away from us through the crowds like a slim, velvety snake.

The scent of lemons wafts towards us.

'Hey,' says Dan with his Pippi-the-dog smile.

'I need a drink,' says Lizzie abruptly. 'You're on your own, Han.'

Dan takes my hand almost before she's left the room. 'Let's go outside,' he whispers in my ear.

'I stood on your garage roof once,' I say, detaching my fingers from his. 'The lights were on but, as they say, no one was home.'

'But I want to talk to you,' Dan says, following me as I try to make my way out of the crowded room to somewhere less lemony. 'I want to know what you want me to do.'

I don't have the energy for this.

'Dan, can you honestly not work this out for yourself?' I say in frustration. 'You are being REJECTED. I *reject* you.'

'You didn't reject me at the beach.'

I flush. 'Maybe not at first, but I got there in the end. This isn't going to change, can't you understand that?'

'But I've never felt like this about a girl before.' Dan sounds quite indignant.

'What am I supposed to do, applaud?'

'But you're so amazingly hot! And your hotness tonight is making me hotter than . . . a Hotpoint. That's a thing, right? A Hotpoint?'

Give me strength. 'It's a cooker, you plonker,' I say.

'Please Han,' Dan says, catching me round the waist. He looks as if he's about to cry. 'This is driving me nuts.'

I am terrified that Lizzie will come out of the kitchen at any minute. If he *dares* . . . If he so much as . . .

'OW,' he yelps, pulling back from my lips and clapping his hand to his face.

I smooth down my dress. My palm is stinging, and I flex my fingers a few times as I rush into the kitchen with as much dignity as I can manage.

Something is flickering outside the dark kitchen door: a large outdoor screen set up at the end of Sol's back garden. I step out into the cold night air with my eyes fixed on the giant black and white images dancing across the screen. I think it's the *Bride of Frankenstein*. A few people are braving the chill out here under the coloured lights and patio heaters, their fingers wrapped around drinks, watching

251

Boris Karloff taking the Bride's little hand and making her scream.

I sit down on a bench tucked underneath a little ivy-covered arbour to one side of the garden and watch. Almost at once I can feel my heartrate slowing and settling. *Movie magic*, I think gratefully, as the silvery fingers of the story dig into me. I don't think about Dan and I don't think about Lizzie and I don't even think about Sol, until he sits on the bench next to me.

'It's all a bit mad inside,' he says. 'Thought I'd come out here instead.'

'Did you find Carmen?' I ask, sniffing. 'To give her the drink?'

Sol peers at me in the darkness. 'Are you crying?'

I rub my nose with my fingers. 'It's a sad story,' I say, gesturing at the screen. 'Poor Monster. He just wants to love the Bride.'

People walk past our bench, obscuring our view of the movie with their flickering shadows. Laura and Jake run giggling into a large bush. Dan sits alone on a chair by the screen with his head in his hands. It feels as if Sol and I are in our own private cinema booth.

'They can't see us, can they?' Sol says.

'Didn't you know?' I say back. 'This is a magic bench.'

'I always knew there was something weird about it.'

'Anyone who sits here is invisible to the rest of the world,' I continue. 'This bench is number twelve Grimmauld Place.'

It would be nice, I think, *if that were true*. As I think about all the things you could do on an invisible bench, my tummy starts aching like I've done too many sit-ups.

'Is Carmen—' I begin.

'Han,' he says, 'do you mind if we don't talk about Carmen?'

His eyes are large and serious and his nose isn't all that far from my own. The arbour we're sitting underneath suddenly feels like it's just grown smaller.

'Um, sure,' I say.

His leg feels warm against mine. There are so many thoughts and hopes and fears flying around my head right now, I half expect them to make pinging noises as they ricochet off the sides of my skull. I want to kiss him.

Ahead of us, the screen flickers silver as the laboratory explodes in a shower of unconvincing bricks. My fingers start creeping up the sleeve of Sol's velvet jacket. I don't know where they're going.

He puts his own hand across mine, halting its progress. I pull my fingers back with a face as hot as a Saharan rock at noon. Thank God for the darkness.

Trixie appears in front of our bench like a bony Egyptian mirage. We both leap to our feet, Sol banging his head on the top bit of the arbour, me gulping at the air like I've been swimming underwater.

'Have you seen Stevie?' she says. 'He said he was getting me a drink and I can't find him and I want to dance.'

Hanna

'I can look for him myself, Hanna,' Trixie says.

'Yes, but four eyes are better than two,' I tell her brightly, 'as the optician once said.'

'What optician?'

Hunting for Stevie proves a surprisingly good distraction. He isn't in the kitchen, or the hallway, or the living room, which has turned into a thumping whirl of sound, full of bodies jerking like they're being electrocuted. The only place left to check is the downstairs toilet. It's occupied, and by more than one person from the sound of the giggling.

Trixie hammers on the door. 'Stevie?' she squeals. 'Who's in there with you?'

The door unlocks and Vashti comes out, straightening her skirt as Stevie attempts to hide behind the door. His efforts are about as successful as a Boeing 727 trying to tuck itself into a garden shed.

'It's not what you think, Trix,' he begins, as Vashti slides away into the kitchen. 'She came in after me. I couldn't get rid of her.'

'Don't you dare bring Vashti into this,' Trixie spits.

Stevie looks genuinely horrified. 'I would never cheat on you. I'm not that kind of—'

'Vashti is my *friend*. She'd never go after you without encouragement, never in a million years!'

'Newflash, Trixie,' says Lizzie, leaning over the banisters above our heads. Her facepaint is heavily smudged. 'Vashti Wong is nobody's friend but her own. You go together perfectly.'

Trixie's little face twists. I feel a kick of dismay. *Don't poke the tiger*, I think.

'Lizzie,' I say nervously. 'Trixie's just had a shock. Be kind.'

'Like Trixie was to me?' Lizzie says with a snort. 'Fat chance. I'd tell you to pick better friends if I thought you were any kind of friend worth having, Trix, but you're not, so . . .'

'Has your *best friend* told you about getting with Dan at the beach yet?' Trixie asks. 'Has she mentioned that? No, I don't suppose she has, have you, Hanna babes?'

I'm sunk. Torpedoed. Blown to pieces. Trixie's expression is so full of spite that she's almost glowing. Stevie, who has been sitting at the bottom of the stairs with his head in his hands, looks up and frowns.

'I hate to be the bearer of bad tidings, Lizzie,' Trixie continues, trembling, 'but that's how it goes. So in future, I suggest you check with your own friends before dissing mine!'

Lizzie lifts her multicoloured eyebrows at me. There's nothing for it.

'I'm sorry!' I cry. 'I should have told you but I didn't want to risk losing you again over nothing. I pushed him off as soon as he . . . Well, I pushed him off pretty quickly, and I've been trying to get rid of him ever since, you've seen me trying to get rid of him, haven't you? I mean, haven't you?'

Raz appears at the top of the stairs, sliding a hand round Lizzie's waist. He's lost his turban, and his face is covered in blue and green paint in all the places where Lizzie's isn't. I stare at him in surprise. What—

'Of course I have,' Lizzie says unexpectedly. 'I'd take my hat off to you, Han, only I'm not wearing one. Hats don't suit me, if I'm honest.'

'I liked your sombrero at the beach that day,' offers Raz.

Lizzie pats him on his paint-stained cheek. 'You should have come over and talked to me then instead of brooding over your book.'

'I was at a good part,' Raz objects.

Trixie stamps her foot in a bid to get everyone's attention back. 'Hanna kissed Dan!'

'Dan kissed *me*,' I say. I think I actually raise my hand here.

'What's one snog between friends?' Lizzie asks. 'I mean that by the way, Han,' she adds. 'Although, in the spirit of honesty, I might have been a bit more pissed off about it if Rasmus hadn't come through for me tonight.'

This is clearly not going the way Trixie had imagined. It's not going the way I imagined either. There's Raz nibbling my best friend's ear for starters, and there's Lizzie looking

256

unfazed by Trixie's bombshell. Is this real life again? You know, as opposed to movies?

'Dan tends to ignore girls he's succeeded with, as I can tell you with some confidence,' Lizzie continues. 'I think it's safe to say that he hasn't been ignoring Hanna lately. It's a bit tragic really, seeing him fail.'

'But—' Trixie splutters.

'Hush,' Lizzie says, raising a finger. 'I haven't finished. You see, Trixie, Hanna has done something in the past year that's completely beyond you. She's learned a *lesson*. And I know she won't go back on that lesson, however tempted she might be. *That* is friendship.'

I think I might cry. I offer a watery smile instead and blow a few feeble kisses at my best friend with my hands.

'Can we get back to making out now?' Raz asks Lizzie's neck, his hands wandering through her long dark hair.

'Yes, Rasmus,' Lizzie says with a nod. 'We can.'

There is an interesting silence as they resume their snogging.

'You're still a bastard, Stevie,' says Trixie, in a bid to recover some ground. She attempts a smile. 'But if you are very good, I might let you make it up to me.'

Stevie rises from the bottom of the stairs, very tall and badly wrapped.

'You have to be kidding me,' he says with awful dignity.

And then he walks away from her.

Trixie folds into something small and scared.

'Stevie?' she whispers at his departing back.

He doesn't look round.

SOL

I haven't moved since Hanna rushed away from me. The movie has looped around to the beginning again, so I stay where I am and watch. Most of the story bounces over my head like a stone skipping across the sea, apart from the bit about how you can't make love happen if it's not there, and my thoughts are all of Hanna's hair hanging like bright gold down her smooth bare back, of Nigel bringing my grandmother to her knees, of vampires and cocktails, of Frank's face as large as Hagrid's on the fridge. Of Hanna's hand on my arm, and my hand on her hand, and her snatching her fingers back as if my touch had burned her.

I sit back down on the invisible bench. It would be nice to have extended its magic somehow, and made it a place where I got to kiss Hanna's long white neck and her gentle mouth and put my hands in her cool, smooth hair and not had to face the consequences. Elsa Lanchester rolls her Rs like bowling balls over my head.

'You look like you need a drink.'

A frosted bottle is placed in my hands.

'Because I tell you, I bloody do,' says Stevie, setting a crate of cold beer down on the ground. 'And I don't drink alone. You're legal now, so get to it.' He chinks his own bottle against mine and drains it.

'Trixie?' I say.

'Trixie,' he confirms.

The beer's not bad. Cold and harsh, the bubbles scraping the back of my throat. The bottle's gone before I realise it. Stevie hands me another from the stash by his feet.

'She was looking for you,' I say, wiping my mouth with the back of my hand.

'She found me,' Stevie says. 'In the toilet with Vashti. We're over.'

We sit there in silence for a while. I select a third bottle, pop the cap off on the arm of the bench and pour it down my throat. A pleasant feeling of relaxation starts to spread through my limbs.

'We weren't even doing anything,' Stevie says plaintively. 'Well, I got a feel of Vashti's breasts, but only because she had me up against the wall. I couldn't exactly miss them.'

'I got the breasts too,' I say. 'At the beach.' I gesture with my beer-holding hand, sending a spray of brown liquid in an arc in front of us. 'She cornered me in the reeds. We pissed off a swan.'

'You pissed on a swan?'

'Pissed OFF a swan,' I repeat. 'IRRITATED a swan. ANNOYED a swan.'

'Terrifying things,' says Stevie.

259

'Swans?'

'Vashtis.'

When I make it to my fourth bottle, it proves harder to open than the first three. I have to try five times before I fire the cap into the neighbouring bush.

'I've been going out with Carmen Mendoza for seven months and I've still got nowhere near her breasts,' I inform Stevie. 'Because her dad is RoboCop and I can only think of Hanna.'

Stevie belches and pats me on the shoulder.

'Seven whole breastless months, and for most of that time I've been unable to think of anything but Hanna,' I continue. 'I'm a coward and a shit.'

'You are, my friend,' says Stevie.

'I think about Hanna's bum a lot,' I confide.

'Most of us do, mate.'

'I have to end it with Carmen,' I say, standing up. The ground tilts, and I put my hand on Stevie's head to stop myself from falling over. 'I have to end it now, even though I've got no hope of ever getting Hanna to love me. I have to break Carmen's beautiful, kind heart and let RoboCop come after me with an Auto 9.'

'Do it,' says Stevie. 'And then come right back here and drink more beer with me.'

'I hear you,' I say. 'I'm going now.'

I head erratically for the kitchen, cannoning off the doorframe like the time Gareth went after Nigel in the fencing helmet. Nigel who almost killed my grandmother and has never asked for a single favour in return. I wish I had balls like Nigel's.

'Has anyone seen my girlfriend?' I shout at the guests. I peer up at the fridge. 'Hey Frank,' I say. 'When did you get so tall?'

'If by your girlfriend, you mean the spectacularly curvy girl in lace looking this way, she's in the hallway at the bottom of the stairs,' Frank tells me.

I lean against the fridge. 'She's gorgeous, isn't she? Kisses like a goddess. I'm about to ruin her life.'

The hallway is further away than it looks. Putting down her drink, Carmen looks curiously at me as I extend my arms towards her.

'God, you're beautiful,' I say with a sudden burst of passion. 'Like a big pneumatic tyre. Have I told you that today?'

Carmen looks at the bottle dangling between my fingers.

'Beer,' I tell her helpfully.

'I can see that. How much have you drunk?'

I wave my beer around. 'Not counting.'

'You need some fresh air. Why don't we go into the garden?'

'I just came from there,' I object.

She puts her arm round my waist and helps me back through the kitchen. I wave at the guys at the cocktail bar, cannon off the kitchen doorframe again, and make it over the hazardous doorstep with difficulty.

'I fell over that once,' I tell her. 'Slashed my head open.'

Talking of slashes, I realise that I need one rather badly. I fumble with my zipper and angle myself towards the wall. I can't think why people are looking at me.

'Thank you for being there,' I tell the wall. 'Thank you

for being so supportive at this difficult time, especially to Gareth's roses.'

Stevie ambles up the garden towards us.

'He's drunk, Stevie,' says Carmen. 'I've never seen him drunk before. I don't know what to do.'

'You should go out with him,' I say, pointing at Stevie. 'He's single now, and much nicer than me.'

'Why are you saying this?' Carmen says in bewilderment. 'Stevie, why is he talking like this?'

'He won't think about other girl's bums when he's with you,' I tell her. 'Stevie's solid. Trustworthy.'

Carmen's beautiful pillowy lips quiver. 'You're being disgusting.'

'I'm sorry,' I mutter, sliding down the wall, where I land in the puddle of my own making. It seeps through my trousers. All the good feelings of the beer have been replaced with a horrible feeling of nausea, physical and mental. 'Carmen, I'm really sorry but there isn't going to be any Baroness. You see, you can't marry someone . . .' I pause to belch, 'when you're in love with someone else. Can you?'

That's a quote, I think. Hanna would know where from. I can't even be original when ruining someone's life.

'Take me home, will you, Stevie?' says Carmen tearfully.

How come he's not drunk? I wonder, as Stevie puts his big paw round Carmen's tiny little waist and guides her back through the kitchen. He's put away at least as much as I have. I pick myself off the ground. The world spins around me like a gyroscope and I keel into a bush.

'Are you OK, Laura?' asks Jake, somewhere beneath me.

Hanna

Trixie is sitting in the corner of the living room, crying her eyes out. Curled up like that on the chair, she looks about six years old. It's the loneliest sight in the world. There's something inhuman about ignoring her high-octane levels of distress so I push through the dancing crowd and stand in front of her with my arms folded.

'I bet you're enjoying this,' Trixie weeps.

'Loving it,' I agree. 'That's why I've come over to see if you're OK.'

Trixie wipes her blue-black kohl eyes, smearing her make up so that half her face ends up slate-grey.

'Stevie dumped me,' she says in dull disbelief.

'Are you surprised?' I should work on the sympathetic vibe but it's hard.

'I thought he loved me. He's the best thing that's ever happened to me.'

'Shame you only just noticed.'

'Don't rub it in, you bitch!'

263

'I didn't have to come over here,' I point out. 'I could have left you alone, like your friends have.'

'Hanna, I have to get him back,' she groans. 'I can't live without him.'

'I felt like that about Dan once,' I say. 'But I've been single now for ten months and it hasn't killed me.'

'Ten months?' Trixie says faintly. 'Single?'

It is quite a long time, I realise. And not only have I been single, in all that time I've had just one snog. That can't be healthy. No wonder I'm mooning so badly over Sol.

'God. Stevie and I were together for longer than that.' Even in the depths of her despair, Trixie sounds mildly pleased with herself. Then the smug thing vanishes and she's in tears again. 'We were together for almost a year. We had sex and everything. It can't just *end*. God! I wish I could rewind this evening.'

'Life isn't a movie,' I say.

Trixie nods, cries some more, nods again. Jake and Laura appear. They are both covered in leaves. Vashti is behind them.

'Sol is wasted out there,' Jake says, thumbing at the garden over his shoulder. He plucks several twigs out of Laura's hair. 'He fell into a bush.'

That's not right, I think. *Sol doesn't drink.*

'Is he all right?' I ask.

'He's in better shape than the bush,' says Laura, giggling.

Vashti glances at the weeping Trixie without interest. 'He sat in a puddle of his own piss,' she tells me. 'It was gross.'

'No one deserves friends like you,' I say in disgust. 'Not even Trixie.'

Sol is still lying in the shrubbery when I find him.

'Foliage is surprisingly comfortable,' he mumbles. 'I should fall into it more often.'

I try to grab his arm and haul him out, but he's too floppy. I wonder where Carmen's gone. 'How much have you drunk?' I ask.

'Not enough.'

I get his arm round my shoulder for better leverage and pull again. My boobs are in danger of popping out of my dress at the exertion. He's heavy, and he smells. Somehow I get him on to his feet.

'Don't tell RoboCop,' he slurs, leaning against me as I walk him back towards the house.

This feels like stumbling along with a wardrobe draped round my neck. Nigel snarls as we make it to the bottom of the stairs. Swaying by the stairpost, Sol looks doubtfully at the climb. I push him from behind, leaning into him, wrinkling my nose at the smell of his trousers. When we're at the top, we somehow make it along the landing and into his bedroom, where I shove him sideways to land face-down on the bed.

'Mrs Robinson, you're trying to seduce me,' he says in a muffled voice as I tug his trousers off. 'Aren't you?'

'You're covered in wee,' I tell him. I feel a bit panicky. Do I have to do his pants as well?

'Carmen's better off with Stevie.'

'Shh, that's not true.' I avert my eyes and tug his pants down his legs and pull his bedcovers over him as best I can. There's a limit to this undressing thing and I think I just reached it.

'Lovely bum,' he mumbles into his moonstriped pillow.

'I'll find a bowl for you to be sick in,' I tell him.

When I return, he is fast asleep with his arms sprawled on either side of his head like he's skydiving. His top half is still neatly dressed in jacket, shirt and tie. His bottom half, as it were, is peeping over the top of the duvet.

I set the bowl down beside his head. As I tiptoe guiltily back to the door, something scrunches under my foot. A small piece of paper scored with lines and angles. I pick it up and turn it over in my fingers, staring at the bent corners and crumpled folds.

I've seen something like it before, but I can't think where.

SOL

14 NOVEMBER

'There was a club at school in the States run by this Japanese teacher called Mr Yamauchi. It wasn't exactly cool to do the class, but I wasn't doing so well with the transition thing from the UK to the States, and the classes really helped. I met one of my best friends there, a guy called Frank. He got beaten up almost as much as I did. We're still friends, although it's not really the same thing online.'

My grandmother's hair is stragglier than it was at the station and her skin is covered in creases, like I've folded her a few hundred times. I glance at Gareth by the window, wondering what he makes of all this information. It looks like he's taking in every word. *At least someone's listening*, I think, as he nods at me to continue.

'We used to make paper rabbits and birds and easier things like that, but it got boring.' I'm feeling increasingly stupid, the longer she stares at me. 'So I asked Mr Yamauchi one time to show us how to make these figures that I'd seen online. Frank never got the hang of it, his figures always turned out like creased alien lifeforms, but mine were usually OK. Figures have a lot more folds and they can take ages, but I like their different characters. I use them in these films I make.'

This lady who I don't know turns her face to the wall, releasing me from the grip of her unnervingly Gareth-like gaze. I stare instead at the way her nose is shaped like mine.

'I've got one here,' I tell the side of her head. 'A figure.'

I put the little figure on the scratchy hospital blanket in front of my grandmother's curled fingers. They don't move.

'It's not the original. I made that a few weeks ago for a film I'm doing, but it got broken so I made another. I think maybe this one is better. I got his arm wrong the first time. I hope you like it.'

What is so interesting about that wall? It's only green.

'Probably best not to tire her out on a first visit,' says the nurse.

We leave, our footsteps loud in the wide white space of the ward. I'm regretting giving the figure to her already. It took me three evenings to make and she didn't even look at it. I'll have to make a third one for the film now. I don't know why I brought it, or why I talked so much. It just seemed like the right thing to do.

The atmosphere is heavy with unspoken things as we peel off the main road.

'Your little paper figure was beautiful,' Gareth says eventually. 'How did the first one get broken?'

I pull my eyes from the darkness outside. 'Someone trod on it after the party.'

'You, most likely. The state you were in.'

The flashbacks, hazy as they are, make me feel almost as ill as the main event. I don't remember much beyond peeing against the garden wall and ending it with Carmen. I don't want to think about how I wound up in bed without my trousers on. I definitely don't want to think about how ill I was in the morning, how anything would have been preferable to the puking and the crushing headache I endured all day.

'I don't want to talk about that.' I fix Gareth with my gaze. 'I want to talk about her.'

'First films, now origami,' Gareth says evasively. 'Is there anything else I ought to know about your interior life?'

'Gareth, she's in the car with us anyway, whether you want to talk about her or not.'

It's interesting to see my dad struggling. I wonder if I look as congested and anxious when Hanna tries to make me talk about things.

'Fine,' he says at last. 'What do you want to talk about?'

Where to start when you have so many questions?

'What was she like growing up?'

'Strict. Everything was black and white, she never saw the grey. She invested her life in me. When the investment didn't turn out the way she expected, she . . .' Gareth considers his words. 'Sold her stock,' he concludes.

'She was at the station that day, so I'm guessing she's local?'

'She lives on Imperial Avenue.'

Dan lives on Imperial Avenue. All those houses with their big gates and their fringed blinds and their silence.

'That's only five minutes from us,' I say.

It's started raining, and the wipers make a hypnotic noise as they leap and swish and bow like ballet dancers. I can't stop the question jumping out of me.

'Am I turning out the way you expected?'

Gareth glances at me. 'What?'

'Will you sell your stock if I study film instead of accountancy?'

Gareth pulls over to the side of the road with such a swerve that the tyres make a squealing noise on the tarmac. He looks as if I've just punched him in the throat.

'I'm not my mother,' he says.

'You're half of her. Like I'm half of you. I ask because . . . that thing you said about not paying for the fees if I do film—'

The rest is lost in Gareth's jumper as he clumsily hugs me.

'I would never do to you what she did to me,' he tells the top of my head.

'OK,' I say, with my mouth full of fluff. I move my head so breathing is a little easier. We stay there for a bit, awkwardly angled over the handbrake, as the wipers swish away at the rain.

'Do you ever wish you knew your mother?'

'Sometimes,' I tell Gareth's armpit. 'Not often though. Maybe I'll get to it later.'

'So we've done OK, me and Andrew?'

'Ask me again when I'm twenty-five. Apparently that's when my frontal lobe will finish maturing.'

Gareth releases me and puts his hands slowly back on the steering wheel.

'I'm sorry I didn't talk to you about the film thing sooner,' I say.

'I understand why a little better now.'

We sit there for a bit, watching the wipers.

'Do you think it's fixable?' I ask when Gareth finally flips on the indicator and pulls back into the traffic. 'You and her?'

'Not sure I want it to be.'

'You've been up at the hospital every day since it happened. Waiting for her to wake up.'

'That's guilt. About Nigel.' He clears his throat. 'You told her you've made some films already. Can I see one?'

I try to quell my usual unease. 'I'm sick with terror about the piece I'm putting together for my application anyway. What's a little more nausea between father and son?'

'Less than you produced in that bowl, with luck.'

'Thank you for that,' I say with a grimace, as we turn into our road. 'And, you know, for getting the bowl in the first place.'

'Wasn't me, son. It was Hanna.'

It takes me a while to realise we've pulled up outside the house. I scramble to unbuckle my seatbelt and follow Gareth to the front door.

'Hanna? Hanna Bergdahl?'

I'm doing the surname thing like Trixie does.

'She's a good girl. Looks out for you. Came to find us in the study around eleven or so that night to ask for a bowl.'

I follow my father into the kitchen. 'But I didn't have any trousers on,' I say, appalled at this fresh vision of hell. 'When I woke up, I didn't . . . She must have seen my . . . She could have seen—'

'I don't suppose you were much of a threat,' says Gareth. 'Coffee? Then we can go upstairs and you can show me a film. We'll take these plans of yours from there, OK?'

Hanna

'Call me,' says Lizzie again, holding on to the train door to keep it from sliding shut.

'I'll call you as soon as I get there,' Raz says.

'Call me on the way.'

'I'll call you before then.'

They're so disgustingly happy. If I didn't love them both so much, I'd be crying. I avert my eyes as they snog loudly in the doorway with the doors puffing and hissing either side of them. If I had a car horn right now, I'd lean on it.

'Phew,' says Lizzie, looking a little cross-eyed as the train pulls away. 'Do I have stubble rash? I can't believe I won't see him for a week. Do you think college would notice if I ran away to university?'

'You run away to sea,' I say. 'You *apply* for university.'

Lizzie adjusts her beanie. She has taken to wearing them in a range of super-bright colours since Raz told her she suited hats.

'I could eat him like a gorgeous custard slice,' she says.

'You already did,' I say, dragging her through the ticket

hall and out into the street. 'He only had half a face left when the train door slid shut.'

'You don't think he'll meet some superbrain at uni this week and replace me?'

'You asked me that last week and the week before. So far, so good. Honestly Lizzie, he's mad about you. Do you want to come back to mine?'

My best friend looks coy. 'Actually, I've got an appointment. I'm going on the pill. We nearly . . . Well, at the weekend things got . . .'

'Whoa,' I say, holding up my hand. 'Brother.'

'How is *not* talking about the sex I intend to have with Rasmus fulfilling your role as a best mate? I might have to talk to Trixie instead.'

Lizzie backs away from me, grinning and blowing me kisses, the November wind whipping up her long dark hair and almost despatching the beanie. Then she flicks a couple of fingers at me and vanishes behind the bus stop. I stand there for a moment, fiddling with my own hat, tucking in a few flyaway hairs. There's a heavy feeling in my stomach. There's nothing like having a best friend in love to make you aware of your own romantic situation. Or lack of one.

It starts to rain as I trudge up the hill, my hands deep in my pockets and my hat pulled down as far as it will go. I've crossed the road by the chippy and have almost made it to the level crossing when a squeal of tyres makes me look round.

A dark blue car has swerved off the road and parked very unevenly by the pavement with its wheels at strange angles.

Sol and his dad are in the front, having what looks like an argument. Sol's face is turned to the window. His face is almost as pale as it was at the party. I freeze where I am.

Gareth is cradling Sol's head against his chest now. I look away at that. It feels like I'm intruding. It's only when the car pulls back on to the road that I start walking again, watching its tail lights up ahead, the brake lights coming on and off as they inch through the traffic. I wonder where they've been, what they were talking about.

Before I know it, I've followed the car all the way to Sol's road. Feeling a little like a stalker, I lurk by a tree a short distance away as Gareth gets out of the car. Sol almost falls out of the car on his side, scrambling after Gareth, asking him something in a loud and urgent voice that I can't quite hear. I wonder what I would say if either of them turned round, and am grateful when they don't.

The door clicks shut. As I am considering whether to walk the long way round to my house or turn back the way I've just come, I catch Sol's green eye in the hallway window.

His pale face bleaches more than I ever thought possible. I am about to smile hesitantly at him in a 'Well, what do you know, just passing, what are the chances' sort of way, when he spins away from the window like I just shot him. I glimpse him taking the stairs three at a time like he can't wait to get away.

I used to be good at this stuff, I think bleakly, as I walk the long way home with my chin tucked right inside the collar of my new coat. How have I got so out of practice?

By the time I have reached my house, I'm remembering

Dan's garage roof and all the fruitless crying in the corridors that followed the disaster of New Year. And realising that, in fact, I'm not good at this stuff at all. I'm useless because I've never had to *do* it. The boys were always doing it for me. Buying cinema tickets, chasing me round swimming pools.

'I've just got in too,' says James, wandering out of the kitchen with a mug of tea in his hand. 'And I'm trying to put on *The Incredibles* for Linus in the snug, but I can't remember how the DVD player works. Give me a hand?'

I think of Gareth and Sol, holding each other in the car. I think of Dad's tyres on gravel; of James's comfortable, steady presence. I put my arms out and catch my stepfather round the middle.

'I said a hand, not a hug,' says James as he holds his tea aloft. 'Not that I'm complaining.'

30 NOVEMBER

Sorry but I can't make movie night this month.

Cant do it this mth anyway

Uni application has taken over my life.

Not a problem honestly

Been meaning to thank you for looking after me at my party. V embarrassed about it.

Said id return the favour 1 day

Maybe a movie next month?

New Years Eve next mth!

What, already?

TANGLED
(2010)

DIRECTORS **NATHAN GRENO** and **BYRON HOWARD**

WRITER **DAN FOGELMAN**

Based on the Brothers Grimm story RAPUNZEL

When Flynn Rider (voiced by Zachary Levi), hides in a convenient tower with a crown he has stolen from the palace, he meets Rapunzel (voiced by Mandy Moore). Rapunzel has lived in the tower all her life, imprisoned there by the witch Mother Gothel (voiced by Donna Murphy), because her magical golden hair holds the secret to the witch's youth. Rapunzel is desperate to see the world, and enlists Flynn to help her escape. When will Rapunzel realise that she is the kingdom's lost princess?

When designing the Flynn Rider character, the directors gathered thirty women from the studio for a 'Hot Man Meeting', in order to make Flynn the most attractive hero Disney ever created. *Tangled* is the 22nd highest-grossing animated film in the world.

Hanna

'You don't think it was devious telling him I couldn't do movie night?'

Lizzie indicates Linus, sucking his thumb peacefully on the sofa in between us.

'He could still have come over,' I say. 'We're watching a movie, aren't we? Babysitting and movie nights go together like popcorn and candyfloss.'

'You couldn't have *done* anything, though,' says Lizzie, with another meaningful glance in Linus's direction.

'Fat chance anyway,' I mutter. 'Don't forget, he sprinted up the stairs because he couldn't stand the sight of me the other day, not to mention how at the party he stopped me from . . .' I stop, wishing I hadn't started the sentence.

'Snogging him,' Lizzie finishes helpfully.

'Snogging,' says Linus.

Lizzie and I are relieved to see that he's watching Flynn and Rapunzel kissing.

'Believe me, Linus,' says Lizzie, observing the scene with a smirk, 'that's not snogging. Animated kissing never gets the lovely, grinding *squish* quite right.' She returns her attention to me. 'The party thing is more likely to have been about timing. You're not that repellent.'

'Thanks,' I say glumly.

'Sol isn't the kind of guy to cheat on his girlfriend even when he has the opportunity. This is a *good* thing, Han, OK? Get him to break up with her, and you may yet be in with a chance.'

I flop my head back on the sofa and wonder if my heart will ever stop hurting. 'He sounded really jealous about Carmen and Stevie, like they had been flirting or something,' I tell the ceiling. 'I think that's why he was so drunk. He's totally into her, Lizzie.'

'Rasmus was really into Leah. Things can change. Do you think Carmen knows you took his trousers off?'

I feel a prickle of alarm. 'I hope not.'

'Me too,' Lizzie says. 'I'd have a thing or two to say to a girl who'd removed Rasmus's underwear without my permission.'

'I didn't *look*!' I repeat.

Lizzie puts her arm round Linus, who's getting sleepy, and stares fondly at the TV. 'Don't you think Flynn Rider looks like Raz?' she asks.

'You know how people have a swear box?' I grumble, reaching for more popcorn. 'We should have a Raz box. Flynn looks nothing like my brother.'

He does look like Sol though. Apart from the fact that his hair is brown and doesn't flop over his face. I study Flynn's eyes. Are they green like Sol's, or brown? Green, I think, and very attractive the way they crinkle . . .

I'm losing it over a two-dimensional character now.

'Hanna,' says Lizzie, 'either you have to go for Sol or you have to forget him. This mooning doesn't suit you.'

'I'm not mooning,' I say.

'I've never seen you moon before,' Lizzie says. Her eyes gleam. 'Although of course, you've seen—'

'—Sol moon before, yes, I get it,' I say as she cackles. 'I'm not mooning, Lizzie, OK? Mooning is what cows do.'

'That's mooing,' says Linus, removing his thumb for a brief moment before inserting it between his teeth again.

'So you could look Sol in the eye if he came to the door and say "Hi!" and everything would be entirely normal?' Lizzie asks.

'Yes,' I say firmly.

Lizzie looks out of the snug window. Her eyes widen.

'Oh my God,' she says. 'Sol's walking up the front path . . .'

I hit the floor at speed, covering my head with my hands.

'You're funny, Lizzie,' says Linus.

'He's not there, is he?' I say from the carpet.

'Get up, you idiot.'

The movie finishes moments after the popcorn does. I take Linus up for his bath, where we play with his Lego and build an underwater lair like the lair in *Dr No*, only not as cool and with more corners. As I wash his curly hair, I think about what Lizzie has said. She's right, of course. I should go for Sol or I should forget him. Deep in thought, I carry Linus in his fluffy towel through to his bedroom, where I stand on a piece of Lego and swear so loudly that he threatens to tell Mum what I said.

He's out cold four pages into *The Official LEGO Star Wars Annual.* By the time I get back to the snug, Lizzie has flipped the TV on, so I sit on the sofa beside her, nursing my injured foot. I can't help thinking about the contrast to the last thing I stood on, how it crumpled so quietly and caused me no trouble at all.

'Excellent,' says Lizzie, sitting up as The Psychedelic Furs blasts out across the snug. 'They don't show this film often enough.'

'I watched this with Sol,' I say. 'In March, I think. Or February, maybe.'

'Good, isn't it?'

I rub my foot. Feeling is starting to return. 'I don't remember much about it apart from the main guy. Andrew someone.'

'I completely love it,' says Lizzie. 'And completely hate it too.'

I squint at the screen as the little guy with the pork pie hat and pointy white shoes rocks up. Sol wore a hat like that, the night we watched this. I sit forward, staring at the screen. Remembering.

'I can't believe she ends up with the rich weasel,' Lizzie says. 'Do you know, they reshot the ending because the general public didn't want her to get with Duckie?'

'Andrew McCarthy's hair is a wig in the last scene,' I say. I can hear Sol telling me that now, like he's beside me, with brightly coloured Smarties in a big bowl on the table in front of us. 'At the end. They had to get him back and he'd already shaved his head for another—'

'Shut up, I want to watch this.'

Blane doesn't look like Dan at all. Having barely noticed Duckie last time round, I can't take my eyes off him tonight. It's like watching an entirely different movie. How does that work? Different memories of that evening drift in with each scene, flipping through my head like magician's cards. Smarties. Um Bongo. Hairspray. Phone. Film. Cogs fit together with an ominous clunk and wheels begin to turn.

Paper figures.

'Lizzie,' I say.

Lizzie waves at me to be quiet. I fumble in my bag with fingers that suddenly don't seem to be working properly. I kept the film, didn't I? I wouldn't have deleted it, would I?

'Lizzie, please,' I say. 'Look.'

I hand her my phone. I've already pressed play. Lizzie gazes at the little film, all eight seconds of it. Two paper figures. A car. Headlights. Not kissing, kissing, not kissing again.

'What is this?' she says, interested now.

I have been so incredibly stupid.

'A Valentine,' I whisper. 'From Sol.'

Pretty in Pink is forgotten. I take a large gulp of air.

'I've just worked it out. He made it for me. He sent it to me. I spent half the evening badgering him for his opinion on it, when he was trying to watch the movie. I didn't know it was from him. And now it's too late because he hates me and he's with Carmen!'

'Slow this down,' says Lizzie as I gulp for oxygen. 'What makes you so sure it's from him?'

'The figures,' I wail. 'The paper ones. I trod on a broken one in Sol's bedroom at the party!'

'I can't believe he made such a perfect little film for you,' Lizzie says, awestruck. 'Boyfriends of the world, beware.'

I take the phone like it's something that will disintegrate between my fingers. 'I asked him if he thought it was from Dan!'

'Tactful.'

I start pacing the snug. It's not a big space so I have to turn round every four steps. Shit. *Shit.*

'Do you think Sol chose the movie that night on purpose?' Lizzie asks. 'Like, he was trying to tell you something?'

'Turn it off,' I say.

She does. We sit there in silence.

'Your timing's a bit out,' Lizzie says finally.

'A *bit*?'

'OK, completely out. But at least there's hope now, right? Even if he doesn't like you at the *moment*, he did once, so he could again, right?'

'He's with *Carmen*.'

'Hanna, we're seventeen years old. Sol is very unlikely to stay with Carmen for ever.'

'Maybe not, but what if they're still together in ten years, like the Beckhams?' I demand. 'What then?'

'Won't happen.'

'So you and Raz are just a fling? Just a brief, uninvested snogathon?'

Lizzie bites her lip.

'THANK you,' I say with a kind of sour satisfaction. 'And now that we're agreed, I think the best thing all round is to forget this ever happened. I'm going to delete it.'

Lizzie reaches for me. 'Don't delete it Hanna, it's too—'

I watch the little masterpiece blink and vanish into nothing. It feels as if someone has just ripped the skin from the inside of my heart.

'Too late,' I say bitterly. 'Like everything in my life right now. It's just too *late*.'

THE GREAT
GATSBY (2013)

DIRECTOR   BAZ LUHRMANN

WRITERS   BAZ LUHRMANN
and CRAIG PEARCE

Based on the novel by F. Scott Fitzgerald

In the spring of 1922, wide-eyed Midwesterner Nick Carraway (Tobey Maguire) moves in next door to wealthy Jay Gatsby (Leonardo DiCaprio), whose elaborate parties are legendary. Meanwhile, across the bay, Carraway's cousin Daisy (Carey Mulligan) struggles in her marriage to the womanizing Tom Buchanan (Joel Edgerton). As his own life begins falling apart, Carraway realises that Daisy and Gatsby share a complicated romantic past that overshadows everything.

F. Scott Fitzgerald's great American novel was published in 1925, and would have been called *Under the Red, White and Blue* if Fitzgerald hadn't left it too late to request a title change. The 2013 film won Oscars for Production and Costume Design. The actress Sigourney Weaver is named after a minor character in the book.

SOL

18 DECEMBER

It's time to stop fiddling, tweaking, shading and filtering, adjusting, reshooting. My past, present and future sit in front of me on the screen, condensed into eighteen minutes. There's nothing more I can do.

'God I'm hungry,' I say as I come out of my bedroom. 'I could eat Nigel on toast.'

'You'd have to get him off the spare bed first,' says Gareth, coming past with an armful of papers. 'Give Andrew a hand, will you? He's been in there for hours.'

Nigel is sprawled at his fullest extent across the spare bed, caught as if in flight. He's showing no signs of moving as Andrew attempts to straighten the duvet around him, although he opens one eye, crocodile-like, when Andrew reaches for the cushion behind his head.

'Is Gareth's mum really coming here?' I ask.

Andrew gives up with the cushion. 'Apparently, yes.'

'I can't believe she's coming.'

Andrew sits slowly on the bed. Nigel still doesn't move.

'It's Christmas, Sol,' he says. He looks fed up. 'Ebenezer Scrooge didn't believe anyone was coming either. How's the editing going?'

'I've finished it,' I say.

'Any further critical advice needed?'

I'm getting better at the whole showing-my-work thing. My parents have liked pretty much everything I've showed them so far, which counts for a lot.

'Probably. But I'd rather watch someone else's masterpiece and feel inadequate by comparison tonight. Could you and Gareth maybe check it through with me again tomorrow?'

'Done,' says Andrew. '*The Great Gatsby*'s on later. Watch it with us if you're not busy.'

We have tea together in the kitchen, me and my parents, as loose and easy as an old pair of pyjamas. I even find the courage to mention Carmen. Or rather, the absence of Carmen.

'That's a shame,' says Gareth. 'We liked her.'

'We never met her,' Andrew says.

'We liked the *sound* of her,' Gareth amends.

'I thought she sounded rather boring,' Andrew says.

'She wasn't boring,' I protest. 'She was nice.'

My parents make near-identical faces.

'She's better suited to Stevie,' I say.

I've warned him about the dinners with her parents and the Costa thing, and he seems fine with it. Excited, even. He played golf with RoboCop last week.

'You did the right thing,' says Gareth. 'Life's too short to spend with the wrong people.'

'Talking of whom,' says Andrew, 'your mother is arriving when?'

Gareth looks grim as I choke into my soup.

'Oh, don't look so disapproving, Gareth, I'm just teasing,' says Andrew. 'Of course she can't spend Christmas alone, not after everything. She'll have to take her chances with Nigel, that's all. We're not putting him in the cattery.'

'The cattery won't have him,' I say.

Once Gareth has lit the fire, we sit together in the living room with large cups of hot chocolate like three boy scouts and watch *The Great Gatsby*. Every now and again, I find myself looking past the twinkling Christmas tree at the armchair by the window. I picture my grandmother glaring in it on Christmas morning.

'Do you think she'll sit there?' I ask.

'I can't see her sprawled lengthways on the fire rug,' says Andrew. 'Will you *look* at that set? It's utterly extraordinary.'

'Daisy Buchanan looks like Hanna,' I say, switching my attention back to the screen. 'Except Hanna's eyes are blue. And her hair is longer.'

'And she's not such an outright bitch,' says Andrew. 'Excuse my language.'

'When are you going to ask that girl out?' says Gareth.

I feel as if I've been having this conversation all my life.

'I'm not,' I say patiently.

'You are going to show her your film though, aren't you?' says Andrew. 'It seems only fair, seeing how it's all about her.'

The room goes still. I go stiller.

'Don't tell me you didn't notice,' Andrew says to Gareth.

'I didn't say that,' says Gareth.

'It's not about her,' I protest. 'It about a guy who likes a girl who doesn't like him back. It's not about Hanna and me. Hanna or me. It's not about Hanna at all.'

My parents wait.

'Is it that obvious?' I ask eventually.

'The thing is, Sol,' says Gareth, 'we know you, and we know Hanna, and so . . .'

'And so it's *blazingly* obvious,' says Andrew. 'It's also completely charming, by the way. She'd be mad not to love it.'

I realise that I've stood up. 'I'm not showing it to her,' I say.

'We're not saying you should,' says Gareth soothingly.

'Thank you,' I say, sitting down again. 'It would be totally awful and I'm not going to do it, so I'm glad we're clear on that.'

'But not showing your film to Hanna is like Gatsby throwing parties for Daisy,' says Andrew in disappointment. 'All that effort for something she never even sees?'

'I didn't *make* the film for Hanna. I made it for my course application. My course tutor will see it and offer me a place with any luck, and that's all that matters.'

'But—'

'Drop it, Andrew,' says Gareth, in a voice I've only ever heard him use once, when Nigel brought a grass snake into the kitchen.

Normal relations are just about resumed by the time Gatsby is lying face-down in his swimming pool. Nigel slinks into the room as the credits start rolling, leaps into the empty armchair and starts clawing the life out of it.

'Imagine if he did that to your mother's knees,' says Andrew.

Gareth silently gathers up the empty hot chocolate mugs.

'It might soften her up a bit,' Andrew goes on. 'If anyone needs softening up, it's her. If I had claws like Nigel's, you can be sure I'd—'

'Will you just STOP?'

Andrew looks shocked and stops.

'I'm looking forward to this Christmas a lot less than you are, and with a damn sight more reason,' Gareth hisses. 'But I'm giving it a go. What have I got to lose? A mother who doesn't like me anyway? And what have I got to gain? A relationship, maybe. Some things are worth a bit of effort, Andrew, OK? Can you make that effort for me? For this family? Can you?'

'Honestly,' says Andrew, a little flustered as Gareth stalks out of the room with the empty hot chocolate mugs. 'That man can be such a drama queen.'

MOVIE NIGHT
(2017)

WRITER & DIRECTOR SOL ADAMS

Sol Adams' stop-animation technique showed its many-folded face for the first time in this short film. Incorporating what critics have described as 'dream puppetry', the tale of the two paper dancers unfolds in the harsh light and natural camerawork for which this director is becoming increasingly well known.

Hanna

31 DECEMBER

'Why are we here?' I say warily, staring at Dan's big illuminated gates.

'Is that a philosophical question, or more of a geographical one?'

Lizzie's looking amazing tonight, in a long purple dress with the kind of fringing normally reserved for grandmothers' lampshades. Among all the other girls swarming for Dan's front door in identical body-con numbers covered in fake-tan tide marks, she stands out like a peacock. Raz is wearing his Lord Byron T-shirt and an extraordinarily tight pair of rock-star trousers, and is holding Lizzie's hand.

'You said we were going to your place,' I hiss. 'You said nothing about coming here.'

'Must have slipped my mind,' Lizzie says airily. 'Come on, Hanna. It'll be more fun this year than last. We're together again, and neither of us will go anywhere near Dan this time. We'll dance, and we'll drink, and we'll bring in the New Year in our own inimitable style.'

'Style?' I repeat. 'I am wearing my Snoopy jeans.'

'And you look gorgeous in them. Much sexier than everyone else.'

I love my jeans. They have Snoopy stitched on one knee and Woodstock on the back pocket and I've had them for ages. For understandable reasons, I don't wear them in public. If I had heels on, I'd dig them into the ground like tent pegs. But you can't do that in Converse. I tug wretchedly at my old white T-shirt. At least it's clean.

'I can't go in there,' I say.

'You can, and you will. You've forgotten how to have a good time lately, Hanna. It's my duty as your friend to show you the error of your ways.'

'But you're *with* someone,' I wail. 'And you look fantastic.'

'And you're with us, and you look fantastic too. Problem solved. Rasmus and I won't leave you alone with Dan, if that's what you're worried about.'

I'm forced to keep up with Lizzie and Raz, or get lost in the flood. I think of the movie she said she had cued up and waiting for us at hers. I think of the popcorn in my bag, and the Brad Pitt and Angelina Jolie masks I packed for a laugh. This is not how I pictured seeing out the old year. I fiddle morosely with the little ping-pong moon in my pocket. I've taken to carrying it around with me like a good-luck charm.

'Remember dancing, Han?' Lizzie says, coaxing me into the hallway, grabbing a drink from the waiter at the door and thrusting it into my hand. 'You used to like it.'

'I'm not properly *dressed*!'

'You've got clothes on. That's the main thing.'

'But—'

'Don't be boring. It's New Year's Eve. Ooh, I love this song. Dance with me.'

If I had turned up wearing nothing but a bobble hat, I couldn't feel more conspicuous than I do right now. My cheeks are burning as Lizzie pulls me into the great glassy living room I remember so painfully. What a lot of changes a year can bring.

'Loving the Snoopy thing, babes,' says Vashti in amusement, whirling past with her bangled arms round Laura and Jake.

Lizzie jigs around me with her fringed bits flying around and her hair in a whirl around her head. Raz joins us, leaping and jumping like a Victorian poetry-loving kangaroo. I want to leave, but I can't now because that would make it look as if I've lost some kind of unspoken competition. There are cultures in the world that dance at funerals, locked into a strange combination of misery and physical activity. I try to emulate them. It's better than nothing.

'Style it out, Han!' Lizzie shouts. 'There you go!'

The dancing isn't helping. I miss Sol in my bones. Being without him is like trying to play tennis with a missing elbow, or rollerblade with a kneecap that's gone AWOL. I can't cover his shoulders in damp mascara every time I cry. I can't hug him or smell him and I can't make him laugh. I can't put my hands on his chest as his muscles shift and move, and I can't smell his woodiness. The lack of all these things suddenly feels so acute that I have to stop dancing and just stand there in the middle of it all and let it run me through like some kind of pain javelin. This isn't how I felt about Dan, all surging rage and howling tears. This goes deeper, like a fissure in a rock.

I leave the crowded room to stand on to the wooden deck. The sky is overcast and it's cold. I wonder if it will snow tonight, like it did last year. Like it did when Sol stood by the bus stop with the light shining around his head and we watched it fall.

There's a football match going on down in the garden around the lion fountain. Stevie raises his arms aloft as the ball smacks off the lion's nose to roars of appreciation from the other players.

'Hello Hanna,' says Carmen, coming up behind me. She's in a killer purple dress that looks as if it's been painted on. 'Everyone's talking about your jeans. Where did you get them?'

'The back of my cupboard,' I tell her.

Carmen laughs. 'I'll tell them that if anyone asks.'

'They should find more interesting things to talk about.'

'Oh, I think they find you very interesting. I find you interesting too. You don't play the game.'

I don't want to feel flattered, but it's hard to resist Carmen's open smile. 'Lizzie is better at not playing the game than me.' I gesture at Snoopy. 'The jeans are more circumstance than rebellion.'

Sol wouldn't let Carmen come alone to Dan's place so he must be here somewhere. I moisten my lips and hope that he doesn't appear on the balcony.

'Thank you for your help in the summer,' Carmen says.

Good work there, Hanna, I think. *Making sure Carmen and the boy you're crazy about have stuck it out through thick and thin.*

'GOOOAL!' yells Stevie down in the gloom.

'I was upset when he ended it of course, but then I worked it out,' she continues.

I've lost the thread now. I frown at Carmen and try to understand.

She watches my face. 'The answer's simple when you know it. To cross the river, you need the right kind of bridge.'

A selection of movie bridges spin randomly through my head. Godzilla smashing through the Golden Gate, a dangling rope festooned with avenging Thuggees, a few broken Colombian planks and Kathleen Turner, *The Bridge to Terabithia.* Did Carmen just say she and Sol—

'And I wasn't the right kind of bridge,' Carmen says.

'The right kind of bridge,' I repeat, staring at the sky.

By the time I think to lower my chin, Carmen's gone. I gaze into the garden, at the figures running from side to side, at the ball as it flashes now and again through the beam of the outside lights. Five minutes later, I've walked round the side of the house, past the showroom garage (a blue Evoque now) and down the drive. I take out my phone, and check it, and put it away again, and take it out again, and text Lizzie.

> **Have to go, HNY xxxxx**

My feet are taking me down Imperial Avenue. I follow them towards the station. A train is pulling in as I climb the footbridge steps, so I stand at the top and watch and breathe and think, and turn my ping-pong moon over and over in my fingers. And when I have done that, I take the steps back down again and start walking.

SOL

It worked at the party so there's no reason why it will fail me now. But still, I check and I check again. Andrew's big screen billows as the wind catches it, the images rippling like reflections in the water. Something is rippling in me as well. I don't examine it too closely, in case it makes me pull the plug and take myself upstairs to hide in the cupboard beside my box of paper figures. But some things are worth a bit of effort, as Gareth said not so long ago.

Of course, there's no guarantee that she'll come. I haven't spoken to her for weeks. She may have left the country to spend New Year on a Swedish beach. This is the loophole that is keeping me going.

We still have the Christmas lights up around the garden. They are swaying in the wind, clinking lightly against each other. It had better not rain.

I take out my phone.

> Are you in Sweden?

> No

Not on a Swedish beach then.

> Are you at Dan's party?

> Not any more

Not dancing the night away in another guy's arms either. Unless, of course, she left the party *with* that imaginary other guy, like the way she left with me last year, only with kissing.

I make myself go on.

> That bad, was it?

> Where R U?

In a mindless state of terror and hope. I can't put that, so I put the next truest thing. Off it goes, flying away into nothing on invisible black wings, telling her everything she needs to know.

> Waiting for you.

Hanna

We had a teacher in Year Two who made us sit in alphabetical order and introduce ourselves to our neighbours.

'I'm Hanna,' I told Sol.

'You're supposed to be Louise,' Sol told me.

Louise Bedlington and I swapped seats and Louise kicked me so hard that my shins were spotted like a dalmatian for days afterwards. I asked the teacher if I could sit next to Sol the following week.

If that story had been a movie, I would have sat next to Sol from the start. But I got kicked in the shins instead and only found my best friend by going the long way round. There's a moral in there somewhere, but, being real life and not a script, it isn't entirely clear.

Risks like this aren't meant to be taken in Snoopy jeans and with a sweaty back. They should be taken in good make up and a great dress, if taken at all. And yet here I am, putting one grubby Converse foot in front of the other without even a detour to add make up. But after what feels like hours of walking around, I no longer have a choice.

If he was interested, wouldn't he have called by now? Just because he's not with Carmen any more doesn't automatically mean I'm going to be next in line. Then I think about him in the snow last year, and I remember the little film with its perfect paper figures, and I think about his words on the station with his face against my neck and I quicken my pace. As I think I've said before, you have to live in hope. Hope needs to count for something.

When I reach the end of his road, I sit down on the wall and briefly press my hands to my stomach. Maybe it would be better for everyone if I just went home now and cued up *Mr and Mrs Smith* as originally planned for Lizzie's, and put on the Brad Pitt mask and cried into my popcorn. The trouble is, Sol's is closer.

Up again. Move forward. Fiddle feverishly with my ping-pong moon. Lean briefly against a tree. The movie director is shouting stuff like 'Who is this idiot? Get her off my set!' and firing his producer round about now.

Beep.

Are you in Sweden?

Why would I be in Sweden? I'm never in Sweden at this time of year. I don't want to answer questions about Sweden now, not even from Sol.

No

I start moving again, pressed forward by the growing sense of urgency.

> **Are you at Dan's party?**

> **Not any more**

> **That bad, was it?**

That rather depends on what happens next.

> **Where R U?**

Glancing up, I see the lights shining through his curtains. My heart lifts and sinks at the same time, which feels so odd that I wonder if maybe I have two hearts running in opposite directions, like hotel lifts. I slide my phone into my pocket and pick up my pace. His front door can't come quickly enough.

I'm jogging up the path. I'm leaning on the doorbell.

He opens the door.

This is the moment in movies when there is a sudden rainstorm and someone does Andie McDowell's *Four Weddings and a Funeral* speech ('Is it raining? I hadn't noticed') and we laugh and cry and fall into each other's arms. It's the moment I've wanted all my life, a perfect closing scene poised and ready for a hundred memory replays.

I gaze into Sol's lovely, speckly, anxious green eyes.

'I'm sorry, but I *really* need to use your loo,' I say.

SOL

'The thing is,' Hanna continues, edging round me, 'I haven't been since Lizzie dragged me out to go round to hers, only we ended up at Dan's party, and we were dancing for about an hour and then I left and I've been walking around for, well, ages really, and so the bottom line – as it were – is that I really need to go now. Sorry. Thanks. Out in a minute.'

In the silence that follows her scuttling into the downstairs toilet, it's clear to me that I have to hide. I open the cupboard, the big one where we keep the Hoover and the ironing board, and I get inside, and I shut the door. *It will all be fine*, I think, in that illogical way of extreme stress. She'll come out again, and she won't be able to find me, and so she'll go, and we can pretend none of this happened in the morning.

Except, thirty seconds into my lonely vigil, I realise that I can hear a train whistle coming from the garden. The film has looped back to the beginning and is starting again. I didn't turn it off when I answered the door.

My palms start sweating. Hanna has been in the toilet for approximately forty seconds, which means she could be coming out again at any time. If I leave this cupboard at the same moment she leaves the toilet, there will be quite a lot of explaining to do. If I stay where I am, she will come out of the toilet and, logically, follow the sound.

Nigel growls somewhere in the darkness by my feet as I hear the toilet door being unlocked.

'Sol?'

It's important to stay calm. I don't have to remain in this cupboard indefinitely. Just until she has left the hallway. I could say that I went upstairs to get something. Except I don't have anything so she'll know I haven't been upstairs to get something. I snatch the dustpan and brush off the little dusty hook on the cupboard door. I now have a dustpan and brush. Good.

'Where are you, are you upstairs?'

The front door is to the left of the cupboard. I strain my ears, listening for the telltale sign that she's moving that way. Nigel pats my foot thoughtfully.

'Can I come up?'

I sag against the cupboard door at the light tread of her feet on the stairs. I can leave now, and turn off the film while she's up there. I put my hand on the cupboard door. Withdraw it as I hear her feet coming back down again.

This is the point where Nigel bites my ankle. Really sinks his teeth in. I sink my own teeth into the padded part of the ironing board as pain hazes through me. I am still holding on to the dustpan and brush. Professional to the last. I hope she doesn't open the cupboard door.

She's in the hallway again now. I can feel her hesitating, wondering what's going on. It's almost a relief when she goes through the kitchen and into the garden. A sense of fatalism descends.

This is it, then. No going back.

Hanna

Up on the screen at the bottom of the garden, two paper figures are twirling at the heart of an ordinary-looking world of bleached light and shaky pavements. They are dancing to music no one else can hear, unless you count the slamming of train doors and the screech and whine of air brakes. They spin like leaves on the wind.

The backgrounds change and whirl like roulette-wheel dreams, although the train noises remain. There's a paper tiger in some reeds, a fight of a hundred folds beside a Venice canal. The tiger is speared by a galloping knight on a paper horse. A paper car, headlights, kissing figures – I know this part. Still the dancers dance.

Rain comes in sheets. The dancers soften and bend under the weight of the water, losing definition, faltering and slipping. There are clouds now, of water or smoke, obscuring the action. When they clear, there is only one dancer left, small and lonely and wet on the ground. Feet pass him by (I know it's a him, don't ask me how), and tread on him, and he grows smaller as I watch, until he is barely recognisable as a figure at all.

Sol comes to sit beside me as the picture fades away. I breathe him in.

'You can't end it like that,' I say.

'Did you hate it?'

I shake my head. I shake it and shake it. 'No one could hate it. It's too beautiful. It's just sad, that's all. What happened to the other dancer?'

'I don't think she wanted to dance with him any more.'

I wipe my cheeks because they are wet. 'Maybe it's not as simple as that. Maybe the rain was making her hair frizz up and that's why she went inside.'

He looks bemused. 'She left him to die in the rain because of her hair?'

'She's been dancing past tigers and knights and speeding cars for the last fifteen minutes,' I point out. 'Getting out of the rain is the most sensible thing she could have done in the circumstances. Rain is a nightmare when you've spent three hours straightening your hair. Boys have no idea. Seriously. There was this one time when Lizzie tried to straighten her hair right before—'

Sol puts a finger on my lips. My heart suddenly feels considerably larger than the ribcage trying to contain it.

'I made it for you,' he says. 'Well,' he amends, 'I made it for my Sheffield application, but I was thinking of you the whole time I was making it. I wasn't going to show it to you because I was too terrified of making an idiot of myself, but

Gareth said something the other day that made me realise how important it is, sometimes, to take risks.'

My lips twitch under his finger. My whole body feels like someone just plugged me in.

'And, OK, this is a massive risk and probably a hopeless question, but I have to ask it because I can't go on not knowing. Do you think – could you ever like me as more than just your friend?'

I already do, I try to tell him with my eyes. *I completely adore you. I've lost my mind over you.*

'It was fantastic being your friend, Han. I loved that closeness we had and all the time we spent together before it all went wrong, and I want it again. But I want it on different terms. Wait, who am I kidding, I've *always* wanted it on different terms. Well, maybe not when we were six, but since I came back from the States and you were there in all that yoghurt and you were so beautiful that you blinded me.'

He removes his finger.

'You blinded me,' he repeats quietly. 'And not because you are unspeakably beautiful, which you are, and especially in those jeans by the way, but because you are kind and funny and you talk too much, and you bring me out of myself. I didn't tell you I loved you out of shock the day Nigel almost killed my grandmother. I told you because I couldn't hold it in any more.'

SOL

No one warns you that once you *start* talking, you have at some point to *stop*. No one thinks to mention that.

'I've been a massive idiot about a lot of things,' I continue when it looks alarmingly as if Hanna might try to join in this one-sided conversation. 'When I let you think I'd been out with Carmen before, that wasn't true. I was just trying to empathise with the whole ex thing in order to make you feel better, or impress you, or something.'

'Sol—'

'Wait,' I say hurriedly, 'I remember now, it was because I didn't want you to talk to Dan. You thinking Carmen was my ex – I don't have an ex, by the way, not in this country, there was Lucy Shapiro but she's in California and that never went much beyond a bit of groping – you thinking she was my ex-girlfriend seemed to do the trick. And I know I was an idiot for not telling you when I went out with her for real, but that was because I felt so conflicted about letting you think I'd been out with her before.'

I stand up. No good reason why, I just do. 'Not talking to you about my films, not talking about my grandmother, they were stupid moves too, but I've never been able to talk about things the way that you can. My grandmother came to convalesce here over Christmas, by the way. It wasn't a complete disaster, Nigel didn't finish the job, she shook my hand when she left and we got a thank you and "best wishes" in the post which Gareth thinks might be a start to something resembling a relationship. And just now when you came out of the toilet and wondered where I was? I was hiding in the cupboard.'

I probably should have stopped at 'relationship'. Stopping there would definitely have been better.

The sky decides to start raining. Not the heavy stuff I have on the film, but that mild mizzly kind that gets down the back of your neck but which you can't quite be bothered to escape. On the big screen the figures are whirling around again in blissful ignorance of what comes next.

I feel Hanna's fingers creep into mine. I fold my hand tightly around them and hope and hope and hope.

'Raz and I had a Christmas card from Dad this year. We got "regards." It might be the start of something too, or it might just be what it is.'

'A Christmas card,' I say.

'Yes.'

We stare at each other.

'I've got something for you,' she says suddenly. 'I hadn't planned this because I'm not as cool as that, but now we're here it seems appropriate. It's always been yours really.'

I gaze at the little ball she is holding out to me and I take it and I stare at the wobbly Sea of Tranquility drawn on one side with a smudged Sharpie. Hanna Bergdahl has just given me our moon.

'I don't know why I ever thought your beautiful little film was from Dan,' she says. 'He couldn't make a paper aeroplane. Trixie's with him now, did you know?'

I put the moon in my pocket. Then I let go of her fingers and lift both my hands and push them through her hair to the cool, damp place at the base of her neck, feeling the little bones at the bottom of her skull and the place where her pulse is flickering.

'I thought it would take her longer to get over Stevie because she was so devastated at the party when Stevie dumped her,' Hanna continues, sliding her arms round my waist and up and under my T-shirt, exploring the muscles in my back and down my sides and making me shiver, 'but after a couple of weeks she was acting all hard to get around Dan, probably after seeing how it worked with him and me, although that was totally not on purpose. They were snogging in the corridor before Christmas. I reckon she's got him until around mid-January.'

I bring my thumbs back in line with her jaw and I hold her there for a second or two, marvelling at the perfect symmetry of her face, her Bunsen burner eyes, the mismatched dimples on either side of her beautiful parted mouth. At the fact that I'm about to kiss her, and that she isn't going to stop me.

'Hanna,' I say. 'Why the hell are we talking about Trixie?'

Hanna

I don't know why it took me so long to fancy him. He's completely beautiful. The lines and planes of him, the height and breadth, the thickness of his hair, the blaze in his eyes, the sweetness of his soul. I reluctantly pull my hands from the warm ripples of his back and catch his face as he leans towards me, feeling the contour of his cheekbones in my palms.

'Wait,' I say, suddenly desperate to make this moment last, to revel in the anticipation of something that I've been wanting so badly for what now feels like a very long time.

'Really?' he whispers against my lips.

No.

Not really.

EXT. SOL'S HOUSE - NEW YEAR'S EVE - 12 midnight

From his position inside the bush, NIGEL observes
HANNA and SOL kissing. After five tactful minutes,
during which they show no sign of stopping, he
emerges, brushes lightly against their legs with
his tail, and is gone.

FADE OUT

ACKNOWLEDGEMENTS

'*Movies are my safe place, my perfect world, where nothing goes wrong that can't be fixed by the ninetieth minute.*' Oh, how I love movies: always have, always will. Unashamedly romantic, I liked sad ones when I was a teenager (*Gallipoli*, anyone?) but find that I seek out happy endings these days. Something about life, perhaps? It was brilliant choosing the movies to fit Hanna and Sol's story. Like Hanna, I'm a little conflicted about *Star Wars*, but *Italian for Beginners* . . . wow. Seek it out if you don't know it, and thank me later.

This book has taken a while, pitched in 2014 and crawling into existence like the world's longest credit sequence. THANK YOU to Naomi Greenwood my editor, who adored the idea from the moment I proposed it. 'I love stories about best friends who fall in love,' she said, and so do I. Polly Lyall Grant and Emma Goldhawk for keeping filming on track in Naomi's absence. Michelle Brackenborough for her beautiful cover and interior design, and especially for paper Nigel at the end. All the best boys and key grips and gaffers in marketing, production, rights and sales doing the invisible but super-important stuff off-set. Stephanie Thwaites at Curtis Brown for her endless encouragement and advice. My niece Delilah Acworth, the first person to read about Sol and Hanna in an early draft of the manuscript and offer advice. And finally Will, who never likes the same films as me but whom I love regardless. Although we need to talk about *Under Siege*.